catch a falling star

KIM CULBERTSON

Point

Library of Congress Cataloging-in-Publication Data
Culbertson, Kim A. author.
    Catch a falling star / Kim Culbertson. — First edition.
      pages cm
    Summary: Carter Moon is expecting to spend a quiet summer working in her
parents' restaurant and hanging out with her friends Alien Drake and Chloe —
but when a Hollywood company arrives to film a movie, her sleepy California
town is suddenly transformed, and Carter finds herself playing an unexpected
part in it all.
    ISBN 978-0-545-62704-7
1. Motion picture actors and actresses — Juvenile fiction. 2. Acting — Juvenile
fiction. 3. Best friends — Juvenile fiction. 4. Friendship — Juvenile fiction.
5. California — Juvenile fiction. [1. Actors and actresses — Fiction. 2. Motion
pictures — Production and direction — Fiction. 3. Best friends — Fiction.
4. Friendship — Fiction. 5. Self-realization — Fiction. 6. California — Fiction.]
I. Title.
    PZ7.C8945Cat 2014
    813.6 — dc23

                                                        2013029467

10 9 8 7 6 5 4 3 2 1   14 15 16 17 18

Printed in the U.S.A.   23
First edition, May 2014
Book design by Yaffa Jaskoll

for anabella,
my sweet stargazer

one

If my life were a movie, it would start with this moment. The scene would open with one of those expansive overhead shots of a vast, forested landscape, the bleached summer sky threaded with clouds. The music would be something rumbling, like thunder, or maybe more liquid as the shot found the curve of our river cutting through granite mountains, its waters famous for their inky green swirl, reflecting all the pine and sky. In that introductory, melting sort of way, the camera would dip in, fastening to the yellow line of the single band of a remote highway leading into our small town tucked into the endless mass of Tahoe National Forest, zeroing in on the passing of a road sign:

LITTLE, CA

3 MILES

Next, the shot would pass that sign and slide into the slender downtown of Little, California. My town. It would move along the pretty pastel rows of Victorian shops and houses, the corners of streets marked with wrought-iron lampposts, past gaggles of people at outdoor cafés or leaning their bikes against storefronts or waving as they crossed the street. It would highlight the way our

1

town had a sort of sunlit glaze in the summer, a slow ease that built the slimmest of armor between us and the rest of the world.

In the movie version of my life, the shot would slow as a sleek black Range Rover turned the corner and made its way like a mirage up our main street, people stopping to shield their eyes from the sunlight glinting off its perfectly washed windows.

The audience would know instantly that nestled inside that air-conditioned car sat someone bigger than our small town.

But this wasn't a movie.

This was my life.

And I still had three more hours before my shift ended.

My friend Chloe, though, could make any moment feel like a movie. So Chloe would make sure to magnify it for both of us. "Carter, that's him!" she shrieked, clenching my arm as we cleared dishes from the patio of Little Eats, my family's café on the main street of downtown Little. A half-filled cappuccino mug slipped from her hand, breaking into two clean pieces on the cement of the patio, the handle separating from its white porcelain body.

"Ouch, Chloe." I unpeeled her death grip, quite sure my circulation had been compromised. "That's coming out of your paycheck, not mine." We watched the onyx car glide by, our café a watery and strange reflection in its tinted back windows. In the front passenger seat, a man in his thirties rested his tanned arm on the rim of the window, tapping absently to music we couldn't hear, his mirrored sunglasses miniature versions of the tinted backseat windows.

The car came to rest at the stop sign right outside our patio.

"Do you think he can see us?" Chloe breathed, drinking in the Range Rover's idling purr.

2

As if in response, the back window slid open, and before we could blink, we had a full view of its famous passenger.

Adam Jakes.

Movie star.

Chloe gasped, her face going slack with shock. Framed in the backseat window, Adam Jakes peered out, his famous blue eyes hidden behind sunglasses. Everyone in the café patio stilled, as if a mountain lion had entered a field and all inferior wildlife held their breath. There, framed in that window, was the same tousle of burnt-sugar hair, the symmetrical face, the same pair of wide shoulders, the slouchy look of his mouth that always seemed to say, Yeah, this is how I look when I wake up. The last time I'd seen one of his movies, he'd been playing some sort of teenage James-Bond-goes-to-high-school. The plot escaped me. Still, seeing him there in the window, I felt a strange ribbon of nerves move through my stomach.

He reached out the window, dumped a cup of ice, and then the window slid closed again, its tint reflecting our astonishment before the Range Rover moved away up the street.

Chloe shrieked, "Get me a cup!"

I shook my head. "Oh, you are not going to —" But before I could finish, a woman with a blond bob tossed the remains of her iced tea into a shrub and thrust her glass into Chloe's outstretched hand. As if she'd unearthed a treasure of gold, Chloe hurried to scoop up the fallen ice.

The door of our café banged open, and my dad emerged with two plates of mango chicken salad for the women sitting near the small fountain in front, the dinner plates like saucers in his large hands. He checked to make sure they didn't need anything else before noticing that one of his employees was in the gutter scooping up dirty ice cubes.

He frowned and glanced at me. "Do I want to know?"

I grinned. "Nope."

He disappeared back inside.

Chloe held up the glass, triumphant, the melted bits of ice glimmering in the afternoon light. She blew a strand of dark hair from her face. "Take a picture."

Shaking my head, I clicked a picture with my phone and sent it to her. "You're ridiculous. Now get back to work before I have you fired." I nodded toward her empty busing tray. "You can start with the glass you're holding."

Her look suggested I'd asked her to move to Yemen. "I'm not throwing this out." She placed it gently on a nearby table. "I'm keeping it."

"It'll melt, brainiac."

Chloe plopped her nearly empty busing tray back on the rack. "I love you, Carter, but I worry about you. This ice belonged to Adam Jakes. *Adam Jakes*. That's going in my freezer. I don't care if your dad makes me pay for this glass, too."

I laughed, picking up the pieces of the broken cup Chloe had abandoned earlier, knowing Dad wouldn't make her pay for either of them. "You're a highly disturbed individual."

She squinted after the departed car, wiping absently at a coffee spill on one of the empty two-top marbled tables near the fence. "Did you see the guy in front? That was Parker Hill, Adam Jakes's manager. He's thirty-two, British, and a Pisces."

I tossed the broken cup into the garbage. "Why do you know that?" I pulled my long brown hair away from my neck. We'd only been outside a few minutes, but already the heat was getting to me.

Chloe handed me a hair tie. "I know things. And how can you not think that was exciting? Adam Jakes just drove right by us. Adam Jakes just dumped his ice on *our street*." She pointed at the small pool of wet his ice had left, now quickly drying in the sun.

I frowned. "Kind of rude, if you ask me. When Crazy Jay dumps his ice on our sidewalk, you think he's disgusting."

She frowned at me. "You're hopeless."

"I know." I grinned, clearing a stack of dishes. "But that's why you love me."

Shaking her head, she leaned against the fence, the tables behind her forgotten.

The café door banged open again, and Dad emerged with two more salads for a different table. Pausing, he caught Chloe idling against the fence. "Funny thing, Chlo — those dishes still haven't learned how to wash themselves."

She pushed away from the fence. "I'm on it, Mr. Moon."

"I'll be inside, not holding my breath." Dad disappeared back through the front door, wiping his hands on the burgundy half apron I almost never saw him without.

I filled the rest of my busing tray with the remaining dishes (sans Chloe's celebrity ice) and checked to make sure one of our regulars, Mr. Michaels, was okay on coffee. He smiled at me from his roost at the farthest table tucked back against the side of the café, his wrinkled face even more dappled with the afternoon light coming through the leaves of the old maple that made umbrellas unnecessary for most of our patio seats. He raised his coffee cup, so I scooted over with a pot of decaf.

He gave my arm a nice squeeze and nodded toward Chloe. "What's all the excitement about?" His voice had that whispery sort of fatigue people got in their seventies, like they'd just gone and talked themselves out over the years and didn't have much left.

"That car that just passed there," I told him, putting my hand on his flannel-shirted shoulder; it was pushing ninety degrees outside, but Mr. Michaels was always in flannel. "It had a movie star in it. Adam Jakes. The one who's filming here for the next few weeks."

Mr. Michaels swirled the remaining coffee in his cup. "I read something about that in the paper. He's filming a Christmas movie?"

I nodded. "Right. For the next few weeks, Hollywood will be filming a Christmas movie. Even though it's June. And Chloe's freaking out because she got to touch Adam Jakes's ice." I widened my eyes, clasping the hand that wasn't holding the coffee over my heart. "His *ice*, Mr. Michaels!"

Chloe scrunched up her nose, a busing tray full of dishes against her slim hip, her face a mask of disappointment at our sad lack of pop culture appreciation. "You both should be freaking out. This is a big deal." She held up the sacred glass, the ice mostly melted now.

"That," I told her, not bothering to hide my amusement, "is a glass of water."

Chloe stomped inside in a huff.

* * *

"He's filming tomorrow downtown. We have to go." Chloe squinted at her laptop, tucking her short hair behind her ears.

"I'm working tomorrow." I sipped some iced peppermint tea and waited for her to finish checking her various celebrity sites. We were late to meet her boyfriend, Alien Drake, for stargazing, but it was no use pushing her until she was done.

Chewing my straw, I stared at the pictures plastered on the massive bulletin board above her desk, a layered collection that spilled off in all directions. Pinned amid magazine cutouts of swoon-worthy actors, at least a dozen of the pictures featured seventeen-year-old Adam Jakes, his six-foot frame always muscular and tan, his hair with just the right amount of tousle, his eyes oceanic. There were a few of him smiling, his face lit up, and one of him obviously laughing. But in the more recent photos, he looked gloomy and distant, his face showing the wear of his recent scandal.

Even *I* knew how much trouble he'd been in. You'd have to live in a hole not to have noticed his face splashed all over *Star* and *Celebrity!* last November, documenting his reckless involvement with an unknown twenty-two-year-old redhead, a fast car (also red), and an amount of cocaine the tabloids kept referring to as "substantial." In one of the larger black-and-white photos Chloe had pinned up, I thought he just looked sad.

She had some other pictures up there, too — pictures of Alien Drake, some of me, and some of the three of us together, usually at one of our star-watching nights. These were my favorites, but it felt strange to see them sandwiched in between all the celebrities, like we could ever be part of the same galaxy. I squinted at a new one I hadn't seen before of me in profile tugging at the end of my ponytail, staring off over the roofline of Alien Drake's house, the sky darkening.

"When'd you take that?" I asked her, pointing to it.

"Hmmmm."

She wasn't listening to me, still focused on the screen in front of her. I scanned the rest of the wall, smiling at the glossy Adam Jakes's glass-of-ice print newly taped over an old picture of Adam Jakes at a Lakers game. Chloe never took anything down. She just kept pasting things over other things, papering her walls like some sort of room-sized decoupage project. Every so often, a pale purple wall peeked through, but only rarely. Many a roll of Scotch tape had been sacrificed in the name of Chloe's wall collages.

One of the things I loved about Chloe was she'd always been a fan girl, pure of heart and obsessed. Even though we'd only started hanging out in ninth grade, her room still held fragments of the girl who'd loved any book, movie, or game featuring fairies or superheroes. Every concert ticket, every play, every actor crush of her past still existed somewhere in the layers of those walls. If you started unpeeling, you'd unearth Chloe's seventeen years of life. Even if I didn't share her Hollywood obsession, I admired her for loving it so completely.

My phone buzzed.

Where the asterisk! are you guys?

I texted Alien Drake back:

C's drooling over Adam Jakes — in case you've been living under a rock, he's in town!!!?

Seconds later:

Gee, hadn't heard. Tell her to bring a towel & get over here.

"Alien Drake's waiting." I picked up the quilt I knew she liked from her bed. Alien Drake was Drake Masuda, my neighbor and best friend of twelve years and Chloe's boyfriend for the last six months. My phone buzzed again.

A cattle prod works nicely.

I laughed out loud. "Your boyfriend suggested I use a cattle prod if you don't get a move on. You ready? I'd prefer not to resort to violence."

"Almost." Chloe frowned at something on the screen, making no move to hurry. As usual. "He has an early call. I wonder what that means?"

Annoyance bubbled up in me. I was trying to be patient but, seriously, we were going to miss my favorite part of the night, when the sky purpled and the stars suddenly jumped out from the velvet dark. I sighed in a sort of overdramatic way I hoped she'd notice.

She didn't.

As much as Chloe was obsessed with this stuff, I was the exact opposite. Why should I care about actors? They just happened to be good at acting, the way some people were good at fixing cars or building bridges. Just because they were splashed all over magazines, television, the Internet, did that mean I should listen to their opinions about the world energy crisis or hear what they ate for dinner? It was so weird.

"I think early call means he has to show up to work early," I told her, hoping to move her along. No wonder Alien Drake had to threaten farm equipment. This girl had her own time zone. "As do I. As do you. So let's go. This is getting ridiculous." Nothing. "Chloe!"

"Fine." She slammed her laptop shut, flashing me her own trademark Hollywood smile, the one that usually came right before she needed something from me. The one I could never refuse. "But you're coming with me tomorrow to see him, right?" There it was.

"Of course I am." Anything to get her out of this room and up on that roof.

yesterday's sightings

Things Are Looking Up in Little, CA

Morning, sky watchers. Last night, we sat on the roof and thought about nebulas.

No, that's not dirty (get your mind out of the gutter and into the sky).

A nebula is where a star is born. It's all the junk that has to come together — dust, helium, hydrogen, ionized gases — to create the right conditions for a star. Think about it: There are so many stars in the sky, we can't even count them — it'd be like counting every grain of sand on the beach. Still, they aren't just up there. It takes something, the exact right sort of condition, to make a star. It got us thinking about how everything in life needs a nebula. If we don't have the right sort of conditions, what chance do we have?

See you tonight, under the sky.

two

The next morning, Hollywood descended on Little. We lived two blocks from the café, but I could already hear the purr of generators the moment I stepped out onto the front porch of our house. I studied the line of pines behind the Victorians across the street, green but dry against a pale morning sky. The air already warm, I took the steps two at a time, giving our black Lab, Extra Pickles, a quick pat where he lay sprawled on our front walk.

My mom was packing our white VW van on the street in front of our house.

"Need help?" I watched her heave a container full of what looked like pretzels into the back. "Are those pretzels?"

"Snacks for the volunteers." She wiped at a glisten of sweat on her forehead and tightened her ponytail, a mirror version of mine. Tall and athletic, her dark hair streaked from days in the sun, Mom could pass for thirty even if that was how old she was when she had me. She never wore makeup and mined all her clothes from the local consignment shops. To me, she always looked pretty, even with her face constantly creased with worry for whatever current cause she'd embraced.

If my mom were a superhero (and she kind of was), she'd be

Activist Mom. Not for a specific cause, but more in a massive save-the-whole-world sort of way. If there was a protest — anti-war, pro-education, save the yellow-spotted tree frog — chances were, my mother was out hoisting a hand-lettered sign above her head. She followed about a zillion blogs, and since I'd started high school she often left for a week or two at a time, coming back with pictures of mounds of protesters curled in sleeping bags on the street, or with her arm slung around some guy who called himself Harvest and was protesting an evil chemical used on crops somewhere flat and brown.

It actually drove my older brother, John, kind of nuts. Not me, though. At least she believed in a better world. Wanted to do something about it. It was a lot better than some of my friends' moms who seemed like they only cared about the theme of the prom or plastering their kids' walls with SAT words. Sometimes, if I wasn't too busy, I went with her. Not in the summer, though. Dad needed me at the café.

She stopped packing, her eyes falling on me, casually taking in my denim skirt and fitted white T-shirt, both finds from one of her consignment raids. "You heading to the café?"

"Yeah."

She tried to keep her face neutral. "I thought maybe you'd want to stop by Stagelights? See what Nicky's up to for the summer?"

Not this again. Nicky had been my teacher at Stagelights, my former dance studio where I'd spent the better part of my child-hood. Until I'd quit. My parents knew enough to stop bringing it up. Or at least they *usually* did.

"It's hard to believe it's been over a year since you've checked in with him," she pushed.

"Mom," I warned.

She fiddled with a pile of blankets in the back of the VW. "It's still just so strange not to see you dancing at all."

"I teach my class at Snow Ridge Senior Living."

She grinned. "And that's lovely, even if they mostly can't move."

I tried to keep the smile out of my voice. "Don't mock the elderly, Mom. It's rude."

"Okay, okay, I was just *asking*. No need to make a federal case out of it." A huge *clank* downtown sounded through the morning air, and we both started, our eyes straying to something mechanical we couldn't see but could suddenly hear. She made a face. "Ugh, Hollywood. Glad I'm heading out." She slammed the back door of the van.

I shot her a look that said, *Please, no Hollywood rants.* While I was indifferent to Hollywood, Mom *hated* it. Chloe had learned not to bring it up at our house when she was over for dinner unless she wanted a six-part thesis on Hollywood's waste, its gluttony, its vapid lack of regard for the *working man*. Of course, Dad would often remind Mom with his easy smile, "There are plenty of working men in Hollywood, Rose, honey. And women."

Sighing, I leaned against the side of the van, peering into its depths; Mom had it stuffed with supply boxes, blankets, sleeping bags, and donated clothes.

Hands on her hips, she followed my gaze. "Maybe I shouldn't go. The café is so busy right now. And your brother might need me." She chewed at her lip.

This was her ritual. She cited reasons for not going, and we assured her it would be fine if she did. I hugged her. "It's fine. Go."

13

Waving out the open window, she drove away down our tree-lined street.

After seeing Mom off, I headed down our street and crossed to Pine, maneuvering through a couple of STREET CLOSED signs. Halfway up Pine, three huge semitrucks loomed giant and white, coils of wire spilling from them and snaking their way toward Main Street. A small crowd had gathered near the Pine View Apartments, everyone whispering and pointing at the trucks.

Among them, I could see Alien Drake standing on the sidewalk, surveying the white trucks the way he studied the night sky. He'd probably walked Chloe to work at Little Eats that morning. Even if they'd been together six months, I was still getting used to him as Chloe's boyfriend and not just as my best friend. He and I had, after all, grown up together two houses away and had sleepouts in my backyard every summer since we were five, when he moved to Little from Maui. Watching him standing there slurping an iced mocha, I tried not to miss the times he used to walk me to work instead of Chloe.

"Morning, stargazer," I called to him, and he walked toward me away from the crowd, waving a greeting. No matter how late we stayed out watching the sky at night, Alien Drake never looked tired.

He wore his usual uniform, a black hoodie and Bermuda shorts that drooped past his round knees. "Loud enough for you?" He motioned to the trucks with his iced mocha. I could tell Chloe had made it for him because it had *I LOVE YOU!!!!!* written in Sharpie across the side.

I gave him a quick one-armed hug. "I just sent you some ideas for the blog."

"Cool." He took a long drink of his mocha, draining half of it.

Alien Drake and I wrote a sky blog called *Yesterday's Sightings* that we'd started last fall as juniors. The blog was mostly the stuff we talked about while we stargazed. Drake was obsessed with the possibility of life beyond Earth (hence his nickname), and even though I'd never fully believed in all his UFO stuff, I didn't *not* believe in it — if that made sense. Plus, stargazing was fun year-round even if it was most fun in the summer when the hot days cooled and we could lie on Alien Drake's roof and "space out." Drake was way into the science versus myth side of it, so we learned stuff about aliens and space, but mostly it was just nice to sprawl out on his roof or a field somewhere, the sky an onyx, jeweled sheet above us. There was nothing quite like the stars to remind me how small I was compared to the vast black sky and, somehow, that nightly reminder relaxed me.

"Speaking of alien life . . ." I nudged Alien Drake and nodded toward the trucks. "We've been invaded."

"Definitely beings from another planet." Even with his wide face, his smile seemed barely to fit it. Alien Drake credited his Hawaiian genes with the fact that he was almost always relaxed and happy. He was like a people version of a therapy dog. Perfect for Chloe. Who often needed relaxing. And therapy. It also made him the world's best friend. He drained his mocha. "You got big plans today? Working?"

"I'm on sandwich duty today."

"Exciting."

"Yes, very exciting. Bread. Turkey. Tomatoes. Lettuce. It's a science." He knew, maybe more than anyone, how much I loved working at Little Eats. And I especially loved being on sandwich duty, the steady rhythm of assembly. Preparing large quantities of food was its own sort of meditation.

"Well, I'm heading to the river." He popped the plastic lid off the mocha and fished out an ice cube to chew on. "You should come out after you finish your scientific duties."

I quirked a half smile. "Your girlfriend is dragging me in search of the infamous Adam Jakes."

He raised his bushy eyebrows. "You going to help her raid his cooler for more ice?"

"I'm just there for support. She'll need me to prop her up when she faints from sheer amazement at his otherworldly presence." I rolled my eyes, knowing I was standing next to perhaps the one person who cared even less than I did about celebrities.

His smile slackened, barely noticeable. "Carter Moon: Celebrity Support. You should have T-shirts made. Even better, you should come to the river."

We stood for a minute, watching the idling trucks. I couldn't believe I'd agreed to go stand around staring at a film set when I could be going to the river. Which is what I really wanted to do. I wanted to sit in a pool of sunlight and read, my feet in the green water.

"For the record," he said, "I'm taking it personally." His eyes scanned a group of guys hauling equipment from the back of one of the trucks. "Your choosing Chloe over me."

I knew he was kidding, but I couldn't help the snag in my belly. I didn't tell him I could pretty much say the same thing to him. Not that Alien Drake and I could ever be more than friends. Chloe knew this, which was why I could be a third wheel with them. Alien Drake and I had tried that once in the winter of eighth grade, a kiss on his roof bundled under his mom's old paisley bedspread as we watched the sky. It had been a total disaster that ended in a fit of giggles (me) and a revolted body spasm (him) that almost pitched him off the roof. Alien Drake was like a brother to me. A brother who didn't get defensive all the time.

Alien Drake rattled the ice in his cup. "Okay, sandwich scientist. I'm off, then. Text me if you change your mind and you decide to ditch Chloe and do something for yourself for once. Otherwise, see you tonight." Waving, he headed back up the street, leaving me staring into the mess Hollywood was currently making of my town.

* ✳ *

To Hollywood's credit, they seemed to work a long day. When I got to Little Eats at eight, they'd already staked out a side street nearby for some filming and had built a wire-infested, camera-ridden den of Christmas cheer: heaps of fake snow, sparkly garland draped in windows, a horse harnessed with a cheery Christmas wreath around its sweltering neck. People in shorts and T-shirts hurried about, and I caught glimpses of several actors bundled in wool coats and boots.

No sign of Adam Jakes, though.

All morning, Chloe kept casting her distracted gaze toward the bustle down the street until finally, after three dropped salads,

Dad threw her into the kitchen on dish duty and pulled me off sandwiches to take her place out front. We were busier than usual, probably because people had come downtown to see the film set, and I did my best to make up for Chloe's sudden absence from the patio. By noon, I was sweaty from racing around refilling iced teas and listening to the general buzz about the "movie people."

During a lull, I leaned against our fence and studied the trailer parked along the street across from us where the film crew seemed to go to get food, emerging with salads, drinks, and other snacks. A man who must have been an actor in the film banged out the trailer door, holding a can of Coke, wearing head-to-toe winter wool as if it were thirty degrees out.

Did it ever throw them off, jumping so quickly between fantasy and reality?

After my shift ended at three, Chloe almost pulled my arm out of its socket dragging me down to the set. At the roped-off corner of the side street leading to Main, we could see crew members moving hurriedly about, actors standing around in Christmas wear, and a few curious onlookers hanging around the edge of the rope like new swimmers. A couple of scruffy-looking guys with cameras slung around their necks checked their iPhones or smoked cigarettes.

"*Paparazzi,*" Chloe whispered. I could almost hear her heart hammering in excitement.

We waited.

And waited. For what seemed like an hour. The crowd around us ebbed and flowed as people grew weary and left, and then new onlookers joined the line. All I could think about was how good the river would feel after a day like this, the cool water tingling my tired feet.

"Oh my God!" Chloe shrieked. "It's *him*," she hissed, marking my arm with her viselike fingers. She pointed spastically, her body having some sort of celebrity-related seizure.

The cameras all lifted in unison. The bystanders took a collective intake of breath.

And, yes. There he was, emerging from the door of a shop, in a full wool coat, designer jeans tucked into Sorels, his hair the same honeyed muss as in all those pictures on Chloe's wall, his eyes bright even from a hundred feet away.

Adam Jakes.

He turned toward us and gave a sort of half wave, half shrug. Chloe let out the kind of squeal a five-year-old makes on Christmas morning and tried to get the zoom function to work on her iPhone. I studied him as he talked with the man Chloe claimed was his manager, the British Pisces. Adam Jakes frowned at something Parker Hill was saying and gave a little neck roll like he was prepping for a boxing match.

"We love you, Adam!" screeched a woman far too old to be screeching at teen actors; she leaned into the rope, waving madly.

Ignoring her, Adam Jakes disappeared back into the shop, like one of those lions at the zoo that makes a quick appearance before going back into the cave to lunch on some sort of severed piece of meat.

Sweat trickled down my back. "Can we go now? You saw him."

Chloe's eyes were fixed on the door Adam Jakes had disappeared behind.

"Chloe?"

She didn't take her eyes off the set. "I'm going to see if he comes out again."

"Then I'm going to the river," I told her transfixed frame. "Blink twice if you can hear me." No blinks. Shaking my head, I left her standing there. I'd grab a drink at Eats and head to the river to meet Alien Drake. That was enough celebrity sightings for one day. Or for one life, for that matter.

* ✳ *

Inside Little Eats, Dad stood at the counter, his back to me, talking to a woman I didn't recognize. He turned at the swish of the kitchen door. "Hey, you. Back so soon?"

"Just grabbing a drink and heading to the river." I filled a cup with ice and tried not to stare at the counter woman.

Her dark hair was shot through with gray and frizzed out around her head like she'd stuck her finger in a wall socket. She had a pair of reading glasses hanging from a chain, wore a pair of purple-rimmed glasses on her face, and had two more pairs of sunglasses stuck into her frizz. She was like a walking LensCrafters. "So," she said to Dad. "You can help me out?"

"I can make a couple calls. Maybe pull off some chicken Caesars, maybe some cheese plates, some cookies." She nodded enthusiastically. Dad turned to me, his eyes the only thing betraying that he'd been here since five a.m. "Can you hang out for a second?"

"Sure." I poured some lemonade over the ice and took a long swallow.

The woman scribbled a number on a napkin. "Here's my cell and, seriously, thanks for this." She hurried out the front door.

"What's up?" I asked, setting my cup down on the counter.

Dad picked up the phone and started to dial. "The movie people need a second meal."

"What was wrong with their first one?" I dragged a busing tray to several of the blond wood four-tops that needed clearing.

He clamped the phone between his ear and shoulder. "They're running overtime and need to contract out for some extra food." He disappeared into the back, emerging again with three huge bowls we used for mixing salads.

I stopped loading up the gray tub with dishes. "For tonight?"

He nodded, then said into the phone, "Henry, it's Mike Moon, over at Little Eats. Any chance you can have Steve run over some romaine heads? Yeah, now. For the movie people." He laughed at something Henry must have said on the other end. "Yeah, right?" He motioned for me to leave the busing. "Can you make some Caesar dressing?"

Bye-bye, river trip. I disappeared into the kitchen.

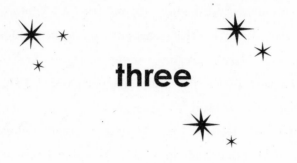

three

After I helped Dad organize the movie people's second meal and did all the dishes, I drove an extra salad over to my brother at the Fast Mart. The night had cooled, and I shivered as bits of stars began to peek through the dark. I watched him through the scratched glass of the storefront. My brother — tall, broad shoulders in an ash-colored T-shirt, his dark hair curling around his ears. He hadn't noticed me yet, so he didn't have a chance to put on the face he'd light just for me. The face he got before saying, "Hey, little sis."

The face he wanted me to think was his real face.

He was on the phone, his features pinched. Turning to lean against the counter, he caught sight of me, his eyes widening. He held up a single finger. *One minute*, he motioned. *Wait.*

I turned from the window, studying the only other car in the lot. A tricked-out white Honda sedan. A group of guys in beater tanks laughed at something they were watching on one of their phones. T.J. Shay's friends. Which meant T.J. was somewhere inside Fast Mart. My stomach clenched.

As if on cue, T.J. sauntered up to the counter, waiting for my brother to get off the phone. He dumped his bag of Cheetos and bottle of Mountain Dew on the counter. T.J. and my brother had been friends in elementary school, but by the time they hit middle school T.J. had traded his Magic cards for 40s stashed in brown paper sacks. By high school, he'd pretty much dubbed himself the king of that certain group of rural white boys who fancied themselves gangsters. He'd tricked out his car and taken to cutting class to hang with his older brother, Cory, who ran some sort of questionable "yard work" business but who never seemed to do much more than occupy his garage.

Suddenly, T.J. reached across the counter and grabbed the phone from my brother, who slouched back against the lottery machine. T.J. nodded, said something to my brother, punctuating whatever it was by chucking the phone at him. Seconds later, he pushed through the doors, clearly not paying for his snacks.

I tried to keep my face blank.

As he sauntered by, T.J. gave me a brief once-over. "Carter," he leered.

"T.J." I didn't look at him. Eye contact with T.J. Shay usually required a shower afterward.

The Honda squealed out of the lot as my brother joined me on the sidewalk.

"Hey, little sis." John pulled me into a bright-faced hug, smelling of cigarettes and mint gum like he always did.

"What did T.J. want?" I noticed the stains of a fading bruise under John's left eye.

"Just needed to use the phone." He angled his eye away from me.

"Did you remind him you talk into it rather than chuck it? I mean, I know he's not the sharpest knife in the drawer, but it's really a simple sort of function." I held my hand to my ear like a phone.

John half smiled and avoided answering. "You see any of the movie people yet?"

"They're all over downtown like ants. You can't miss them."

He lit a cigarette behind his hand, as if it was the thing being kept secret. "Did you see the famous one, the actor?"

I shrugged. "Chloe dragged me to the set today, and he came out of a shop for about five seconds." A stray lock of hair had escaped my ponytail, and I tucked it behind my ear.

"That is so cool. I bet he's loaded. How much money do you think he has on him at all times?" John stared off in the direction of T.J.'s exit.

I shrugged, not at all liking the direction of this conversation. "I'm not really privy to Adam Jakes's financial habits."

John flicked some ash in the general direction of the outside garbage can. "Maybe he'll come into the café."

"Actually, Dad and I ended up making a bunch of salads and stuff for the set tonight." I'd smell like garlic for two days to prove it.

He looked impressed. "Seriously? Like working for them? You should have called me."

"You were here." I didn't mention Dad wouldn't have offered him any work even if it hadn't been last minute. "We just helped out — some salads, a cheese plate, some cookies. We had about an hour to pull it off. It's not like we're dining daily with Adam Jakes and his entourage." I coughed loudly and made a show of waving the smoke away from my face.

He blew the next stream of smoke to the side. "Can you

imagine having that much money? How much do you think he carries around with him?"

"What did T.J. want?" I asked again.

His eyes darkened.

"Who was that on the phone?" I tried to get him to look at me.

He stubbed out his cigarette, turning serious eyes on me, his body tense. "You a reporter now? You doing a cover story?"

I watched the sky as it bruised with evening, slipping toward black, a thin slash of pale light still lining the horizon of pine trees like a halo. Even from the crappy Fast Mart, our town could be so beautiful. No wonder they wanted to shoot a Christmas movie here. Maybe they came just to film that sky. I held up the salad. "Have you eaten? I brought you some extra."

He relaxed his shoulders, tapping out another cigarette but not lighting it. "I can eat something here."

"Nutritious." I chewed my lip, already feeling the air loosening between us, and held the salad to him. "Come on, despite the obvious appeal of a Ho Ho and Funyuns dinner, you love Caesar salad."

He pulled his free hand from his jeans pocket. "Thanks, sis," he said, taking the bag. "I do love me some Caesar."

The phone began echoing inside the Fast Mart, its trill muffled. His eyes darted toward the sound. "I gotta get back."

I didn't stick around to watch him answer it.

I preferred my brother's fake face.

* ✳ *

The light in my closet had burned out. I ran to the basement, grabbed a box of bulbs, and, returning, scooted a chair close enough so I could replace it. Extra Pickles watched me intently from his perch on my bed, his tail thumping. "There," I told him, the closet flooding with light. He wagged his approval. I searched the shelves for the old quilt I wanted to bring for star watching tonight. As I pulled it from the top shelf, a pale satin bag slipped out with it, landing first on my head, and then on the floor beside me. A familiar tug pulled at my chest. Reaching down, I picked it up, the fabric slippery in my hands.

My dance bag.

I'd shoved it back there over a year ago, not wanting to throw it out with some of my other dance stuff. I turned it over, running my fingers over the frayed dark blue stitching of my name in the bottom corner. Inside, I could feel the rounded lump of my first pair of pointe shoes. Mom had made the bag out of the costume I'd worn in *The Nutcracker* the first time I danced Snow, the ice-blue satin almost white. She'd stitched my first name and appliquéd a lemon slice of moon next to that, a few bright stars pocking the fabric around it. I'd carried it to class almost every day for five years.

I tried to push the ache back down, away from where it pawed at my heart, remembering Mom's suggestion about checking in with Nicky. When I'd quit, I'd filled two black garbage bags with leotards, costumes, shoes, and posters, and told Mom to donate them, but I couldn't get rid of this bag or those shoes inside it, so I'd pushed them far and away and forgotten about them behind the quilt.

"Carter? You coming?" Chloe called up the stairs. "What're you doing?"

"Nothing!" I hid the bag between some hanging clothes. "Be right there." Extra Pickles cocked his head, his ears alert. "Don't look at me like that," I told him, clicking off the light.

* ✳ *

"How's John?" Alien Drake settled down next to me on the quilt. Chloe peeked out from behind the telescope he'd positioned for her, eyebrows raised.

We didn't usually talk about my brother, but they knew I'd just seen him. I studied the stretch of dark sky above me, my eyes soothed by the dim twinkle of stars, the cool bath of night air. "It's been pretty mellow for a while, which worries me. You know John. He goes through waves."

Alien Drake gave my arm a squeeze, then moved on to dig through the grocery bag we'd hauled onto the roof. After extracting a bag of Doritos, he popped them open, the air infused with sudden nacho cheese. Next door, the neighbor's sprinklers went on, drowning out the sound of the creek behind the house. "Did he end up seeing that counselor? That one your mom found?" He chewed a handful of chips. Alien Drake always seemed to devour food rather than eat it, huge quantities disappearing in seconds.

"He did. At least we think he did." My parents didn't go with him to the meetings anymore. "He said he did."

I didn't miss the look Chloe and Alien Drake exchanged.

At sixteen John had been diagnosed as a compulsive gambler and had spent the last three years in and out of various support programs. He'd burned through too much money to count and had severed most of his relationship with my parents when he'd stolen

27

from the café safe at the end of my sophomore year. Chloe and Alien Drake had gone through most of it with me, talking to me when I wanted to talk, but also just knowing when to *not* talk about it.

Right now was starting to feel like one of those times.

"That's good," Chloe offered, peering back into the telescope.

Alien Drake must have sensed my unease because he changed the subject. "Oh, I was going to tell you, I had a great idea for our blog."

Relieved, I sat up. "What is it?"

"Well, obviously we should mention something about Hollywood being here. Sky stars. Movie stars. It'd be a good topic." Chloe and I waited for him to elaborate; sometimes it took a while to see where Alien Drake was going with an idea.

Crunching chips, he said, "So I was reading on *Universe Today* that the most massive stars are often the shortest lived." He went on to explain that we could write about how many movie stars often burn big and bright but flame out. "It's an interesting comparison, right?" He tilted his head, waiting for our response. "I mean, especially considering what a mess Adam Jakes is."

He had a point. I pulled a notebook into my lap so I could jot down some ideas. Adam Jakes was the most famous thing to walk into our town in the last decade partly because of his storied past. Chloe had already informed us that one of the reasons they were shooting a Christmas movie in June was because Adam Jakes had been in rehab the past few months.

Chloe, always quick to defend her beloved Hollywood,

frowned at us. "You know, a lot of celebrities get better. I read somewhere that Adam Jakes is really trying to focus on his career again. That's why he's doing *A Christmas Cheryl*."

We stared at her blankly.

"The movie they're shooting right now." Annoyance crept into her voice. "It's a remake of *A Christmas Carol*. It's supposed to be a really sweet family movie."

"A really sweet publicity stunt." Alien Drake stuffed another handful of chips into his mouth.

Chloe shrugged. "You don't know that."

Alien Drake chewed. "Sure I do. This is his management's serious attempt to get him through phase four."

Chloe rolled her eyes. "Is this the Alien Drake Five Phases of Child Celebrity theory?"

He grinned. "Why, yes, it is. Thanks for asking."

A theory of Alien Drake's I hadn't heard? "What is that?"

Chloe groaned. "Don't encourage him."

Alien Drake chewed another mound of chips. "Phase one: adorable child actor in a well-known series or film."

"Check." I smiled.

"Phase two: branches out, enters teen years, people who care about that sort of thing hold their breath." He nodded exaggeratedly at Chloe, who stuck out her tongue at him.

"Check." I held up two fingers.

"Phase three: the train wreck of predictable behavior. Clubs, drugs, depression, rehab. Fill in the blank with disorder of choice."

Chloe was trying not to laugh. "You're a very cynical young man, Mr. Masuda."

I held up a third finger.

He grinned at Chloe before continuing. "Phase four: the comeback."

"A lot of them make comebacks, real ones," Chloe insisted. "People like a comeback story."

"Did you read that in *Celebrity Comebacks*, the paperback edition?" Alien Drake crumpled the chip bag, stuffing it back into the brown sack.

She made a face. "Some of us *who care about that sort of thing* do like a comeback. You know, real, honest-to-God comebacks. Not everyone hates Hollywood like you two."

"Hey, I love movies!" I told her. "We don't *hate* Hollywood."

"Yeah, we do," Alien Drake said. "I love movies, too, but Hollywood and movies are not the same thing." He reached for Chloe's hand. "But we definitely adore you."

Chloe popped open another bag of chips, keeping it just out of his reach, but then she slipped her hand into his and tilted the chips toward him as a peace offering. "I know."

"So Adam Jakes is clearly in phase four?" I asked.

"Obviously," Chloe said, grinning at Alien Drake's bemused look. "What? Even I have to admit, it's a pretty good theory."

"And what's phase five?" I sipped my water, waiting.

Alien Drake hesitated, twining his fingers tighter around Chloe's. "Phase five has two branches. Either they figure it out, or they burn out, supernova style. In which case, the only place we'd ever see them again is on some third-rate reality TV show."

"So phase four is kind of the key, sort of determines if the star burns out," I said, and Alien Drake nodded, staring up at the dark sky.

I thought about Adam Jakes, emerging like a zoo animal from the shop today, barely blinking away his bored expression; thought about all his bad press, his strained face all over the magazine covers. "Given the particular movie star in our sky right now, I think it's a great idea for the blog. The life cycle of a star."

Was that what we saw today? The fading embers of Adam Jakes?

four

The next day, Hollywood returned. Only this time, they caused a bit more of a stir, shutting down two main streets and blocking access to a stretch of shops. I could see the flurry of activity from where I stood in the patio of Little Eats. I knew our locals and it wouldn't be long before they started getting grumpy.

Little was named after Daniel Little, a miner who'd struck it rich on gold in the 1800s. The Daniel Little house, now a hotel, sat like a sky-blue Buddha at the top point of Main and Pine Streets, the arms of the Little triangle meeting Gold Street at the bottom. Each year, tourists flooded Little, taking pictures of it, painting it, or just wandering through its restaurants, shops, the winery's tasting room, or Mountain Books. "Where are the billboards?" they would wonder as they sat in our patio, stabbing at a Cobb salad. "It's so cute," they would sigh to me as I refilled their iced teas. "You must love living here," they would say.

Thing was, I did love living here. And I didn't mind the tourists the way some of the locals did. They were a huge part of our café, and they gave me a constant reminder of how lucky I was to live here.

A flurry on the sidewalk caught my eye. Speaking of locals, I watched six of them, backs straight and packed like bowling pins, storm by the café, their arms full of poster boards taped to yardsticks. Protesters. Already?

Then I noticed Nora Trent, thin as a birch tree and six feet tall. John sometimes joked that Nora could just fasten her protest poster to a hat and she'd actually look like a picket sign. Nora was a constant fixture at our house, and she often helped Mom with some cause or another; still, she always seemed to resent being second in command, and with Mom off in the Central Valley, Nora could run her own show.

And now she was heading toward the movie set.

Mom would never have wasted her time on a soft issue like Hollywood. Gripe about it? Sure. Roll her eyes at it. Absolutely. But *protest* it? Never. Mom wasn't a bumpkin, and she wouldn't act like it by toting a picket sign down to a movie set. Rose Moon would see the bigger picture, would know the kind of money coming into Little would be good for future causes like parks and stream cleanup. So unless Hollywood started mistreating animals or dumping chemicals in the river, Mom would stay out of their way.

It wasn't like I was siding with Hollywood, but they didn't need Nora Trent gumming up their set, and honestly, it was embarrassing to Little. Maybe it was the sweet card that Debra (the frizzy-headed stressball from last night) had left taped to our window this morning gushing about the salads, or maybe I just felt like Nora was getting a bit big for her britches with Mom gone; either way, I pushed through our gate, following Nora and her gang to the edge of the roped-off section of Main.

"Hi, Nora." I tucked my hands into the pockets of my shorts. "Pretty cool, huh? A movie being filmed here."

"Hmmm," Nora replied distractedly, holding her hand flat like a visor, scanning the busy crew, her eyes flicking like some sort of human tracking system, cataloging the number of cables, vans, lights, set additions, and mentally calculating their total environmental impact.

I tried a different tactic. "I thought you were going with Mom."

"No, no. Someone needs to stay here." She directed the five other women to set up next to Foothill Realty.

Nodding, I noticed Adam's manager standing near one of the vans. Parker Hill. He watched us, his glasses pushed into his hair, his eyes narrowed. "Sure, okay. Make sure Hollywood doesn't push its big-business attitude around here, right?"

Her face brightened. "Exactly." She patted my shoulder.

"Keep corporate out of Little," I added.

She gave a quick nod. "Your mom's doing a good job with you, honey."

Parker took a couple steps toward us, obviously listening.

I cleared my throat. "Um, okay, no offense, Nora, but where is everyone? I mean, six of you? Seems like an off day for you, really."

Nora bit her lip, her eyes sliding to the five women, one of whom was using her sign to fan her face. "Carter, I don't have to explain to *you* that protest is about being a voice, even a small one."

I nodded agreeably. "Totally, of course. But don't you want to plan a *bit* more, figure out what it is you're trying to say?" I motioned to a short, wiry woman almost as tall as her sign. "I mean, her sign's in pencil," I whispered. "That's kind of amateur hour, Nora."

Nora's sign dipped.

"You guys should come up to the café. I'll pour you some iced tea and you can strategize. I mean, what are you even protesting?" I asked, motioning to a sign that just read: NO, HOLLYWOOD, NO! "No what, Nora? No what? It's not very well thought out." I started up the hill a few steps, hoping I could pull her with shame and the offer of free drinks.

Nora hesitated, just a moment; then she turned on a heel to round up her drooping group. Shaking my head (that was too easy), I started for the café, but not before catching Parker's eye. He tipped an imaginary hat at me and gave a little bow.

* ✳ *

I flipped the sign to read CLOSED (COME TOMORROW!) and lowered the front shade. A few seconds later, a tap on the door startled me, and I zipped the shade back up, coming face-to-face through the glass with Adam's manager, Parker Hill, his green eyes smiling, his hand raised in greeting.

I let him in. "Did you need a drink or something?"

He stepped into the cool café. "Actually, I need to speak with you. It's Carter, yes?"

"Yeah." How did he know my name? My cheeks warmed at the way he said it in his charcoaled British accent. I was such a sucker for it. Too much PBS *Masterpiece* and Jane Austen movies.

"You have a moment?" He let his gaze float around the café.

"Sure." I motioned to a table, my stomach fluttering.

He sat, slipping his iPhone from his pocket and resting it on the table.

I chewed my lip. "You want something? I just turned the machine off, but I could make you an iced tea."

"Lovely."

I hurried to pour some lemon tea over ice, garnishing it with a fresh sprig of mint, and setting it on the table in front of him.

He didn't touch it. Scrolling through his iPhone, he motioned for me to sit across from him.

I slid into the chair, gazing at all the busing that still needed to be done on the other tables around us, at the bulging piles of dishes already on the busing cart. I would be here a while tonight.

He looked up from his screen. "Charming place." He made a vague motion in the air with his hand. I studied all the pictures on the walls, all the paintings and photos Dad had collected — different shots of diners or cafés we'd discovered over the years. No matter how many we found, he just kept hanging them up, so not much wall space remained. The collection must be well over a hundred prints by now. I almost didn't notice it anymore.

"We like it."

Parker's eyes fell on me. "That was quite clever today. With those protesters. Thanks for helping us out."

"Believe me, I was helping them out, too. They were about to look like idiots."

"Anyway, the point of my visit is that it got me thinking." When I didn't respond, he cleared his throat and leaned on the table with his forearms. "Listen, this is going to sound a bit strange, and I'm hoping you take it the proper way because it's really a compliment."

My neck prickled the way it did when John was about to lie to me about something. "Okay."

Parker glanced around the empty café as if making sure it wouldn't suddenly turn into a massive recording device. "We'd like to hire you."

"You mean, like more Caesar salads?" They must have really liked my dressing.

He gave his head a little shake. "Not exactly. I mean *you*."

"Me?" I picked at an unused napkin someone had left on the table. "I'm not really an actor or anything."

Nodding, he leaned even farther forward, comically forward, like he might take a nap right on top of the table. "Which is why it's bloody perfect. It's not acting. More like just your average make-believe. Do you fancy fairy tales, Carter?"

"I guess."

"Well, you're about to be the princess in one, if you say yes." He took a deep breath. "We'd like you to pretend to be Adam's girlfriend while he's shooting in Little."

Had I heard that right? "*Pretend* to be his girlfriend?"

He studied me closely, narrowing his eyes. "Just for a few weeks."

"From what I've read, Adam Jakes doesn't have a hard time getting girlfriends." The normal hums and clicks of the café grew suddenly loud around me. I gave a nervous sort of laugh. "I mean, he's a movie star."

Parker's face shifted like clouds gathering. "Then I'm sure, if you've read about Adam, you know he got into a right spot of trouble a few months ago."

I almost laughed; from what I'd read, "a right spot of trouble" was like saying the *Titanic* hit a bit of an ice cube. "Um, yeah."

Then Parker launched into what could only be described as a sales pitch. Adam's "people" thought it might be good for his image if he spent some time with a "small-town girl with proper values." Someone, Parker explained, who'd make it look like he was mending his ways, someone people could really fall in love with. "We think you're the girl, Carter. You're a perfect cast."

"I wasn't aware I was auditioning." I stood, crossing to the rack of chips and granola bars, fiddling with them just so he wouldn't see my hands shaking.

He leaned back in his chair, appraising me. "It's not dirty or inappropriate. Strictly PG stuff. Pure Disney. Hand holding. Some walks with your dog."

He knew I had a dog?

Standing, he slipped his iPhone back into the frayed pocket of his jeans. I'm sure he'd paid extra for that fraying. "We're just asking you to hang out with the bloke for a few weeks. Millions of other birds would kill for this sort of offer."

Ugh. Everything bad about Hollywood started with some version of that line. "I'm not millions of other *birds*." Okay, that also sounded like something a girl in this exact position was supposed to say. I crossed my arms, shrugging. "Look, this is really weird. And . . . flattering, I guess. But I'm sorry. I'm just not interested." I forced myself to make eye contact with him.

The pale light swirling through the windows bathed his face. "Might be some good connections, too. You'll be a senior in the fall, yes? Could be a good way to see what life has to offer outside this place."

Now he was just being condescending. I started collecting the plates someone had left on the counter. "Some people do actually *choose* to live here."

He looked like he might say something else but thought otherwise. "So, you're saying no?"

"Right. I'm saying no." I dumped the plates in a busing tray.

He gave me a look close to respect. "Well, that's new. We're not used to hearing no in Adam's world. Rather, when it's not coming from a studio. I mean, if they could fuel their Priuses on the collective desperation in that town, we'd solve a major global crisis." He chuckled at his own cleverness. Pausing, he cocked his head to the side. "Is it Priuses? Or Priusi?" More chuckling.

Geez. This guy was in love with himself. I migrated back to the perfectly stacked granola bars. If he were any reflection of Adam Jakes, I wouldn't want to hang out with Adam for three minutes, much less the next three weeks.

Parker nodded as if I'd asked him to leave. "Listen, love, take the night to think about it. No need to decide now. We'll ring you in the morning. Or you can ring me." He left a cream business card on the counter. "Oh, and we'd appreciate your discretion."

"You don't want people thinking Adam can't get his own dates?" I tried to sound glib, but my voice shook.

He heard it. With a wide smile that didn't reach his eyes, he told me, "I'm just asking for a little discretion. This was merely an idea we thought we'd look into." He looked around the café. "This can't be an easy place to run, and I understand you've had some, well, financial trouble with your brother. Perhaps this could help with that."

Heat flooded my face. "I think you should go."

"It would be easy work, and we'd pay you quite handsomely." He handed me a slip of paper with a number on it. A *large* number.

I balked, staring at it. "Is this for real?"

"Please." He frowned, slipping his sunglasses down off the top of his head, turning his eyes to mirrors. "Of course it's real, love. What did you say earlier to that protester? It's not amateur hour."

The paper felt heavy in my hands. "You know, entire families in Little live on this kind of money for a whole year."

He grinned. "Not in my world. Cheers." Then he left, the café bell jingling behind him.

The lights in Chloe's pool cast the world in a pale green glow. Behind us, the drip system for her mother's rose garden whispered on, soaking the dirt rings around their gnarled trunks. I drifted in the center of the pool on a clear raft, the interconnecting pockets of the raft also glowing. Chloe had some soft indie folk I didn't recognize playing low on the stereo and it glazed the air around me, putting me in a trance.

Something cold hit my back. Chloe was chucking ice cubes from her Diet Coke at me. "Did you hear me? Earth to Moon." This was one of Alien Drake's and Chloe's favorite things to say to me when I zoned out. Of course, with a last name like Moon, I'd heard far worse.

"I heard you." I flipped over, the raft swaying in the night water.

"Okay, so you're just ignoring me."

Above me, the stars arched their twinkling backs. "How long does it take him to heat up a pizza? I told Dad I'd be home by midnight." I watched the door, where Alien Drake had disappeared almost a half hour before. We hadn't seen him since.

"He's probably talking to my dad about the UFO sighting in Scotland," Chloe said, an ice cube plunking into the pool next to me. "Did you see him today?"

"A UFO?"

Another near miss with an ice cube, this one with more velocity. "I was at that stupid set for two hours and no sign of him."

The night had cooled, and I shivered on the raft. I paddled my way toward the side. "You sure it was the set that was stupid?"

Chloe was curled up on a squishy lounge chair, a huge towel around her. She lowered her voice. "Come on, Carter, I can't talk about him around Drake. He gets mad."

"Because you're lusting after a guy who isn't him? How dare he." I grabbed at the side of the pool, steadying myself.

"He's a *movie star*. He obviously has nothing to worry about."

"Drake or Adam?"

Chloe glared at me through the shadows. I couldn't actually see her, but I could feel her glaring. "Well, not everyone can be so above it all, Ms. Small Town U.S.A."

The back door slammed, the smell of pizza drifting across the pool. "Right now, I'm Ms. Starving U.S.A." I pulled myself onto the side of the pool, the raft drifting away like a ghost to the center again. I went over to where Alien Drake had rested the pizza on the low brick wall that ran the length of the pool. "Mmmm . . . Want one?" I held out a slice to Chloe, a saucy peace offering.

"Yes, please! Yum," she said, taking a bite, then giggling as a long string of cheese fastened itself between the slice and her chin. Alien Drake handed her a napkin. He settled into a lounge chair next to her, half the pizza in a heap on his plate.

I listened to them chewing and talking about the UFO sighting in Scotland. In the ease of the moment, here in the night glow of the pool, I almost told them, Parker's offer bubbling up like lava, but I stopped myself. I knew I couldn't tell them. Chloe would freak out and think I should do it, and I'd never hear the end of the surely relentless mocking from Alien Drake.

Sighing, I chewed my piece of pizza and stared out over the pool. Alien Drake shot me a look. "You okay?"

Before I could answer, my cell buzzed. I reached for it. Dad calling. "Hello?"

"Where are you?"

My skin tingled at the tense tremble of his voice. "I'm at Chloe's."

"Is John, by any chance, with you?"

"No."

Dad sighed into the phone. "Okay."

"Why? What happened?"

"Just come to the café." He hung up.

* ✳ *

Someone had thrown something through the front window of the café, the part with the cream-and-black etching of LITTLE EATS. When I got there, John sat on the curb in a pool of light from the streetlamp, his face in his hands, and Dad spoke with a dark-haired

42

policeman I didn't recognize. Dad had turned on the lights inside the café, but most of the outside felt shadowed and strange. It wasn't often I saw the café at midnight.

I sat down next to John. "What happened?"

He motioned behind him. "Someone threw a brick through the window."

Obviously. I forced my voice to sound patient. "Do we know who?" I watched Dad, his face sagging, his gaze clouded and sad.

John's eyes darted like bats away from mine. "How would I know?"

He knew. My brother's eyes did that every time he lied. Once, after Halloween when I was six and he was eight, he ate every last Snickers out of my candy bag and then lied about it, said they hadn't made Snickers in Fun Size that year, his eyes laser-tagging all over the place.

Lately, I just called him on it, a recent development he did not care for. "You're lying."

"Shut up, Carter." He sank his face into his hands again.

Maybe it was the shadows. Or the dark quiet of downtown. Maybe it was the stretch of glinting sky that didn't change above me no matter what was happening down here on Earth, but I asked him, for the first time, "How much money do you owe T.J. Shay?"

He pushed himself up, scowling. "Don't get involved. This is none of your business, and it's not Mom and Dad's business."

Next to me, the moon shimmered in shattered pieces of glass on the ground, the sky insisting on its beauty even in the broken places. "It seems like a brick through their window is their business."

43

I had pushed it too far. His face went slack, as if his eyes, nose, mouth, cheeks, and chin just sort of collectively gave up, and he turned and headed down the middle of the dark street.

* ✳ *

At home, Dad opened a beer, slumping into a chair at the kitchen table. I put a kettle on for tea and slipped into the chair next to him. "Did you call Mom?"

"No."

"No?"

He sighed. "You know how she gets."

Over the last four years, I'd watched the situation with John slowly deplete both of my parents. At first, they were confused, determined. Then, angry. Neither of them yelled, so the fights with John about his gambling, about his lying, about his stealing, stretched into the taffy-tight air of the house, low murmurs in the night when they thought I was asleep, John's voice oscillating over the years between pleading, defensiveness, apology, fatigue.

Then, after he stole from the café, something just broke, and he was "living somewhere else" or "not around for a while." In his absence, our family lived in an easy space. No drama. No tension. Just the daily rhythm of the café, of school, of regular life.

I loved my brother, but I preferred the ease of his absence.

Mostly, though, I missed our old family, the one before John started lying, stealing. Before he started betting. We were a different-shaped family then. When I was little, John was the sort of big brother all my friends wished they had. He built fairy houses with me under the shade of the old maple in the yard, hanging

44

wind chimes and scattering colored drops of glass he called dragon tears through the salt-and-pepper gravel, the light dappling him through the feathered green leaves. All through middle school I'd find notes in my dance bag taped to Snickers bars, Post-its on the bathroom mirror with funny animal pictures; and every Christmas morning, he'd wake me up early, before Mom and Dad got up, and we'd sneak downstairs and rearrange all the presents. The first time, it totally freaked Mom out because we both knew she'd never really stopped believing in Santa. Not really.

Then, somewhere along the way, it just began to change shape. Not all at once, which is why I didn't notice it at first. Like a perfectly round ball of dough that sinks and flattens, he changed our shape. I was too old for fairy houses, but everything else stopped, too. The notes stopped. The Post-its stopped. The Christmas mornings stopped. Every week, it seemed, he slipped out pieces of the life he'd built with us, breaking it down like a bird's nest in reverse, one small ribbon of string or branch at a time unwoven and carried away.

I stood now in the dim light of our night kitchen and poured hot water over a mint tea bag in a blue ceramic mug. The clock ticked on the wall. The crickets sounded through the open window of the kitchen. I stared out into the black of the backyard, at the monster form of the maple tree, at the silhouette of our garage. "Dad?"

"Yeah?"

"If T.J. doesn't get his money, will he just keep throwing bricks, or something worse?"

Dad hesitated. Occasionally, he and Mom talked about John's

gambling in passing, the way you would about something you read in the newspaper or overheard at the café. But they never really talked to me about it. About the darker pieces. They hid it away, as if it were contagious, so it didn't infect me, their whole, functioning daughter. "Much worse, honey."

"Why don't you tell the police?" My hands felt cold, even holding the warm blue mug.

"It's complicated." Dad's standard answer when he didn't know the answer. "Besides" — he pulled from his beer — "it might be easier to just pay T.J. off — get John a fresh start."

My stomach turned. I'd heard that before. How many fresh starts was a person allowed? Two? Ten? As many as it took? "Maybe we could get him back into treatment." Six months ago, he'd emerged from a place in Napa, his face smooth, his eyes two bright spots of promise, a look I recognized from days when he and I would lie in the grass and make shapes out of clouds. Like the time when cloud watching seemed entirely enough to him.

"Yeah." Dad sighed again, finishing his beer. He set the clear bottle on the table, rolling it back and forth in his hand. "I'm afraid that's a bit out of our range right now."

I pulled Parker's paper from my pocket and pushed it across the table to him, my stomach a fist. "Maybe not."

five

The next morning before we opened, Parker knocked again, and Dad let him in. Dressed casually in jeans and a T-shirt, he smiled eagerly at both of us. "All right, then? You're a go?" He didn't even seem to notice the window, the huge piece of black plastic taped over it.

"Guess you get to fill up your Prius," I mumbled from behind the counter, my hands cupped around a steaming cup of coffee.

Dad shot me a strange look, looking tired and rumpled in his Little Eats T-shirt and khaki shorts. Dad wasn't a small guy, his broad shoulders still echoing his stint on the Little football team in high school, but today he seemed like someone had taken an eraser to all his edges, diminished him.

Last night, he'd said no right away. "It's offensive."

Was it? It had weirded me out, but I didn't feel *offended*. "They're not asking me to do anything other than sell an image." Of course, I wasn't totally sure how I felt about that part of it.

"That makes you sound like a Pepsi commercial." Dad had frowned at his empty beer bottle. "Your mother would flip out."

She would. I thought about how I could explain it to Mom. "What if I was just doing it as some sort of social experiment?"

Dad widened his eyes at me. "God, have we been such horrible parents that you'd think there's a way to spin this?" He tossed the bottle into our recycle bin.

But I could feel his moral boundaries growing mutable like gum, so I pulled my last card. "I'm a responsible person, Dad. I've always been responsible. You have no reason not to trust me."

"I know." He studied a spot behind me on the wall, turning it over in his mind. "It doesn't sound like they're asking you to do anything other than hang out with the guy." He sighed. "I mean, it's not something *I'd* want to do."

"No offense, Dad, but I'm not sure that's the angle they're going for."

His gaze rested back on me. "Okay. But, before you say yes to this, I need you to think about something. You're a private girl. A *really* private girl. I'm not sure you'll like getting wrapped up in that world. It'll be very intrusive, Carter. Not just to you. They're going to dig."

"I know."

"I'm not sure you do."

"I'm not that interesting."

"You'll be who Adam Jakes is choosing, and for some sick cultural reason we'd need your mother to explain, that will make you interesting enough." He stood, the chair scraping the floor. "But I do trust you, so I'm going to let this be your call."

Now, Parker stood near the drink cases of our café, calmly reading our specials board still left over from yesterday. Catching my eye, he said, "We'll wait for Adam and go over the ground rules." He checked his phone.

"Adam's coming here?"

"Yes."

"Now?"

"Is that a problem?" Parker glanced up.

"Nope." My voice came out a squeak. I moved from behind the counter to one of the tables, sipping my coffee, the confidence I'd felt last night draining from me.

Several minutes later, Parker let Adam Jakes in through our kitchen door. Seeing him move into the café, sunglasses flashing even though the morning light was still more the blue haze of dawn than bright, anxiety flooded my body, and I wanted to take back the phone call I'd made as soon as I had woken up at four thirty this morning.

This was definitely not okay, social experiment or otherwise.

Adam Jakes stopped, pushed his glasses up into his tousled hair, and, for the first time, looked at me, a look that clearly said he'd rather be anywhere else in the world but here. I managed a wobbly smile. What must this tabloid boy — this fast-car, fast-girl, rehabed movie star — think of the brown-ponytailed small-town girl standing in front of him? Me. Carter Moon. I had knobby knees, an uneven tan, a slow car, and the hardest drug I'd ever tried was an oregano cigarette in fifth grade that made me swear off pizza for six weeks.

"Um, hey," I mustered awkwardly. "I'm Carter."

"Hi, Carter," he purred, the lights from the drink cases reflecting in the mirrored lenses perched in his hair. "Let's get the basics down; you should pay attention." His eyes darted around our café. "Do you need a minute?"

"Why would I need a minute?"

"Sometimes girls need a minute after they've met me. You know, to get over the shock." He flopped into a chair at a nearby table, suddenly absorbed in his phone.

I glanced at Parker, who sort of half frowned at Adam. Maybe I should tell him I needed a minute to get over the fact that I'd just committed to spending a huge chunk of my summer with a guy who seemed to have the social awareness of a two-year-old. Biting that gem back, I asked instead, "Do either of you want something to drink?" I shot a glance at Dad, who stood quietly behind the counter, eyes narrowed, watching Adam with the same look he got watching his 49ers botch an important football game. I could feel his mind changing, too.

Adam didn't look up from his phone. "Parker will hook me up."

Parker hurried to order a drink so long and with so many stipulations I lost track somewhere between "chai" and "soy" and "nonfat" before I refocused on Adam. My *boyfriend*. I let out a laugh that sounded like a parrot hiccupping.

This got his attention. "Something funny?"

"This."

"What?"

I made a motion with my arms as if to say, *Everything*. "This whole thing. It's pretty funny." He didn't seem to think it was too funny. I let my eyes wander the café, suddenly aware of how small it was, how some of the pictures on the walls sat askew, how the trim around the doorway leading to the bathrooms needed new paint.

Adam drummed his fingers on the table. "Are we going to do this or what? I'm in makeup soon." He motioned to the chair across from him, his eyes already back on his phone, and mumbled, "Have a seat. Don't be nervous. I know it's weird to finally meet someone you've thought about but who has no idea who you are." This was clearly something he'd said before; it had the dry-edged tone of rehearsal.

But I wasn't *nervous*. That was *not* what I was feeling. More *nauseous*. I thought about telling him where he could put his fame and his attitude; I thought about telling him I didn't think about him. The way I didn't think about my dentist or the guy who worked at the gas station. Not unless I was having my teeth cleaned or filling up my car. I wanted to tell him that, but I couldn't seem to find my voice. Adam obviously thought I was just another stupid, starstruck girl. Which made sense. Girls probably acted like idiots in front of him. Probably tossed their panties at him or worse.

Well, my panties were staying on, thank you very much. "I'm not nervous. It's more just weird than anything else. You being here. With me. This — whatever it is we're doing." I tried to laugh, but it sounded like a balloon popping.

Adam looked up from his phone, a smile twitching his mouth. "And what is it you think we're doing?"

My cheeks burned. "Nothing! We're doing nothing. We're totally PG." Great, now I sounded like Parker.

Adam's eyes flashed. "I mean, I'm open to ideas."

Behind me, Dad dropped whatever drink he'd been making. I heard the cup clatter to the counter. My tongue knotted up. Okay, fine, I was nervous. Stupid, gorgeous, stuck-up movie star. I wanted to telepathically suggest to Dad that he make Adam Jakes a nonfat-soy-chai-cyanide latte.

Parker handed Adam a white mug. Apparently, that hadn't been what Dad had dropped. "Charming banter, you two, but we really need to talk ground rules." His voice was smooth, low, like talking to a kitten. I nodded in what I hoped was a reassuring, confident manner. Most likely, my head bobbed like a chicken. As much as I hated to admit it, I couldn't seem to find my confidence. Adam Jakes, jerk or not, was still a movie star, and he just seemed to take up all the space in the room.

"Let's talk," I managed, my chest tight.

Fifteen minutes later, Parker had done all the talking, and Adam hadn't looked up from his phone. Not once. Finally, Dad showed them both out through the kitchen door, where the black Range Rover sat idling in our back lot. After closing the door behind them, Dad sat down next to me at the table, his face worried. "Maybe this isn't such a good idea."

I hoped my face didn't reflect his worry right back at him. "It's a little late now, don't you think?"

He hooked a thumb in the direction of their retreat. "I don't like that guy."

"Which one?"

"Both of them."

"They certainly love themselves." I sipped my coffee, almost cold now, and put my hand on his arm. "It'll be fine, I promise. I'll back out if I need to." I glanced at the clock. We needed to start getting ready to open. I stood. "We need more mango iced tea if you want to make it."

His gray eyes followed me. "Mom thinks she should come home."

I brought out a stack of clean mugs for the top of the espresso machine. "She doesn't need to do that." I squinted at one to see if it was too chipped to use, decided it was fine, and added it to the stack. "It might be easier if she didn't."

He bent to pick at something in the hardwood. Smashed gum. Lovely. Using a napkin to pull it up, he said, "She's a mama bear, for sure."

"More like Mama Militia Coordinator." Only that wasn't totally fair. On the phone last night, I told Mom that I was going to pose as Adam's girlfriend, and I'd expected a lecture on the moral vacuum that was young Hollywood, but instead she heard me out, heard my reasons, especially after what had happened with John yesterday. She'd been quiet for a second, then said, "You sure you want to do this?" I could see her, curled on the bed of the van somewhere in central California, legs bare, hand covering her non-phone ear like she always did, even when it wasn't noisy.

I told her I knew what I was doing.

She pretended we both thought this was true.

Dad started making the mango tea. "She still gets to worry about you."

"She's worried about the whole world. And I mean, seriously, why should she be here babysitting me and some guy when she's making sure farmers get the support they need?" I checked that the garbage had a fresh bag in it.

He watched me the way he sometimes looked at pictures of toddler me, of first-day-at-school me, that dreamy sadness, then said, "She can't possibly wonder where you get it from."

I studied Dad's back as he went out through the front door to set the tea in the sun. It wasn't always easy when Mom was gone.

He would never admit it, but I think he sort of wished she'd pick a cause closer to home.

I plucked a slippery blue Windbreaker from the back of a chair. It belonged to Mr. Michaels, who should be rolling in in about twenty minutes, wearing another jacket just like it over his flannel shirt. He'd been leaving a jacket on one of our chairs for as long as I could remember. I hung it on the coatrack and studied Dad's face as he came through the door. The creases were back. I asked him, "You're sure *you're* okay with all this? You can tell me if you're not."

He leaned forward, splaying his palms on the counter. "I think you can handle this, I do. It's just that you're so private. And you're not one of those kids who cares about this stuff. Like Chloe. No offense, she's a great kid, but she's a nut about all that celebrity and fame stuff. And you're not. You're going to have a bunch of cameras in your face, a bunch of people in your business. I'm not sure you know what you're getting into."

I started writing out the special sandwich for the day on the board while Dad unwrapped the fresh pastries we had delivered each morning by a local bakery. "Dad, I'm not sure people ever really know what they're getting into. And you know why I'm doing this." I met his eyes.

Sighing, he shrugged his large shoulders, but his eyes smiled. "Are you sure you're seventeen and not forty?"

"You claim you were there." I breathed in the opening of the day. I loved the time when Little Eats was just about to open, everything bright and clean, the coffee-infused air, the slight glow of the refrigerated drink cases, the smell of the pastries, the early-morning light coming through the tall windows running the length of the outside patio. Dad had laid all the wheat-colored hardwood on the floors himself ten years ago, and each year they got more scuffed and worn. All the scratches from the chairs, the feet of our customers, dropped plates. Each scratch, a tiny piece of history.

Dad sighed again, bringing me back.

"What?" I capped the dry erase marker.

His eyes rested on me, sad and tired from last night. "I just wish he didn't seem like such a jerk."

"I know." I flipped the sign to OPEN, COME IN! "But it's only a few weeks. Besides, it'll be easier that way. Just a job."

Dad set out the last of the pastries in the glass case by the front counter. "I hope your brother appreciates this."

His voice told us we both knew he wouldn't.

yesterday's sightings

Things Are Looking Up in Little, CA

Morning, sky watchers. This week, we sat on the roof talking about atmosphere. The layers of protection it allows, the energy it absorbs, why all of us crave being a part of it, and it got us thinking about another sort of star. Movie stars. Celebrities. This is a hot topic in Little right now because (just in case you've been living under a rock and don't know this already) we've got a star burning bright in our town this week. Adam Jakes. James Bond Jr. Child wonder. Sports-car-crasher. He's here shooting a Christmas movie (in June . . . because Hollywood makes its own sort of sense). No matter, he's here, creating an atmosphere. And (for better or for worse) we're all absorbing some of his energy.

Maybe that's why we like looking up at night. For a moment, our immediate atmosphere shifts on us and reminds us we're all part of something wide and far.

See you tonight, under the sky.

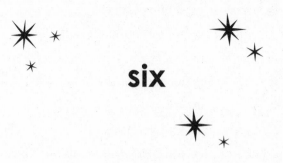

six

After work, I drove to pick up some groceries so Dad didn't end up eating Wheat Thins for dinner. Again. You'd think he'd just eat at the café, but he never seemed to make the time. Turning onto Sixth Street, I saw the light on at Stagelights. Mom's words before she left tugged at me. Had it really been over a year? Funny how time could pass so quickly but leave you feeling like it had been decades.

Impulsively, I pulled my dust-colored Jetta into one of the slots in front of the studio, got out, and peered through the glass, my stomach buzzing with nerves. Nicky Fritz, my former teacher and the owner of Stagelights, was dancing in one of the back studios. I could see flashes of him through its open door, wearing a tank top and black shorts. Nicky didn't seem to age, his black hair still cropped in the same short buzz, his face unlined. At forty-five, he was as lithe and muscular as when I used to stare up at him, a dazzled five-year-old.

When I could tell he'd come to a pause, I tapped on the glass. He hurried into the lobby of the studio, mopping his face with a hand towel. He unlocked the glass door and pushed it open, letting me in. "Well, well, if it isn't our prodigal daughter."

He let the door swing shut behind us.

"I saw the lights on." The familiar smell stabbed me, that strange combination of lotion, sweat, leotards, and feet. It sounded gross, but it wasn't. The perfume of my childhood. "Am I interrupting you?"

Nicky dabbed his forehead with the white towel. "Never, darling. Just surprised to see you." He squinted at me. "You okay?"

I shrugged. "I just pulled in, didn't really even think about it." For years, I didn't go more than a few days without being here and then I just stopped, like sealing off the door to another universe.

He disappeared behind the counter, emerging with a white paper shopping bag marked *Carter — do not throw out!* "Here, I'm not running a storage facility."

Flushing, I took the bag. Inside, a few pairs of tights, a pair of trashed jazz shoes, and a wrap hibernated. "Thanks." I nodded toward the studio. "You working on something?"

He shook his head. "Just trying to get some exercise. We got so crazed with Spring Showcase, but that's done. Just trying to catch up on some workouts before summer session starts. We had fourteen in Beginning Combo this year. I don't know how Lisa does it. They're lunatics."

I laughed at his expression of horror. "They're four years old!" My body relaxed, easing into the comfort of this place, its wood ceilings, the hum of the air-conditioning, the photos of past shows lining the pale pink hallways. If I tried to count all the pictures with me in them, I'd lose track. My eyes pricked in that itchy way that meant tears, and I tried not to look at the photos.

"Right," he said with a shiver. "Lunatics." He came out from behind the counter and leaned against it, studying me. "You dancing at all?"

"I'm teaching at Snow Ridge, but I wouldn't call it dancing." I dropped my gaze, knowing he'd seen the gloss in my eyes. I knew where this line of questioning was heading.

He nodded slowly, his dark eyes hard to read. "I heard that. That's great. Those old folks keeping you on your toes, I hope?"

I fiddled with the handles of the bag. "Oh, they're fun." It wouldn't be long before he drove down Carter's-Messing-Up-Her-Life Lane.

But surprisingly, he didn't say anything at all. Outside, the late-afternoon sun turned the windows of the restaurant across the street into bright sheets of light. I couldn't look at them. After a moment, Nicky began to say something, then hesitated. Finally, he said, "You want to dance a bit?"

"Now?"

"Why not? You can help me with a bit of choreography for the intermediate jazz summer session. Want to work out some kinks with me?" Without waiting for an answer, he headed toward the back studio. Soon, music permeated the space, a song Dad would have recognized but I couldn't place, a rock ballad from the eighties. I leaned through the open door. "Actually, I have to run — I'm meeting someone."

"Suit yourself." He was already working out some steps, his eyes on the mirror, but I couldn't help but notice a flicker of concern cross his face.

I'd been seeing that look a lot for the last year.

* ✳ *

I waited on a cement bench in the green backyard of The Hotel on Main. Out on the street, a film crew broke down all sorts of equipment, their faint voices and movements echoing in the lush cloak of the garden. Tucked under the shade of a low-hanging tree, I checked my special Adam phone for the tenth time. Parker had told me to have it with me at all times just in case they needed to contact me. Tonight, Parker said they'd *go public* about Adam's relationship with me, whatever that meant, but first we'd meet to *get our game faces on.*

Their game faces were both late.

I fiddled with the frayed hem of my cutoff Levi's and wondered if I should have washed my hair. I pulled the end of my ponytail in front of my eyes, frowning. My hair matched my eyes almost perfectly. Mom referred to it as auburn probably because she thought boring brown (which it actually was) would hurt my feelings. Dad liked to say I was the sort of girl who made men hum "Brown Eyed Girl." I liked to tell him that fifty-year-old men humming an ancient Van Morrison song gave me the creeps. But having matching brown eyes and hair was its own sort of invisibility cloak. I could blend into ordinary surroundings like one of those leaf butterflies I once saw at the zoo.

Which was probably why Adam Jakes just walked right past me.

Watching him, my breath caught. Even though he wore real-people clothes — a pair of skinny jeans, a faded maroon T-shirt, flip-flops, and the mirrored glasses he'd been wearing at the café — he really did seem otherworldly. He ran his hand casually through his hair (leaving it perfectly tousled, of course) and checked his iPhone. In that moment, as if he knew to position himself perfectly in a fading slant of early-evening light that cast a pale rosy glow, bronzing him, he laughed at something he read on the screen, his smile like flash lightning in a purple storm sky.

He was beautiful.

I should have washed my hair.

"Adam?"

He jerked his head toward me, his hand coming over his heart, the smile vanishing, leaving just a dark sky. "Why are you lurking in the shadows?"

Lurking? I glanced down at the smooth bench. "I was just sitting here. Weren't we supposed to meet?"

"I didn't see you."

"Obviously." I didn't get up. "I hope your tardiness is not an indication of how you plan to treat me during our courtship."

He tilted his head, no trace of smile at my joke. I assumed he was studying me, though I couldn't see his eyes behind those mirrors, just flashes of green from the garden. It was a bit late in the evening to be wearing sunglasses. He didn't respond to my comment.

We listened for a bit to the sound of a hidden fountain. Finally, he asked, "Where's Parker?" Annoyed, he typed into his phone. Clearly, Adam Jakes wasn't used to waiting.

I squirmed on the bench. "I'm sure he'll be here soon."

"He should be here now, Cary."

Cary? Was he giving me a nickname? He didn't get to do that. "It's Carter."

He nodded as if that was what he'd said the first time. "Interesting name."

I fiddled with the strap of my bag. "My mom named my brother and me after presidents she admired, who she thought made real social change."

"What's your brother's name?"

"John."

"As in Kennedy?"

"Yes."

"Why isn't his name Kennedy?"

"My dad thinks Kennedy sounds like a girl's name."

"That's true." He smirked. "Funny choices, though."

"Why?"

"Well, one was shot and the other had a one-term presidency." He stretched his arms over his head.

"That's not a very respectful way to talk about our former presidents." I meant it as a joke, but it came out just as flat as my earlier one. He didn't seem to notice anyway, barely disguising a yawn. This wasn't going well. "What can I say? Mom's an idealist." I stared at his mirrors. "So, are you staying here? Bonnie's a sweetheart."

"Who?" He'd started fiddling with his phone again.

"Bonnie, who runs this hotel." I had the feeling I had maybe three percent of his listening capacity at the moment.

He glanced up. "What? No, I'm not here. They got Parker and me a house. Some of the crew's here, though." He typed furiously into his phone. "Where is he?"

As if on cue, Parker materialized into the garden out of a back door of the hotel. "Shooting go all right today?" he asked Adam, ignoring the beeping of his phone, clearly texts from Adam.

Adam stopped accosting his phone. "Where were you?"

Sidestepping the attitude, Parker asked, "You two getting to know each other?" Adam ignored the question. Parker wore a cream linen jacket over his jeans, a pale T-shirt silk-screened with some sort of beer brand logo, and what appeared to be the standard-issue flip-flops. Taking in the lushness of the garden, he nodded at me. "Carter."

"Parker." We sounded like the two leads on a remake of a seventies buddy-cop show.

He held out a thick stack of white pages bound with brads. "Look this over. We can sort out the details."

I took the pages. I'd been briefed on the "ground rules" already — no unscheduled kissing (*yeah, right*), no talking to the press without direction, no other boys, no unapproved tweets or social media posts, even though I didn't have a Twitter or Facebook account — so I wasn't totally sure what other details needed sorting, but I was a good employee, so I smiled and said, "There's room over there." I motioned toward a weathered iron table with three chairs, sitting as if waiting for us. Which, I realized, they probably were. I had a feeling Adam's life was often staged well before he entered the scene.

Confirming this suspicion, the moment we sat, Bonnie appeared at our side with chilled glasses, a carafe of sparkling water, and some cookies. "Hey, sweetie," she whispered to me, setting the glasses down, her gray eyes bright, her blond hair piled high on her head as always. "I made these. Chocolate chip." She glanced at Adam. "I read they were your favorite, Mr. Jakes." Her flushed cheeks showed she was trying really hard not to burst with pride. Her little hotel garden, harboring a movie star.

Adam flashed her a million-watt smile. "You're a dream."

Gag. A dream. What a phony. I bit into a cookie. "Thanks, Bonnie."

She clutched the now-empty tray to her chest. "I just can't believe it! You two right here in my garden. Imagine!"

I tried to keep my smile stuck to my face. "Well, you know, life's funny. . . ."

Adam reached across the table and rested his hand over mine. "You never know where you'll find someone, really connect, you know? I thought I was just coming to shoot in some backwater town, business as usual, but instead, I met Carter."

Bonnie beamed. She was totally buying it.

Backwater town? My smile faltered, the cookie turning to paste in my mouth.

Giving a last little hop of joy, Bonnie hurried off into the house.

Adam retracted his hand. He leaned across the table and, in a stage whisper, asked Parker, "You made sure she has a Twitter account, right?"

"Why do you think I picked this place?" He nodded smugly in Bonnie's direction. "She tweets constantly."

"You think she'll just run in right now and tweet it?" I set the rest of the uneaten cookie back on the table in front of me. "I'm sure she has better things to do."

Parker messed with his phone for a minute, then, smiling, held it out for Adam to read. "See? Brilliant."

He'd logged onto The Hotel on Main's Twitter page, and right there, seconds old:

The Hotel on Main @BonnieOnMain

OMG! Adam Jakes is in MY hotel garden with a lovely Little local! Can you say LOVE AT FIRST SIGHT?

#uhearditherefirst

I shivered. "How'd you know she'd do that?"

Parker tapped the pile of pages in front of me. "Scene one, love. Adam goes public with Carter. Hotel garden."

I flipped to the first page, trying not to cringe at the (working) title.

A LITTLE LOVE STORY (working title)

On the next page it read:

EXT. HOTEL GARDEN — DAY

Adam and Carter sit in the garden together. They met the day before at Little Eats and had an instant connection. Leak news to Bonnie (Twitter-obsessed proprietor).

"Wait . . ." I flipped through some more pages. "Is this a script? A script for . . . us?"

"It's our story. What the public will see." Adam leaned forward, pushing his sunglasses into his perfect mess of hair. "Genius, right? Parker's also a screenwriter."

Parker shrugged, feigning modesty. "It's more of a treatment, really, an outline." He crossed his arms and leaned back in his chair. Down by the thick edge of trees and shrubs blocking the back of the garden, a sprinkler came on, its *hush-hush-shush* sounding, at first, like rain.

I flipped through some pages. "What is this?" I motioned to the odd heading of a scene: *INT. LITTLE EAT'S — DAY.*

Parker leaned over. "Those are slug lines. They tell whether a scene is inside or outside, where it is, and the time of day."

"But how did you write all this already?" I scanned the sixty or so pages. "I only just agreed to this." I noticed he'd mentioned specific things about me in some of the scene headings — the dance class I taught at Snow Ridge, Sandwich Saturdays, and even Extra Pickles. Apparently, we'd be walking him in scene five.

Parker and Adam exchanged amused looks. "The script's been written for a while, love," Parker explained. "We just added your name and some details."

As I flipped through it, I noticed several places where it just simply read *SMALL-TOWN GIRL.* The garden echoed in my ears, the fountain gurgling, the sprinkler shushing, a slight breeze rustling the leaves of an old maple above us. My head buzzed. "It just seems so, well — staged."

Parker frowned. "None of this can be accidental."

"Can I keep this copy?"

Parker reached for the script. "No, I need that. It's our only copy. Can't have this getting into the wrong hands. Besides, there are always rewrites. I'll be texting you scene-by-scene updates."

"Okay." My face must have betrayed my swirling nerves, because Parker's face creased the way Dad's had earlier.

He leaned in, pushing his own glasses into his hair. His eyes were river-water green. "You all right? No cold feet?"

Swallowing, I tried for what I hoped was a bright, easy smile. "I'm ready."

Adam gave me the sort of slap on the back my brother had stopped giving me when I was eight. "Excellent. So, next scene."

Parker flipped open the script. "Little Eats, the café."

Adam rubbed his stomach. "Great. I'm starved."

Funny, I felt like throwing up.

*　·　✳　·　*

I should have warned Chloe that Adam was coming.

Twenty minutes ago, we walked into the café, and in what seemed like a month but was probably five minutes, the following transpired:

Chloe, steaming some milk at the espresso machine, saw me. Smiling, she gave a flip of her hair and, without taking her eyes off the frothing milk, began greeting me in her usual way, which was to start halfway into a sentence as if we'd already been talking for several minutes. This time it was clearly about Alien Drake. "So, okay," she said over the espresso machine. "We're going to try to find a spot in the field up past Hounds Pond, but I told him we're leaving if the bugs get too bitey." Another flip of her hair, her pixie face fixed on the frother. When the milk finished, she glanced up and, finally, noticed Adam. Her expression, like one of those stop-motion videos, went through about twenty emotions — confusion, surprise, recognition, delight — before she entered into full-blown spaz mode.

She screamed, the stainless cup leaping from her hands and clattering to the floor, dots of frothed milk scattering the walls, espresso machine, counter, and Chloe herself. Obviously, Chloe + Adam Jakes = dropping things. "Oh my God!! Adam Jakes!!" she screeched, a huge blob of milk foam sliding down the wall behind her.

That Adam didn't react, didn't even flinch but rather grinned, established how often he dealt with this sort of teen-screech reaction.

The rest of the café, however, did not. At the moment of Chloe's shriek, several people dropped the mugs/forks/items they were holding; two men leaped out of their chairs as if stung, knocking the chairs to the ground; and a woman just trying to enjoy a glass of icy lemonade and a novel while holding a sleeping baby tightly to her chest now had to contend with a wailing infant and a spilled drink. Dad hurried out from the kitchen. "Good lord, Chloe, what on earth . . . ?" Then he saw me. And Adam. "Oh, right. We close in twenty minutes," he told me, nodding to the clock over the door.

"Chloe," I sighed as I helped a shaky Mr. Michaels back into his chair. Then I added, rather unnecessarily, "This is Adam."

Adam nodded, clearly enjoying this. "Hey. Chloe, is it?"

At the sound of her name cradled in the mouth of this movie star, Chloe swallowed audibly and huddled close to the espresso machine, her arms cemented to her sides. "Okay, wow, hi." Then, sneaking glimpses of him from beneath her shaggy bangs, she scrambled to pick up the milk frother. Dad mopped up the various bits of foam with a towel, then set about trying to make sure everyone else recovered, refilling coffees, righting chairs, pouring a new glass of lemonade. As I helped him, the woman took her baby outside, but not before smiling in a sort of daze at Adam.

Now, things settled, Dad brought Adam an egg, spinach, and goat cheese bagel sandwich to where we sat toward the back of the café. Parker positioned himself at a nearby table, a sort of human shield, his phone glued to his ear. The rest of the café had taken to sneaking quick glances at us, pretending to go about their conversations as usual, but clearly texting about us, adding barely sneaked photos of us to their Facebook pages. Adam didn't seem to notice, though he kept his glasses on. He ate the bagel sandwich with a ferocious intensity, and people watched as if he were performing surgery.

I fiddled with the straw of the iced tea Dad brought me and watched Adam eat. "So, that happens a lot, I guess."

He glanced over at where Chloe studied him from behind the counter, her mouth slightly open. When she saw him look, she hurried to finish erasing the daily specials board before disappearing into the kitchen. "You mean your friend there?" He chewed a piece of sandwich. "Yes. Yes, that happens quite a lot."

"Must get annoying."

He shrugged, shoveling the last of the bagel into his mouth and pushing the plate away. In seconds, Parker had it cleared. "It's always been like that." Adam slipped his glasses off, laying them on the table like an upside-down crab. I noticed how his blue eyes, always so electric in the movies, were almost turquoise up close, shot through with some green and framed with thick, short lashes. He had a smattering of freckles on his nose that didn't often show up in his movies, either. Little flecks of deeper brown against his already-tan skin. He really was some sort of human work of art.

Adam checked his phone. "You have about thirty seconds, just in case you want to brush your hair or something."

"Excuse me?" I leaned a bit closer to him, which caused Chloe to gasp from where she'd been peeking over the napkins and straws counter.

Looking up from his phone, he said, "Before they start showing up."

Moments later, two men in jeans and old T-shirts, cameras slung around their necks, pushed through the doors of the café, the one in front already shooting pictures of us.

"Hi, Stan," Adam said, leaning back in his chair and putting his glasses on again.

"Adam," he said, nodding casually as he took a few more pictures. "You care to comment on your relationship with" — he checked what looked like a napkin in his chest pocket — "Carter Moon. This her?" He frowned at me, clearly puzzled. I guess I should have brushed my hair.

"We're just hanging out, Stan. Her dad owns this café. They helped out with some crafty for the shoot." Adam shot me a smile that suggested we were doing just a little bit more than hanging out. Even though I knew it was a fake look, it still caught me and I felt my cheeks warm. Stan took a few more pictures he could title *Carter Moon blushing like an idiot*.

"How'd you meet?" chirped the smaller guy behind Stan. He wore a dirty mustard-colored trucker hat and a ratty T-shirt that might have once been black.

Adam stood up, Parker a split second behind him. "I don't know, George — how do people meet each other?" Cupping a

70

hand under my elbow, he led me toward the kitchen. "Nice seeing you boys."

We passed by a stunned Chloe as Dad held the kitchen door open for us. We hurried into the warm, sun-drenched space. I said a quick hello to Jones, the ex-con who'd been helping Dad out in the kitchen since I was a baby. He didn't give Adam a second look, just kept prepping for tomorrow. Adam, though, gave a small jolt when he saw Jones, probably because Jones had more tattoos than half the NBA and a face that looked like it had been used as an ashtray. In truth, he was a huge softy and taught yoga at Juvenile Hall every Thursday, but Adam wouldn't know that. On our way out, I gave Jones's arm a little squeeze, and his smile softened the rough edges of his unshaven face.

Outside, small crowds were forming — on the patio, in the two parking spots just outside the back door — mostly familiar faces, but also some clones of Stan and George. Raggedy guys, cameras dangling over stained T-shirts. My heart felt tight. How had it all happened so quickly?

The black Range Rover zipped into one of our two parking spots, nearly missing a squat photographer. In the driver's side sat an enormous wrecking ball of a man who could only be described as some sort of Nordic god. He hopped out, surprisingly agile, to open the doors for Parker, Adam, and me.

As Adam slipped into the backseat with me, he gave me a nudge. "You ready for this?"

Something told me, suddenly, I was not.

* ✳ *

The Nordic god dropped me off at home a few moments later, jumping out to open my door for me. Adam leaned over. "We'll pick you up in the morning. Parker will text you the time." The door slammed, and the Range Rover pulled away as quickly as it had arrived.

Dazed, I looked around my neighborhood. My neighbor trimmed his roses in the warm evening light, a lawn mower buzzed somewhere in the distance, the smell of barbecue tinged the air. Nothing had changed.

And everything had changed.

For the next few weeks, I would be a self-absorbed movie star's girlfriend. I sat down on the front steps of my house, my head spinning. A few minutes passed before I became aware of footsteps padding up the hill, the huffing sound of someone walking quickly in my direction.

Chloe.

"See, this is what I'm talking about," she gasped before even reaching me, her short brown hair sticking out in tufts. She must have closed the café in record time. Either that, or Dad had let her go. Probably the latter. She stood in front of me, her hands on her hips. "One of those times a text is in order? Oh, guess what, Chloe? I'M DATING ADAM JAKES!!! All CAPS!"

I smiled weakly up at her. "Nothing so far really calls for all caps."

"Not the point."

"It happened sort of fast." From the angle where I was sitting, Chloe's whole head was highlighted by sky, the sun just starting to color the stretch of clouds pink behind her.

"*How* did it happen? is what I want to know." She blinked at me,

72

waiting. "How did you go from *It's just ice, Chloe* to, oh, um — *I'm going out with Adam Jakes*?!"

"Now I can get you Adam ice whenever you want," I tried brightly.

"Spill it."

"The ice?"

She narrowed her eyes at me. "You're stalling."

"Okay." I practiced what Parker had told me to say. "After we made those salads for the crew, he asked to meet me."

She shook her head, confused. "Salads? He wanted to meet you because of salads? That's the dumbest thing I've ever heard."

"You asked!"

Her eyes were now slits. "And . . . ," she prompted.

"And so we hung out and got to talking." The stain of clouds deepened behind her. I took a long breath, trying to steady the dizzy spin of my head, the jolt of guilt at lying to her.

Chloe tapped her foot, impatient with me. "What did you *talk* about?"

"Um." I licked my lips. I couldn't tell her that we talked about the script that would be dictating the next few weeks of my life. "Just stuff. Movies. My dog."

She crossed her arms. "Extra Pickles?"

I improvised. "He likes dogs. He wondered about his name, and I told him our first dog was named Pickles so this one was Extra Pickles."

"That," she sniffed, "doesn't sound interesting at all."

I shrugged, knowing Chloe didn't mean it how it sounded. "It's the truth."

Only it wasn't.

Sighing, she plopped down beside me, deflating like a balloon. "I can't believe it. He asked to meet you? *You?!*"

"Now you're just hurting my feelings."

She gave me a withering look. "You know that's not what I mean." But it kind of was what she meant. And in her defense, it was basically true. I'm not the type of girl guys notice. In my entire high school career, I'd had one date junior year with Tad Ballard, a lunch at Subway and a matinee of a superhero movie. He was nice enough, told me he liked my eyes, but he never called me again. A week later, I saw him making out with Stacy Merchant next to the girls' locker room. Subway Tad and that lame kiss with Alien Drake in eighth grade. Not exactly the ideal setup for dating Adam Jakes. It was like asking a fourth-grade swimmer to suddenly take a shot at the hundred-meter freestyle at the Olympics.

My phone buzzed in my hand.

Chloe's eyes widened. "Is that *him*?!"

I showed her the screen: *8:30.*

"What's that mean?"

"That's what time he's picking me up tomorrow morning. We're, uh, hanging out again. Before he starts shooting." I couldn't actually remember what we were doing and didn't have the script to tell me.

Sighing as if I'd told her we were flying to Hawaii in a private jet, she sank down onto the steps next to me, her chin falling into her hands. "You are the luckiest girl in the world."

She was right. It was luck. Only not at all how she meant it.

✳

Later that night, someone tapped on the door to my room. I looked up from the book I was reading. "Yeah?"

Chloe poked her head in. "It's me."

"You knocked?" Chloe never knocked.

"Well, you might be making out with Adam Jakes," she told me, coming into the room with a red shoe box and, after pushing Extra Pickles out of the way, sitting next to me on the bed.

"I'm not." I smiled, tossing the book aside.

"So I was kind of a spaz earlier and I'm sorry. You know I adore you for a billion reasons and Adam Jakes will, too. So, to show you I'm sorry times infinity, I brought you something." She set the box in front of me.

"A present?"

"Sort of." She opened the lid. "It's a Celebrity Survival Pack." She pulled out a pair of Audrey Hepburn *Breakfast at Tiffany's*–style black sunglasses. "You'll need these, trust me."

I tried them on; they felt like wearing a couple of salad plates on my face. "They're huge."

She studied me. "They look awesome."

I slipped them off, setting them on my nightstand.

She pulled other items out of the box: a flowered cell phone case for my Adam iPhone, a bottle of "smoothing" conditioner for my hair, some lipstick, a picture frame — deep blue and spotted with stars ("for a picture of you two!") — and a pale pink silk scarf.

I held up the scarf, my face questioning. A breeze came through the open window of my room, carrying the smell of night — barbecue, wet grass — and fluttering the scarf, just slightly, in my hand.

seven

The next morning, the Range Rover pulled up to my house at 8:35. I slipped into the backseat with Adam, who was once again lost in his phone. Seriously, if any girl in this world wanted to trade places with me, she should really wish to be Adam's iPhone. That would be a deep, meaningful relationship. Parker sat in the passenger seat, also in iPhoneLand. "Morning," Parker mumbled, not looking up.

Adam said nothing.

I decided to go for cheerful. "Good morning, Adam. Good morning, various iPhones." No reaction. I eyed the Nordic God in the front seat who'd driven me home yesterday. "Good morning, um, guy driving us."

"That's Mik." Adam typed away. "My bodyguard."

"Good morning, Mik." I smoothed my skirt over my knees.

Mik nodded but didn't take his eyes from the road. We headed toward town in silence, and I snuck a glance at the movie star sitting next to me.

Adam Jakes had been a childhood sitcom star since he was five on a successful family ensemble show called *All of Us* that ran for eight years. Sitting next to him in the plush backseat of the Range Rover, it struck me that he'd been raised a bit like a goldfish, swimming through his childhood in the same bowl, alongside a tank of bigger, flashier fish. I'd only seen some of the show, but it streamed on Netflix, so I'd tried to watch a few episodes last night. Adam's role was the typical cute but pesky little brother who said precocious things and fell into sticky situations the older characters were forced to get him out of. (In one, he spent the entire episode locked in a toolshed talking to an initially scary but ultimately epiphany-inducing spider.) Overall, he was good at his part, sweet and convincing, had won some awards, and was noticed for small roles in movies by the time he was ten. In the last couple of years, he'd ditched the goldfish bowl and now swam freely in the ocean of stardom.

Until recently.

Over the last year or so, he'd had a stormy relationship with the Disney star Ashayla Wimm that ended in an ugly public breakup. In most of the recent candid photos I'd found online, he'd either been scowling or staring sadly away from the camera much like in some of the photos on Chloe's wall. Watching him now, I had to push back the impulse to ask him how he was feeling, to put my hand on his designer denim—clad leg and just say, *How are you?* It seemed like he might need someone to ask him that and actually listen, not just fish for a sound bite. As if reading my thoughts, he glanced at me, barely disguised a sigh, and returned to his staring out the window.

My throat started to close up and, blinking into the morning sun, I tried to imagine myself through Adam's eyes. Small-town girl in an old thrift-store skirt and a messy ponytail. He must be wondering how he got stuck with some hick barista. I liked who I was, liked where I was from, but it was incredible how suddenly dull I felt being flung into Adam's sparkly waters.

Mik turned the Range Rover onto Old Greenway, the road that snaked away from downtown, but twisted abruptly into the empty, fenced McKenzie property. A two-minute drive from downtown, the McKenzie property felt a million miles away. Rumor was, Mr. McKenzie was former CIA. He'd been kind of a sight around town, in his dark glasses and vests with too many pockets. The people who didn't believe the CIA story thought he must be some sort of journalist or adventure photographer, always leaving town for months at a time, never really talking to anyone. Whatever he was, he'd been a total security nut. His five-acre property was completely fenced with sleek boards topped with barbed wire. Prison chic. Over the years, many a teenager had been busted for trying to sneak over that fence and past Mr. McKenzie's cameras. He didn't even have a house, just a gleaming Airstream and five dogs that looked bred to eat people. When he left town last year, pulling that gleaming trailer behind his massive truck, most people assumed he'd been sent on some sort of government assignment. Dad said that was way more fun than admitting he'd probably just decided to live out the remainder of his years on a golf course in Florida.

After punching in the code for the main gate and passing through it, Mik bumped the car along a dirt road secluded by thick pines on either side. Finally, he pulled into a clearing where a series of trailers sat in filtered sunlight.

"What is this?" I gazed through the windows. The trailers were the size of small houses, each with the bright green words *Star Shacks* scripted across their sides.

Parker gave a general wave toward the trailers. "Base camp. Cast trailers. The director, producers' trailers —"

Adam interrupted him. "Stop showing off your big Hollywood terms, Park. She doesn't care that it's called base camp."

Parker's shoulders tensed.

Mik stopped the Range Rover next to the largest of the trailers. I nodded at it. "This is where you're living?"

Adam shook his head. "This is just where we hang out during shooting." He quickly pushed his door open. "Come on. I'll show you. It's got a gym and a milkshake maker."

✳ ✻ ✳

Every kid loves a good fort. I begged my parents for years and, when I was nine, finally got a pretty respectable tree house in the low limbs of the old maple in our backyard. It had smooth plywood walls and floor, a real ceiling, a rope ladder, even some curtains Mom made from a green tablecloth hanging on the one wide window. I had a rug in there, bookshelves full of found treasures like river rocks and smooth acorns with their little hats, and a white plastic table where I could set a vase with a rosebud or maybe a slim branch of dogwood blooming. I didn't use it as much as I had when I was younger, but I still liked to sit up there sometimes, especially at night, and watch the stars emerge through the large window.

Adam's trailer was nothing like my tree house.

His fort was on steroids. In fact, I knew quite a few families in Little who could move in and live out the rest of their years in a place like this. Hardwood flooring gleamed, a sprawling dark blue suede couch faced a flat-screen TV, and off to one side was a mini-gym, complete with treadmill and weights. The kitchen had a microwave, cherry cabinets, a fridge, and, as promised, a stainless contraption that clearly made milkshakes.

"You want one?" Adam motioned toward it. "I can send out for fresh strawberries."

I shook my head, wondering who would get that job — strawberry fetcher. "I'm okay, thanks." The whole place smelled too good, something muted and spicy. Boys' rooms weren't supposed to smell this good. Alien Drake's room always smelled like Doritos and stale pizza. Which was better than how my brother's room used to smell — old sponges and, inexplicably, rotting limes.

Parker plopped down on the couch with his phone, kicking his feet onto the coffee table. After scrolling his thumb along the screen, he told Adam, "You don't shoot until noon, but you wanted to run one of the hospital scenes."

"Oh, right." Adam opened the fridge and pulled out a blue glass bottle of water. He kicked his flip-flops in the direction of what appeared to be a bedroom. They thudded against the cherry-wood door frame, leaving scuffs, and landing splayed out in the hallway. "Carter can read Cheryl."

"Who's Cheryl?" I sat on the edge of the couch, and Parker handed me a script much thicker than the one detailing my fake relationship with Adam.

Adam leaned against the kitchen counter, sipping from the blue bottle. "She's sort of the Tiny Tim figure in the movie." He went on to explain that the movie was a retelling of *A Christmas Carol*. He played Scott, the Scrooge character, who was the teenage son of the largest donor of a small-town hospital. Cheryl was a teen girl with cancer. Her father, the Bob Cratchit figure, worked for Scott's father. When he talked about the film, Adam's face lost its usual sullen haze; it brightened the room. "I need to run the scene where I come to her hospital room. The one before she gets to go home."

"Page 102," Parker added.

I flipped to it. "Wow, you guys are already near the end?"

"We're at the hospital tomorrow, so we shoot all the scenes there," Parker told me.

"Out of order?" I scanned Cheryl's lines. Mostly, she said things like, "You can be my first Christmas present," which made me cringe but probably sounded better in context and would make me sob like a baby when I saw it in the final version of the movie, with all the music and lighting.

"You shoot based on location," Parker told me, pushing himself off the couch and helping himself to some blue bottled water from the fridge. "We have the hospital for only two days."

Adam cleared his throat. "Let's run it." He motioned to the script.

I frowned. "I'm not an actor." My mouth felt dry, like I was about to give a speech at school. "Maybe Parker could do it."

"I'd rather run it with a girl." Adam plopped down next to me on the couch. "Don't think too much about it. Just read it." He cleared his throat again. *"I brought the music box, Cheryl."*

"Don't you need a script?"

He shook his head. "No, I know it. Go ahead. Say the line." He leaned forward, saying his line again.

I swallowed, wishing I'd asked for one of those bottles of water. The script said *(whispering)*, so I tried to whisper *"Scott? Is that you?"* but I sounded creepy, like an old woman in a horror movie. Adam and Parker exchanged a look.

"You're thinking about it too much," Adam said, giving me a flicker of a smile. "Just read it." Morning light filtered through the trailer window, tiny dust motes catching in the air around us. Outside, I could hear other people coming and going, trailer doors opening, closing. A dog barked.

Licking my lips, I tried the line again.

Adam nodded, his eyes locked to my face. *"It's me. I'm sorry, Cheryl. I'm sorry for all of it."*

I forgot to look at my script. "All of what?"

He frowned. "That's not the line."

"Sorry." Scanning the page, I read, still whispering, trying for my best sick voice. *"I didn't think you'd come."*

"I've changed."

I had a question. "How can you be Scrooge if it's not your money? It's your dad's money."

He shook his head, letting his earnest face drop away, replaced with a wash of annoyance. "It's a *retelling*. We're turning the story on its ear. It's a teen version. I'm the *son* of the wealthiest man in town, and I'm the one who has let money dictate my life. My dad's not the jerk in the story. *I'm* the jerk in the story. I don't care about the right things. I've lost sight of what matters. Partying all the time. Sleeping around . . ."

"This is a family movie?"

"They don't show any of that, really," Parker interjected from his perch by the fridge. "It's backstory."

Adam explained, "It's Christmas Eve, and Scott's just screwing around, making things hard for the working people at the hospital, forgetting about what really matters in life. . . ."

"Which is what?" What could a guy hanging out in a decked-out trailer with its own milkshake machine and private gym know about real "working people"? I thought of Mom, off somewhere fighting for farm aid, while I declined a freshly made strawberry milkshake in a tricked-out fort. Not a proud moment for the Moon family.

Adam seemed caught off guard by my interruption. "Um, well, like family and stuff, I guess. And love."

"And he loves Cheryl?" I studied the pages as if they'd answer for me.

"He doesn't realize it until this scene." I listened as he described his part, the way he saw Scott as this lost soul, how this Christmas Eve everything would change for him, and it struck me that he really seemed invested in Scott's story. Maybe it wasn't just some stupid blockbuster to him. Then it hit me. It wasn't just having me as a girlfriend that would try to change his public image. He wanted to be seen as Scott. The guy who got emotionally body-checked by three visiting ghosts and realized he'd been screwing up his life.

Kind of like Adam.

It wasn't subtle. Did they think the public was that gullible?

"And so he's visited by three ghosts who teach him these things." I was ready to go back to the script, but I'd unleashed something in Adam.

Adam stood, pacing the small room. "Sort of ghosts, but not like in the original story. We're not taking a paranormal angle with it. It's different. Contemporary. I run into a kid from my elementary school days, and he acts as sort of a reminder of Christmases past." It took me a minute to register that when he kept saying "I," he meant his character, Scott.

"Then, I see my history teacher from school, who acts as a sort of Ghost of Christmas Present, and finally, you see my future. Me as an old guy — like thirty-five — who has lost the love of my life because I was greedy and shallow. I get to wear old-guy makeup."

I frowned. "Won't that be paranormal? You seeing a future version of you?"

He shrugged, finishing the last of the water, tossing the bottle into a blue trash bin. Everything in the trailer was polished wood. Or blue. Like it had all been designed to match his eyes. Which it probably had been. "I don't know. They have people to figure that out."

I struggled to remember the story. "So the movie won't show your own death?"

He clutched his hand to his chest. "Just the death of my heart. It's ultimately a love story. It's going to kill at the box office."

"A love story?"

"A *Christmas* love story. With Cheryl. We're going to crush."

Parker stood up, brushing out some wrinkles in his linen jacket. "He's brilliant in it."

"I'm sure." Truth was, I'd watch pretty much anything if you sprinkled some snow on it and lit up some twinkle lights — I loved Christmas movies, loved the way they glowed — but I still wondered how some rich movie star who'd spent his whole life in L.A. could really understand a small town enough to convince us

85

he'd gone through some big life awakening. What I'd seen of Adam so far didn't convince me he could look much beyond his own nose. Still, they called it *acting* for a reason.

I'd read somewhere that actors often did research, studied a character to get to know them, walked around in their shoes and all that. And we happened to have a Scott right here in Little.

"Adam?"

"Yeah?"

"You want to see the guy you're playing in the movie?"

* ✳ *

From the open window of the Range Rover, Parker told us we had about forty-five minutes and then we needed to get back to town. "We have to make sure we get in a few more sightings of you two today before Adam starts shooting." He peered up at the hillside. "This looks too private. No one will see you." This was not in the script, and I could tell it made Parker itch a little. Mik handed us the picnic basket that had magically appeared in the back of the Range Rover. "No more than forty-five minutes," Parker reminded us before he had Mik park the car in the shade of some trees.

"Is he your manager or your babysitter?" I smiled so Adam would know I was kidding.

"What's the difference?" Adam shrugged, looking suddenly young, like a kid who'd been told, No, we won't be stopping at the pet store today.

He followed me up the narrow footpath that snaked its way along the green hillside at a mellow angle. It was warm, and the ankle-length grasses around us had browned on their tips. When we reached the top, Little High stretched out below us. Here, we looked directly down on the new football stadium, its rubberized track a black eye surrounding the expanse of green field. Stadium bleachers rose in a metallic blossom all around it. Directly across from us, a crisp white-and-blue sign read: BRYCE FIELD.

"Zack Bryce," I told Adam, "is who you are playing in this movie of yours. Well, except so far he hasn't had any ghosts smack around his conscience."

His hands in the pockets of his jeans, Adam stared at the sign. "Zack Bryce, huh? That's cool. I want my character to be relevant." His gaze drifted in the direction of the library, the clump of classroom buildings near the cafeteria, and the theater, a sad, plain building in need of a paint job.

I explained to him that Zack Bryce was the oldest son of Travis Bryce, who was the son of Don Bryce — a chain of cash, at least by Little's standards. Adam could probably buy them all before lunch and then fly a private jet back to L.A. "The Bryce family owns a good chunk of this town. Travis Bryce donated the stadium to the school. You know" — I shrugged — "so his kid didn't have to play on a crappy field."

Adam nodded. "That was awesome of him."

I frowned. Maybe he really wasn't going to see the connection. How did you describe Zack to someone just like him? Rich. Entitled. Ridiculously good-looking. If you were into the kind of boys who spent longer staring at their own reflections than you did. Which I wasn't. "Yeah, I guess his dad's pretty generous. Donates to a bunch of local charities and stuff. But Zack's sort of a jerk."

"Still, the school got a sweet track out of it."

This wasn't going well; he was missing my point. "I guess Zack doesn't know how to be anything other than what he is," I conceded.

Adam looked sideways at me. "Do any of us?"

"What?" My stomach flipped. I wasn't used to him looking directly at me.

"Know how to be anything other than what we are?"

"I guess not."

Rubbing his hands together, Adam took a step toward the picnic basket. "What do we have for eats?" He flipped open the lid, digging around inside until he came out with a couple of sandwiches, some chips, and two sweating bottles of lemonade. I recognized them as Little Eats Treats and To Go items, the premade things we kept stocked in a low refrigerator case in the café for people who didn't want to wait for made-to-order food. He handed me a sandwich. "Hungry? These pesto ones rock."

I blushed. "I made those."

"For real? They're good." He peeled off the white paper and bit into one. "What do you use for the cheese?" He plunked down onto the grass, kicking his legs out in front of him, and inspected his sandwich.

"Gruyère."

"Tasty." He took another bite. "So, where's this Zack?"

I scanned the track. "There." I pointed to the lone figure stretching at the edge of the track. Zack practically lived here, so I knew we'd see him. "He trains *a lot*."

Adam gave him a little salute. "Good to have discipline. I don't have that sort of discipline. Just parties, girls." I wasn't sure if he meant his character Scott or himself.

I unwrapped my own sandwich. "Oh, Zack does plenty of that."

"But there he is." Adam motioned to the track. "Running his laps."

"He's just not very nice," I mumbled into the white wrapper of my sandwich.

Adam scanned the expanse of Little High below us and gave a small shudder. "Man, school looks a lot like jail."

"It's not too bad." I settled next to him, popping open a bag of barbecue chips. Little High was deserted except for Zack's lone journey around the track. Funny how schools turned into graveyards in the summer, all the busy day-to-day energy gone, the space left humming with emptiness. "Have you ever gone to school?"

"I've had tutors," he said, shrugging, his face guarded again. "The show kept me pretty busy. And now movies."

"Do you ever wish you'd gone to regular school?" I imagined Adam wandering the halls of Little High, waltzing into algebra, going to football games. It would probably seem pretty lame to him. And they'd make him put his phone away.

"I don't think about it." Then he seemed to do just that. "I mean, I probably would have thought it was cool at first, the whole high school thing — parties, football games, dances. Of course, none of those things are really school, I guess." He took a drink of his lemonade. "Actually, I don't think I would have liked it at all. It sounds boring. Always having to be somewhere every minute, packed into rooms too small for half that many people. Always having to ask permission to do anything." He shook his head. "Yeah, no — I would've hated that."

"Well, not all of us can be calling our own shots at age eight." I stared at my uneaten sandwich, noticing his was already gone. "You still hungry?" I motioned to where my sandwich sat on its white paper in the grass.

"You sure?"

"I'm not very hungry."

He eyed me for a minute. "You're not one of those girls who doesn't eat, right?"

"Oh, believe me, I eat. I'll split it with you." I plucked half the sandwich off the open paper, grabbing a stray tomato slice before it fell.

He polished off his half in three bites. "I dated this actress. She ate, like, wheatgrass and tofu cubes. Disgusting."

A shiver went through me. He meant Ashayla Wimm, real-life Disney princess. They had dated for a while, and then, according to *Celebrity!* he dumped her in a horrible, public way. At a Lakers game, if I could remember Chloe's recap of it accurately. She'd told me she'd almost taken down all the pictures of him from her wall when she'd read about the Lakers game breakup. Almost. It was weird to sit here with the guy whose pictures were plastered all over Chloe's wall. Right now, he seemed almost normal, but he could sneeze and it would be news on some online magazine.

I swallowed the rest of my sandwich. "My dad runs a café. You can always count on me to make food a huge priority." I cleaned up our wrappers, stuffing them into the picnic basket.

He leaned back on his elbows. "I'm glad I didn't end up having to fake-date some starry-eyed idiot, speaking of boring. Not that

I'm glad your brother's in trouble or anything, but at least you had to take our offer."

My skin iced over. "What do you know about my brother?"

He must have sensed the temperature change, deciding to tilt his head toward the sun instead of answering me.

I let a minute slip past, then stood and gathered the picnic basket together.

"Where are you going?" He sat up.

"It's probably been forty-five minutes." I found the trail, my eyes trying to focus on the ground, the sun hot on my back. "I'm not sure this was really that helpful," I called behind me. "I don't know anything about acting."

He followed me down the path, so when I turned, trying to still my heart, he almost crashed into me. I didn't like him thinking he *knew* something about John. He didn't know him. Or me. And we weren't some plot point in Parker's stupid script. "I would prefer we didn't talk about my brother. That's one of *my* rules."

He put warm hands on my shoulders. "Okay, whoa." A breeze rustled the grasses around us. "Relax, okay?"

His hands sent a warm wash through me, and I held tight to the basket as if it could steady me. Up close, I noticed that spicy scent again from his trailer, and it struck me that you had to be really near someone to smell them. Nearer than I wanted to be right now. "You don't know him." I slipped out of his grasp and started back down the path.

"Carter?" He called out to me, silhouetted against the bright sky. "For what it's worth, I know what it's like to have people assume they know you. In my experience, they're almost always wrong."

eight

downtown was the opposite of Little High; this time, the hum came not from empty space but from the pressed-in bodies of hundreds of people. Apparently, everyone from Little had shown up to watch the filming and brought along about five extra friends. Mik had trouble maneuvering the Range Rover around the throng at the base of Gold Street, but finally, two men let us through a barricade and onto Main Street. At that point, they'd roped off the sidewalks so the crowd wasn't allowed onto the street.

As we moved up Main Street, I recognized two girls from my Spanish class, half the football team, and Beckett Ray, Little High's own version of a movie star. Beautiful, out of touch with real life, and a total pain in the butt. She often told people, "R-A-Y, like a ray of light," in that whispery, high voice of hers that was some sort of Marilyn Monroe derivative. Now, she had her pale, willowy legs planted in the street near Mountain Books — I could spot that spill of black hair anywhere — chatting with a young police officer who had somehow decided the roped-off areas did not apply to Beckett Ray.

When she saw me in the Range Rover, her mouth actually dropped open. I'd never seen that before. Only read about it in books. But her jaw went slack. I saw teeth. Her dark blue eyes followed our passage up the street, her mouth never closing, and I couldn't help but smile. For the most part, I got along with pretty much everyone, but something about Beckett Ray brought out the dark bits in me and I wanted to start hurling knives. Ever since she'd moved here in seventh grade, she didn't miss an opportunity to remind us she was just biding her time until she could get out again. She *hated* Little, constantly told us what a prison sentence it was to live here and how she couldn't wait to leave for the real world (aka Los Angeles), which seemed about as real to me as Neverland. Once, in sophomore English, our teacher, Mr. Gomez, pointed out that Shakespeare's Dark Lady "probably had hair a lot like Beckett's." She'd flipped her glossy mane over her shoulders and said, totally seriously, "Oh, probably not, Mr. G. I put a lot of time into it, and they just didn't have the product then that we have now." So, yeah, I took just a tiny bit of pleasure in watching her stare after our car, Adam Jakes at my side.

Mik pulled onto the side street near the bookstore, away from the crowd, and jumped out to open Adam's door. Turning, Parker studied the swarm of gawkers behind us. "Your people don't have anything better to do on a nice day?"

"My people?"

Adam already had one leg out of the door, mumbling, "Parker can fill you in on the schedule," as he scrambled out of the car.

Before I could open my door, Parker turned in the passenger seat to face me. "I need you to not change up the schedule like that again."

My hand paused on the door handle. "What?"

Parker's chilly stare rivaled the air-conditioning. "That little visit to the high school. No more improvising. Stick to the script. If you want to make a change in the future, run it by me, okay, love?"

I dropped my gaze like a scolded child. "Okay."

He dug through his bag and handed me a white envelope. "Here. Some cash to hold you over. You'll get the rest at the end."

Peeking in, I could see a thick stack of one-hundred-dollar bills. Parker pushed open the driver's door. "And some advice: Don't get too attached." He didn't wait for my response before he slammed the door and disappeared up the street.

I'd never held that much money in my hands before.

It felt awful.

Later that night, I felt even worse. After finding my way out of the crowd in town, I had tracked down T.J. Shay. He met me at the back of the Taco Bell parking lot, whipping his white Honda into the hot shade of a tree. He rolled down the window, a smile playing at his lips as I handed him the envelope. He counted the hundreds. "Does that cover it?" I'd asked. "For now," he'd said, already putting the car in reverse. I had expected to feel lighter after paying him, elated, but I only felt a sour squeeze in my stomach as he drove away.

Now, I pinned the phone between my shoulder and ear, calling my mom. As it rang, I reached for a bowl for my Raisin Bran. Like father, like daughter. I guess I shouldn't give Dad such a hard time about his Wheat Thins.

She picked up on the third ring. "Hi, sweetie."

"Hi, Mom." I could hear the sounds of traffic behind her voice. She must have been standing on a street somewhere. "Is the world a better, shinier place yet?"

She chuckled. "Hardly. Though we're making good progress with some of the local legislators."

"Excellent." I poured cereal into my bowl.

"You doing okay?" Her voice sounded weird. Motherly.

"I'm good." I tried to sound light and airy.

Her voice told me she wasn't buying it. "Is Mr. Movie Star behaving himself?"

"He's fine. You know, when he's not being a narcissist." *Which is nearly all the time.* I opened the fridge and took out the milk.

"Figures." I heard someone sidle up and talk to her. She held the phone away to mumble something. "Well, keep an eye on him," she said to me.

"That's what they're paying me for," I told her with a hollow laugh.

"I'm not sure how funny I think that is yet." But her voice was smiling. "Oh, and, Carter?"

"Yeah?"

"You tell me if you need me to come home, and I'll drop everything and come home. You know that, right?" She sounded serious, the way she got when she was talking to the city council about garbage in our parks or something.

Warmth flooded me. "I know." Then, I said good-bye before she could hear the threat of tears in my voice.

* ✳ *

Extra Pickles was not behaving himself. Adam and I walked my dog on the small loop near my house at Hawkin's Pond, an oblong stretch of still water shaped like a kidney bean. A couple of years ago, a local conservation company put in a trail and small signs detailing the history of the pond and the wildlife that made it their home. We, however, had only made it a few hundred feet down the trail, Extra Pickles straining against the leash, zigzagging and doubling back, and once almost yanking me into the pond in pursuit of a squawking duck he'd flushed out of a low bush.

"Can't he just walk next to us?" Adam glanced around nervously, most likely for signs of paparazzi (who, frankly, would most likely welcome taking pictures of me trying to control a ninety-pound Lab while Adam wandered helplessly beside me).

"He's not used to the leash. We usually just let him run on the Liberty Trail." I gave too hard a yank and Extra Pickles sat suddenly, his eyes wide and wounded. "Maybe we should just turn around. I think this is hurting his feelings."

Adam crouched down beside him. "Hey, guy." He gave Extra Pickles's head a rub. "You need to chill out so we can get some good pictures, okay? Stop being such a jerk."

"Don't call my dog a jerk!" But Extra Pickles just wagged his tail in the dust of the trail.

Adam cupped his hands around my dog's face. "See, you like it, don't you, jerkface?"

Before I could defend his honor, Extra Pickles wrested his head out of Adam's hands and leaped after a blue jay that had landed several feet in front of him, dragging me a couple of feet forward. "Whoa."

"Let me do it." Adam took the leash.

"Fine." I resisted the urge to push Adam into the pond. "Though I feel I should mention being mean to my dog is not winning you any points in the public eye."

"Naw, we're instant best friends," Adam said, starting along the path again. Within seconds it was clear he wouldn't be faring any better than I had with the ninety pounds of spaz on the other end of that leash. Finally, when his arm socket had clearly had enough, we stopped at a wood bench. Extra Pickles happily took the chew bone I handed him and settled down next to us.

"See, he loves me." Adam stretched his arm along the back of the bench. I leaned against it, feeling it graze against my bare shoulders. What a nice picture we must be, a new couple relaxing on a breezy summer day. Even if I couldn't see them, I could hear the snapping of cameras. The paparazzi layered the woods around us like ninjas. This whole outing was, after all, for their benefit, carefully crafted in Parker's script.

I felt a stab of guilt. How many pictures showcased this sort of lie? How many made the viewers imagine a fantasy? Not just for Hollywood but for regular lives, too. Every year, people mailed holiday cards, posted on Facebook, pulled pictures from wallets — millions of faces grinning into a lens. How many of those smiles were true? Did that family in the smiling Christmas card mostly scream at one another? Was that couple with the small baby getting any sleep at all? Did that little dancer in the pink tutu really want to be dancing? I tried to push the watery feeling down, bury it away in the back shadows of me. Maybe we grinned into cameras in the hope that we might remember we could be happy.

Maybe it just helped sometimes to have a reason to smile.

"He seems good now." Adam nodded at Extra Pickles, who was absorbed in his bone.

"See, not a jerk." I leaned down and patted his head. "Well, most of the time."

Adam shot me a sheepish smile. "I was mostly kidding."

"No, you weren't."

"You're right. I wasn't. He was just so . . . so . . ." He caught my eye, and we burst out laughing.

"Annoying?" I finished for him. "It's fine; he is terrible on a leash." A small sliver of the strangeness between us melted. "Maybe your next movie should be about a regular guy who has to train some sort of clearly untrainable animal. Like a sloth? Or a platypus?"

He grinned, his body relaxing into the bench. "Very nice. You could do development for studios."

I made a face. "No, thanks."

He gave me an odd sideways look, one that made his eyes crinkle at their corners. "You don't like Hollywood very much, do you?"

"Oh, no — I like movies," I started.

"Not movies," he interrupted. "Hollywood. Our world." He rested his forearms on his legs. "It's pretty clear you don't think too highly of me."

I watched a duck dive into the center of the lake, gliding into a bobbing float. "I don't know you."

He gave me another lopsided grin. "Look, don't get me wrong, it doesn't bother me. It's just . . . unusual for me." He stared out over the pond. "I'm used to people clamoring to get close and, well, you're just really guarded. You haven't asked me anything about . . . well, anything. I'm not used to that."

I thought about what it was I would ask him given the chance, given an opening like the one he'd just handed me. My brain whirled with questions: the drugs, the redhead, the Lakers game breakup, but I found myself asking, "Where are your parents?" I knew he was seventeen and that Parker acted as a sort of guardian, but it seemed strange that his parents weren't around at all.

He sat back, surprised. "Oh, well, they're in Hawaii right now. With my younger sister. At least, I think they are."

"You don't know for sure?"

"We're not . . . super close." There was that look again, the one from the tabloid pictures, like a stage light dimming to black.

"Were you once?"

He thought about it for a minute. "Yeah." A distant rumble sounded. Extra Pickles stood, his tail wagging, his ears alert. Adam looked to the sky. "What was that?"

Something shifted in the air. "Thunder." Above us, a swell of purple cloud covered the sun.

In minutes, the sky opened up, rain pocking the lake, a wind coming up, carrying the fresh scent of wet air, dampened earth. We hurried under the cover of a leafy maple, watching the patchwork of purple cloud cover blue sky, hearing the trees shiver in this unexpected shower. The light dimmed but seemed to sharpen in the rinsed air, like someone had just outlined a watercolor in black ink.

"Where did that come from?" Adam shook water from his hair and wiped droplets from his sunglasses with his damp shirt.

"We get these sometimes." Even as I said it, the rain stopped, the cloud moved on, the sun hit the world, sparking a million glittering shards of light.

"That" — Adam shook his head, his face washed with surprise — "was beautiful." Even wet, his hair stayed perfect.

I watched him take in the sky, the trees, the pond, its surface smooth again, the ducks tracking ripples through its middle. "It's a beautiful place," I told him.

* ✳ *

"I love the sky after a rain." I reached for another jelly bean from the candy bag Chloe'd brought to the roof, lying back and letting the spilled-glitter night wash over me.

"Where's Romeo?" Alien Drake poked me in the side. "He too good to hang with us?"

I waved him away, grimacing at the buttered popcorn bean I'd just eaten. I stuffed a few more in my mouth. "Don't call him that. And, no, he's just working. He has a *job*, you know."

"At ten o'clock at night?"

I shrugged. Technically, I was off duty right now, but I knew enough to know he had said he was working. "Actors have weird schedules."

"Yeah," Alien Drake said. "All those yacht parties must keep him real busy."

Chloe chewed a handful of jelly beans. "Seriously, though, when do we get to meet him?"

"You *did* meet him." I shielded my eyes against a flash of headlights coming down the street.

Chloe groaned. "Ugh, don't remind me. I'd like the chance to redeem myself, thank you very much."

Alien Drake shook his mop of hair. "That, I would have paid to see."

She threw a jelly bean at him. "Shut up."

"I'm surprised you didn't hear her," I said, giggling.

Chloe stuck a jelly-bean-blue tongue out at me.

Alien Drake pretended to grab at it. "Nice. Does that also come in neon green?"

"I was surprised, is all," she pouted, picking out a licorice bean and tossing it over the side of the house.

"I would have eaten that," Alien Drake told her, staring after it.

"I know." She smiled widely at him.

Down the street, the car that had passed parked in front of our house. I sat up, watching a dark figure slip from the passenger seat and quietly shut the door. The driver waited as the shadow made its way up our walk and into our house.

John.

Chloe and Alien Drake noticed, too. "What's he doing?" Chloe asked, her voice low.

I shook my head, the mood spoiled. Whatever it was, it couldn't be good.

* ✳ *

Our basement always smelled like laundry detergent and rain. From the steps, I could barely make out John's shadowy form moving along one of the back walls. I pulled the string for the overhead bulb.

He jumped. "Carter!"

"What are you doing?" I watched as he picked through a pile of boxes and mounds of black plastic garbage sacks. I wondered if one of those bags held the remains of my dance career, if Mom hadn't actually donated them like I'd asked her to. As I watched him heave aside a wooden dollhouse that I used to love and hadn't thought about in years, a twinge moved through me at the thought of my dance stuff still down here, abandoned. Basements could be sad things, a subterranean limbo.

From behind the boxes of Halloween decorations, he unearthed a guitar case, dusty and plaited with cobwebs. "Here it is."

"Your guitar?" He hadn't played his guitar in years. Mom had hidden it, actually, so that he wouldn't try to sell it. Which was probably what he was doing here. "Why?"

He brushed at the case, frowning, the light of the swinging bulb barely reaching his face. "Because I thought no one was home, so I wouldn't be hit with a customs inspection. I'm allowed to get my guitar, okay?"

"I know." I watched as he unzipped the case, pulling the slick wood guitar from its tomb. "You going to start playing again?" I could try to be hopeful, could try to imagine him moving forward, this guitar a sign he was finding bits of that old self to patch back together.

"Yeah, I think so." His voice held the hollow echo of a lie.

Maybe I could just hand him a few of the pieces, just to get started. "Remember when we took that trip to Santa Cruz and you played on the beach next to the fire? I think about that sometimes."

He stuffed the guitar back into the case, zipping it up. As he passed me on the stairs, he mumbled, "You're a sweet kid," and then I could hear the front door and the hum of the car moving away down the street. Lately, my view of John was always of him leaving.

nine

The next morning, the doorbell rang.

I finished filling Extra Pickles's food bowl with his favorite kibble, then, wiping my hands on my jean cutoffs, answered the front door.

Parker stood there with a woman. She had slick dark hair, olive skin, was barely five feet tall, and seemed covered in circles — huge white sunglasses, bracelet-sized gold hoops in her ears, bangled wrists, and a tunic dress covered in multicolored spheres. Even her heels had a bubble print.

"Hi!" Circles said brightly.

Parker pushed his glasses to the top of his head. "Can we come in, love?"

I stood back from the door, letting them both into the entry. "I'm sorry, did we have a meeting?" I closed the door.

Parker gave the house a quick glance, then motioned to the woman. "This is Jewel."

"Not short for Julia," she clarified, spelling it for me. She plucked off her sunglasses, perching them stylishly in her dark hair.

I blinked. "Okay." Her circles were making me slightly dizzy.

Parker put a hand on Jewel's shoulder. "Jewel's going to help you put some outfits together, teach you some basic makeup stuff, just sort of ensure you're prepared."

"Prepared?" I glanced at the bright orange duffel bag Jewel carried that was big enough to fit a person. Or a dead body.

Parker checked his phone. "Brilliant. I'll let you ladies take it from here."

Jewel patted his hand that was still on her shoulder. "Terrific, Parky — thanks."

Parky?

He let himself out.

Jewel dropped the orange duffel on the tile in the entry. "Okay, so we're going for small-town girl next door, which you clearly have down." Pursing her lips, she let her eyes scan my cutoffs, my tank top, and my face and ponytailed head. "We just need to *polish*. File off the edges." She reached out and fingered the end of my ponytail. "Get rid of your split ends, that sort of thing." She rubbed her hands together, her nails white-tipped. "Where's your room?"

I held up my hands, feeling as though I needed to defend myself. "I'm really fine. I'm not much of a makeup girl, and I don't really own that many clothes."

Jewel picked up the duffel. "Honey, you're now in major magazines, dissected online. People can be brutal. Let's just spruce you up a bit. We're not talking mega-makeover." There was that full-body eye scan again. "Just punch you up a bit, a more *defined* version of you, that's all. Nothing fancy. Besides, we have Adam's image to consider." Her subtext was clear. *And you'd hurt that image with that split-ended head of yours.*

We headed upstairs.

After two hours, my room looked like the dressing room of an understaffed bargain store. Every inch of space had been taken over with various outfits Jewel would hang up or drape (*yes*) or toss in a heap (*don't wear — ever*). "Oooooh, this is cute," she had exclaimed, yanking out a short-sleeved peasant blouse I'd worn in a dance my sophomore year, or saying things like, "Um, don't wear this," about an olive canvas skirt I'd always kind of liked. "You're not a Girl Scout." Every shirt, skirt, pair of pants or shorts, tank top, bra, underwear, and pajama had been yeaed or nayed. Mostly nayed.

"Some great pieces," she kept mumbling, her circles spinning. "The key is pairing them with each other. Like this," she said, holding up a tight black T-shirt, "with this." She held up a flowing paisley jersey skirt. "But not with jeans. Boooooring." She hooked the skirt to the shirt and looped the shirt hanger over my bedpost.

My math final had been easier than this.

"Now, makeup." She unzipped her duffel and brought out a tackle box. "The key is to apply fresh, glowing makeup, so you brighten without looking painted. It's summer and it's hot, so nothing complicated." Dozens of tubes, vials, brushes, and creams emerged, spilling onto the hardwood floor. She unfolded a portable table and set everything onto it.

This wasn't complicated?

Fifteen minutes later, she held up a mirror. "You have great skin," she told me, capping a gloss and leaning back to admire her work.

"Thank you," I breathed. I had to admit, I looked positively dewy. "How did you, um, get my cheeks to do that?"

She handed me a tube. "Apply right at the end. So easy and the results are amazing." She proceeded to set out new tubes of the various things she'd applied and the paper she'd filled out along the way to show me how to do it myself. I would never be able to do this myself, but I might get close.

"If you two plan to go to a club or something, just call me. I'll show you how to manage the look for nighttime." She folded up the table, tucking it back in the duffel.

A club? "We don't really have clubs in Little."

She paused, frowning. "Well, for whatever nighttime spots you have. And, here." She handed me a business card. "We scheduled your hair for eleven this morning because we know Adam has the signing at two. Just call Parker and he'll send a car."

I took the card, thanking her again. She packed everything up and heaved the duffel over her shoulder. It probably weighed more than she did. She stepped back, studying me. "You're adorable. It's about time he picked a cutie like you."

Blushing, I held the mirror back up, my dewy face staring back.

* ✳ *

"Carter?" Adam squinted at me. Huddled with me at a table in the back of Little Eats, he frowned. "You look a bit shaky."

Shaky didn't come close.

Adam gave me a sympathetic smile.

About an hour ago, we had stopped in for an iced coffee after an afternoon of signing autographs outside Mountain Books and, somehow, the café had suddenly flooded with people. At first, Adam kept signing autographs at a back table while I made us iced coffees, but soon the crush of Adam admirers became too much for Dad. He'd turned the lights off and helped Mik wave everyone out, closing the café early. It had taken twenty minutes to clear out the last starry-eyed fan, and my ears pulsed with the sound of Adam's admirers. Seriously, twelve-year-old girls could let out sounds that were just not human. Now, Mik stood guard at the door, his arms two tree trunks crossed across his chest, but I could still see them out there, milling around like sharks.

I blinked at Adam. "How many autographs did you sign? Like, a thousand?" I ran my finger over the sweating glass of my empty iced coffee. Adam's was still full, the ice melted. He hadn't had a minute to take a sip.

"Maybe a couple of hundred." He had a thin sheen of sweat on his forehead. He told me he'd been up since four a.m. for shooting, but I couldn't tell. "That wasn't too bad." He glanced at his sweaty, watery drink. "Could I get you to make me a fresh one of these?" He disappeared toward the bathroom.

"Please," I muttered, rolling my eyes, but grabbed his drink and crossed behind the counter. I made a double shot of espresso, dumped in some nonfat milk, and topped it with ice, giving it a quick stir with a butter knife. I had it on the table before he returned from the bathroom, looking damp, like he'd splashed water on his face.

He sat, taking a long drink. "So good, thanks."

I slipped into the seat across from him. He'd written his name *hundreds* of times. Written in ink. On napkins. On head shots. In little books people had in their bags. "What do you think people do with them?" I asked him.

He took another long drink, finishing most of it. "I think it depends on the person. Some people collect them. I think others just end up losing them, tossing them. I think it's more the whole ability to say, 'Look what I got. Look where I was.'" He chewed a piece of ice, staring out the window at the low branch of the maple in the side yard, its green leaves shivery with an unfelt breeze. "Maybe it makes people feel like they've recorded something in their life, a memory or something."

I wiped at the ring of water his glass had left on the blond table surface. I did notice that tendency in people even in smaller things — an invite to a party, the good news of a friend, an inside joke at work. All these ways of time-stamping our inclusion in the world, our need to say, I was there. I was part of something bigger than me. "Does it get old?"

He brushed at a stray lock of hair, pushing it out of his eyes and back onto the tousled top of his head. "Sometimes I wish I could just go to the grocery store and pick up a snack or something." He grimaced. "Of course, people hate that. Poor movie star wants a normal life, blah blah blah." He gave a wave of his hand. "People don't get it."

I shook my head. "Those people didn't just see you get mauled by that pack of screaming girls."

"True." He laughed, a low, sweet laugh I hadn't heard before.

The sound of it made me smile. "Besides, sometimes living in a small town, you just want to go to the grocery store without running into someone who knows you, who wants to talk to you. I mean, they're not clamoring for my autograph, but they're still connecting. Connecting takes energy. And it's nothing against that specific person. Sometimes, you just don't want to connect all the time. Or at least I don't." I followed Adam's gaze where it had returned to outside, noticing a couple of photographers, one kneeling under the tree, his lens angled our direction. "Oh, give me a break." I pulled the shade.

Adam caught me lightly by the wrist. "Hey, I meant to ask you, did Parker make sure Jewel found you today?"

"Can't you tell?" I teased, taking a step back, giving him a better view of my ensemble, the black T-shirt and jersey skirt from Jewel's workshop this morning. I'd even gotten a thumbs-up from Chloe earlier when I'd texted her a picture after my hair appointment.

His eyes moved over me, his face brightening. "You look fantastic. She does good work."

Was that compliment for me or Jewel? "Thanks." I tucked my newly glossed and trimmed hair behind my ears, pretty sure any dew that remained on my face after the afternoon we'd had was sweat.

The bell on the door jingled. Mik let Alien Drake and Chloe into the café, waving off a few brave girls attempting to talk their way inside, a tiny flock of bright birds, each in a different version of the same short-shorts-and-halter-top ensemble.

Chloe spotted me and widened her eyes. "I don't act like that, do I?" she asked, hooking a thumb in the direction of the girls wiggling like puppies out front.

Alien Drake slipped an arm around her. "Well —"

"Of course not," I assured her. "Hey." I smiled in Drake's direction. "Come meet Adam. Adam, this is Drake."

Alien Drake sauntered over, his face round and smiling, a black backpack slung over his shoulder. "Loved you in that teen Bond knockoff."

Adam stood and gave Drake a friendly nod. "Five bucks if you can remember my character's name."

Alien Drake's grin widened. "Sorry, just being polite."

Adam laughed. "Don't worry, I can't remember my character's name, either." He parked himself back in the chair.

"Erik Simon!" Chloe piped up, lacing her small fingers through Alien Drake's. She flipped her hair and smiled sheepishly at them. "What can I say? I'm a fan."

"Aw, thanks, Chloe." Adam grinned at her.

She flushed to her ears, dipping her head, eyes averted.

Alien Drake noticed, frowning, and he shifted awkwardly from foot to foot. "Is it cool if we grab sandwiches here?" he asked me. Then he tilted his head, his eyes scrutinizing me. "Did you cut your hair?"

"Carter got a makeover," Chloe gushed. "Doesn't she look amazing?"

Alien Drake's eyes flicked over me. "I liked your hair before."

"Don't listen to him. He has boy vision. It looks great," Chloe said to me.

I flashed her a weak smile as I crossed to the cold case. "So, sandwiches, right? We probably have some premades left." Erasing *Today's Special Sandwich* on the whiteboard, I wrote:

Dad — took sandwiches and chips for dinner.
Going to Drake's! xo — C

110

I grabbed three pesto chicken sandwiches wrapped in white paper and a couple bags of chips from the basket next to the case. "I'll hold these for later if you want," I told Alien Drake.

Outside, the crowds had thinned.

"You coming tonight?" Chloe asked Adam, still having trouble meeting his eyes.

Adam gave me a sideways look. "What's tonight?" We didn't have anything in the script today except the autograph signing.

"We're stargazing." I hadn't asked him because I couldn't imagine him wanting to sit on Alien Drake's roof with a sandwich and a bag of Doritos. Not very glamorous. Also, Parker had insisted, *Stick to the script.* "We go almost every night. You know, actual stars. We like to sit on Alien Drake's roof with a picnic and talk until it gets dark enough."

"*Alien* Drake?" Adam asked.

Chloe stared up at Alien Drake, her face awash with affection. "We've been calling him that since forever because he's obsessed with aliens."

Alien Drake winced. "I'm not *obsessed.*" He gave Adam a funny look. "Watching the stars with a star. Yeah, that's going in the blog."

I rushed to explain. "Drake and I write a blog about the sky. Stars, comets . . . the possibility of life on other planets. It's called *Yesterday's Sightings.*"

"A blog about aliens?" Adam looked interested. "I was in an alien movie once."

"It's about a lot of things with the sky," I explained. "Sometimes it's about aliens."

"More like the possibility of aliens, of something *other* than us, you know, out there." Alien Drake's voice had gone sort of low and quiet. Was it just me or did he seem nervous? It wasn't likely that he would be — Alien Drake cared less about Hollywood than I did — but normally you couldn't shut him up about our blog or his extraterrestrial theories. Was it possible even he was a little starstruck?

"So you believe in the *possibility* of aliens?" Adam clarified.

Alien Drake opened his backpack and started packing the sandwiches and chips I'd set on the counter. "I believe in the possibility of a lot of things. Believing something is *possible* is not the same thing as believing in it."

Adam seemed to be genuinely trying to understand. "I guess I don't really see the difference."

Alien Drake thought about it for a minute; I could see him choosing his words carefully. "Belief is a rigid thing. Yes or no. Possibility allows for all options to exist at the same time. I'm just not a black-and-white sort of person." He zipped up the bag. "I've got to go get some things squared away with the scope. You guys want to meet me there? About nine to eat?" He looked at Adam. "You can come if you want, but I'm sure you have better things to do than stare at the sky with us." Without waiting for an answer, he pushed through the door, Chloe's concerned gaze following his retreat. She glanced at me, eyes wide.

Adam's phone rang and he stepped away to answer it.

"Are you guys in a fight?" I asked Chloe quietly, moving closer to the counter, away from Adam. "Why's he so grumpy and annoyed?" Two things Alien Drake almost never was, and certainly not at the same time.

Chloe shook her head, watching Alien Drake cross the street outside and head toward his house. "I honestly have no idea what that was about." She gave me a puzzled look. "I'm going to go talk to him. See you later, okay?" Before I could say anything, she left the café. I watched her dart across the street, hurrying to catch up with Alien Drake.

Adam came up alongside me, giving me a playful nudge with his shoulder. "So, am I invited or not? Come on, I usually don't have to wait this long for an invite to a party," he teased.

I tried to ignore the instant stomach flutters that seemed to emerge every time Adam did that with his voice. "Drake invited you."

"I want *you* to invite me." This time he gave me only half a nudge, letting the side of his body lean into mine. Okay, utterly impossible to ignore the flutters now. People called them butterflies for a reason.

I chewed my lip. "Honestly, I didn't really think you'd want to come. And it's not a party at all. We just sit on a roof and eat chips. You'll be bored."

"I like stars. The *real* kind. And I like chips." He tucked his phone away, his marine eyes pulling me in like a whispered secret.

"It's not in the script."

"You knew there'd be rewrites." He grabbed my hand and squeezed, sending the flutters away from the safe roost of my belly and migrating south, north — *everywhere*.

She grinned. "In case you ride in a convertible, so you won't mess up your hair."

Guilt welled up in me, finding small channels I didn't know I had. But I couldn't tell her, I couldn't. I'd promised Parker that only my parents would know. Too many potential leaks, he'd said. It couldn't get out or it would ruin everything. I reached over and hugged her. "Thanks, Chloe. You're amazing."

"It's nothing, really," she said, pulling away and fiddling with the items, packing them back into the box, before letting her eyes rest on me. "I'm so excited for you, Carter. This is huge." She pushed the box toward me on the bed, half the scarf lolling like a tongue out the side.

I picked carefully through it again, examining each item closely, mostly so I didn't have to meet her gaze, hoping she couldn't sense my apprehension. Folding the scarf neatly into the box, I tried to sound light and hopeful when I said, "We'll see."

Talk about not being in the script.

"Then you should come," I managed.

"Then I think I will."

∗ ✳ ∗

The creek behind Alien Drake's house rushed, still full from all our late May rains. We stretched out on the sloping roof, warm from the day of roasting in the sun. I loved night in the summer, the sky gone black and star-spotted, the air tinged with pine and a sudden coolness. Around the neighborhood, barbecues smoldered and people had lit their fire pits, but a hush had muted the world, giving into crickets and whispers.

"Tell me again why people wish on stars." Chloe tossed the ball of white paper she'd made of her sandwich wrapping from one hand to the next, her legs crossed at the ankles. Its whiteness stood out in the dark as if lit.

Alien Drake fiddled with his telescope, his body a shadow even several steps away. "We can thank the Romans for that, though I'm sure, like with everything else, there are different answers to that question."

"Let's not forget Jiminy Cricket." I collected the chip wrappers and folded them into the bag I'd brought. Chloe tossed me her white paper ball.

Alien Drake nodded. "Yes, thank you, Mr. Cricket, for decades of star-wishing."

Adam leaned back on his forearms. "What did the Romans have to do with it?" It was so weird to have him sitting up here with us, so normal in a pair of shorts and a UCLA hoodie.

Peering into his scope, Alien Drake didn't answer, so I jumped in, my heart strangely racing. "You can't see it very well now, but Venus often appears as the first bright star of the night. I mean, it's a planet, not a star, but they didn't know that. The Romans would look to Venus and wish for love."

"Love?" Adam sat up, his head angled to the sky. "Not fortune? Fame?"

Alien Drake sat down next to Chloe, putting an arm around her waist. "I like to think that love came before all those things."

Chloe made gagging noises. "Ugh, you're such a girl sometimes," but she wriggled close to him, smiling.

Adam watched them. "Love as the first wish." He tugged at the hem of my shorts I'd changed into until I looked at him. "It's like what I was saying about my movie. It's a love story."

"Everything is," Chloe said, curling tighter into Alien Drake. Clearly, they'd made up after whatever that was at the café earlier. I studied them in silhouette, the way their profiles feathered with night. Yin and yang. I opened a bottle of water and took a long swallow, avoiding eye contact with everyone. Too much talk about love. It made me feel squirmy.

"What's it like to be so famous?" Chloe peered through the night at Adam.

"Chloe!" I couldn't believe she'd just come out and asked him.

"Yeah," Alien Drake added, ignoring me. "Is it like being a really fancy pet?"

"Sort of," Adam said, his head tilted toward the sky, the crickets pulsing around us. Finally, he said, "It feels very lucky and very lonely."

I passed Alien Drake a water bottle. "Why lonely? Aren't you at parties and clubs all the time?"

"Oh, sure." He pulled his knees into his chest and wrapped his arms around them. "You're never alone. It's just, when people always have something to gain from you, you never really know if they like you or . . . whatever it is they think it means to hang out with you."

Chloe sighed. "So, basically, it's like high school."

Adam opened his own bottle of water. "I guess. I wouldn't really know."

"It's about atmosphere," Alien Drake said, pulling his sweatshirt out of his backpack and slinging it over Chloe's shoulders.

"What do you mean?" I asked.

Alien Drake settled back in next to Chloe. "I think people attach themselves to certain people, certain events, because those things have energy; they create an atmosphere. And there is a certain amount of energy that gets absorbed by an atmosphere. Look at the sun."

"Um, we're not supposed to look directly at the sun," Chloe teased.

He shook his head, melting into blogger-philosopher mode. "No, I mean, a certain amount of the sun's energy is absorbed by our atmosphere. Just being on Earth, we get those benefits."

"Not for long." Chloe pulled the sweatshirt closer.

"It's a metaphor, Chlo — not an environmental impact report." Alien Drake stood and, kissing her on the top of her head, went to check the scope again. He seemed his usual self now, not twitchy and grumpy like he'd been earlier at Little Eats. Maybe it had been too weird to meet Adam. Chloe *did* have pictures of him hanging up all over her room. That had to unnerve even the most solid of boyfriends.

I thought about what he'd said about atmosphere. Most of us floated around seeking energy so we could just swim around in it, bask in it. And we didn't always want to produce it ourselves. Maybe that's why people wanted all those autographs from Adam earlier. Proof of atmosphere.

Adam stretched onto his back, his hands tucked behind his head. "You guys always talk this much?"

"Oh, we're very deep." Chloe stood, crossing to where Alien Drake stared into his scope. "Our own little brain trust." Chloe was warming up, losing some of the nerves that had kept her acting so silly around Adam.

I was glad Adam got to see her like this and not mute with her arms plastered to her sides. "Yeah, we're real deep. When we're not throwing water balloons at the Smiths' trampoline." I motioned toward Alien Drake's neighbor, the ghost of the netted trampoline dark. "It's pretty funny when they bounce and freak out his cat."

Adam sat up. "Next time — can we do that?"

I smiled at him, forgetting for a minute that we weren't just an ordinary group of friends, that he wasn't a movie star. It was in that small bubble of ease that I heard myself say, "Sure. You're clearly not afraid of getting arrested."

"Carter!" Chloe's eyes, even shadowed, widened.

I flushed. "What? It was a joke."

Alien Drake let out a low whistle through his teeth, his hand cradling the scope. "Wow, Carter, don't pull the punch or anything."

117

He started to take the scope down, slipping pieces of it into its bulky black bag.

Adam watched me, his eyes unreadable, dark like the sky. "It's fine," he said. "I'm sure I had that coming."

I hurried to fix it. "I'm sorry. . . . I really meant it as a joke."

A car slid by on the street below, lighting our faces for a sluggish second. In the passing wave of yellowish light, Adam's face held a sadness that wasn't just shadow, the look frozen in so many tabloid photos. Then our eyes met and he brightened slightly, the sadness rinsed, and he said, "Forget it. You were just being honest. Believe me, that's rare."

yesterday's sightings

Things Are Looking Up in Little, CA

Morning, sky watchers. I know we've talked about this before, but last night there seemed to be so many dark, blank patches in the sky that it made us think of the Hubble Ultra Deep Field. Years ago, some scientists decided to point the Hubble telescope at a blank spot in space and leave it there for ten days. This might not seem like a big deal, but it was really brave because the time you get on the Hubble is really competitive and they were taking a chance they might not see anything at all. But what they saw was intense beyond their wildest expectations. They found, once they processed the data, that the blank space up there, that "nothing," was actually over three thousand galaxies — hundreds of billions of stars. So, here these scientists pointed the telescope at nothing and found huge unknown worlds. They took a risk, and it majorly paid off. And, that's our star-thought for today. Even when you think you're looking at nothing, what you might not be seeing is whole galaxies.

Think on that.

See you tonight, under the sky.

ten

adam had to shoot the whole next day, so I didn't see him. I felt terrible about my comment, and he wasn't answering my texts, so it clearly wasn't as okay as he'd tried to make me believe sitting there on that roof. Last night, I'd sent another text, *Just saying hi. Hope you had a good day.* It seemed the sort of thing a girlfriend would do (even a fake one), but he hadn't answered.

By the time he picked me up this morning, I'd grown anxious that I'd messed something up, mucking up the thaw that had been deepening between us over the last couple of days, but Adam seemed fine as I opened the door. He handed me an iced latte as I slipped into the backseat. "Sorry, it's Starbucks. Is that allowed, Ms. Indie-Café?"

I pretended to frown at it. "Oh, I don't drink corporate coffee." When his smile dimmed, I grabbed it. "Don't be such an easy mark. Despite the other night, my manners really aren't that bad. This is nice — thanks." I pulled the door shut. "And speaking of that night, I'm sorry I was so rude."

He blinked at me, his eyes confused.

I lowered my voice. "About the 'arrested' comment."

He waved me off. "You worry too much. It's fine."

I swallowed my reply. I was clearly making a big deal out of nothing. Mik revved the SUV's engine, and Adam motioned for him to go. "So, what's in the script for us today?" His phone buzzed in his hand, and instead of diving into it, he clicked it off and tossed it onto the seat between us.

I took a quick sip of my coffee before answering. "When I checked in with Parker yesterday, he said you wanted a tour of Little." I leaned forward and gave Mik a few quick directions.

Adam rested his hand on my knee and leaned close. "Well, you keep talking about how beautiful it is here. I thought you could maybe show me."

My heart caught like a fish in the breathy net of his voice, at how warm his hand felt on my knee. Was he flirting with me? There weren't any photographers around. Clearing my throat, I tried to remember what Parker had said about making sure we positioned ourselves for good photo opportunities. "Parker thought we might get some good publicity shots together." I tried to sound as professional as possible.

Letting his hand slip from my leg, Adam tugged at his seat belt, a flash of annoyance crossing his features. "Look, don't worry about all the publicity stuff, okay? Let's just hang out. Parker can get a little —" He paused, taking a slurp of his own Starbucks. "Well, let's just say he takes his job a bit too seriously sometimes. Don't worry about the photos. Let's just have a good day."

"Okay." I pulled a sheet of heavy stock paper from my purse. Yesterday, I'd had an idea, something fun for Adam that would show him our town but also be a little silly. So after Little Eats, I'd stayed up until two a.m. finishing it. Now, clutching the handmade tour map I'd made, my idea seemed babyish, and I had a feeling it was one of those ideas that seemed brilliant at midnight but totally lame in the daylight.

"What's that?" He grabbed at it.

Sighing, I handed it over. "It's stupid."

He scanned the page. "Did you *make* this?" Now he was really laughing at me.

I tried to grab it back. "Don't laugh. I made you a Little Star Map. You know, like those Hollywood tours. Only it's some of *our* most famous spots, famous people, famous legends. Parker said you wanted a tour of Little and, well, this is what I thought we could do. It didn't take me very long." I swallowed, embarrassed. He didn't need to know I'd spent hours on it. "Forget it, it's dumb. We should do something else."

He shook his head, holding the map out of my reach. "We are *not* doing something else; we're doing this. I don't think anyone's ever made me something like this before." He stared at the paper again, his eyes serious, a shy smile on his lips. "I can't believe you made this." He settled back into the seat, his gaze following a group of kids on the other side of the street racing down the sidewalk, dressed in already-drenched swimsuits and armed with Super Soakers, before letting those eyes, like the tide coming in, fall back on me. "Thanks," he said.

"Sure," I managed, struck with the sudden, odd sensation of floating.

* ✳ *

'Standing beneath the shade of a monster oak, I pointed at the Victorian house and Adam followed my gaze, staring up at the old house, the yard quiet in the filtered morning light.

I leaned into the white waist-level fencing. "This is the Crowley house, hence the name of the street. Anne Crowley lived here in the late 1880s, and while it was officially a boardinghouse, most people around here know that Anne Crowley ran a pretty success-ful brothel out of it."

"So our first stop is a brothel. I like your style." Adam peered up at the house, its green paint starting to peel at the edges. "It's not *still* a brothel, is it? Because this might not be the best publicity spot for me, given my track record."

"No, it's a private house now. But I chose it as our first 'Star Tour' spot because it's one of our more famous ghost stories in Little. And since you're currently starring in a movie about ghosts, I thought it'd be perfect." I pushed through the white gate, motion-ing for him to follow.

"Um, are you allowed to just walk on in there?" Adam grinned at me from the sidewalk. He seemed at ease, loose, that usual dark curtain drawn away from his face. With his hands stuck in the pockets of his knee-length shorts, it struck me that at this moment he could be any other guy at Little High. I guess, had life dealt him a different hand, he might have been.

I held the gate for him. "It's fine. The Roan family owns it now, and they're gone for most of the summer. I go to school with Jack Roan, and he won't care if I show you."

"Show me what?" Adam raised an eyebrow at me. I felt myself

blushing and quickly turned away. He followed me around the side of the house and into the backyard. Fringed with dense trees, the yard formed a sort of skinny, sheltered triangle, one slender point of which ended at a weathered shack with no windows.

I walked to the middle of the triangular patch of lawn. "Okay. Stand here. By me." He joined me, and I closed my eyes. "Close your eyes."

"Seriously?"

"Do it." I opened mine to make sure that he was following directions.

Shaking his head, he closed his eyes.

"Feel how warm it is here?"

"It's a pretty hot day," he told me, his voice edged with amusement.

"Right. Okay, here's how it works; I'll lead you. Don't open your eyes." Opening my own, I led him toward the shack. Somewhere, someone was cooking bacon, the smell of it drifting on the air. I guided him slowly, the way Jack had done with me for the first time back in sixth grade. Right at the point where the lawn met the path in front of the shack, the air temperature dropped suddenly by twenty degrees.

Adam's eyes snapped open. "Whoa." He looked around. "What is that?"

I'd been here dozens of times and it still rippled my arms with gooseflesh.

As quickly as we felt it, it vanished, warmth flooding the air around us.

"Weird, right?" I let go of his arm.

He rubbed it absently, turning slow circles, studying the yard. "Seriously, what *was* that?"

"That was Henry."

He stopped turning, his hands finding his pockets again, his eyes finding mine. "Henry?"

"The ghost." At Adam's bemused expression, I hurried to explain that Henry used to work at Anne Crowley's house as a cook and gardener and all-around handyman, and the legend was that he was desperately in love with one of the girls who lived at the house, a sixteen-year-old girl named Emeline who was a part-time dancer and a full-time employee of Anne's. "Sick with jealousy," I continued, "he burst in on her during one of her, er, um . . . sessions, and there was a chase, and then the guy she was with killed Henry. Stabbed him right here on this path."

Adam pointed at the ground, a smile twitching his features. "This exact path?"

"Well, this spot anyway." I shrugged. "It's fine if you don't believe me, but you felt him. I saw you."

His phone buzzed. "Mik wants to know if we're dead. Should I tell him, no — just consorting with them?"

"Next stop!" I headed toward the Range Rover. "Bye, Henry!" I called over my shoulder, and I could almost hear Adam smiling.

* ✳ *

We stopped at three other spots before lunch. First, we drove to see Cleo Smythe, a woman who'd lived in the same house for 103 years. "Born in that house, gonna die in that house," I told Adam. "Her words. Hi, Mrs. Smythe!" I waved at her where she sat in her squeaky porch swing, and she waved back, holding a sweating glass of iced tea.

Second, I took him to see the old jailhouse, now housing a gallery dedicated to Gold Country lore and photography. "Creepy," Adam had said, peering at a yellowed ancient picture of the gallows, two open graves near it waiting for the hanging bodies. "People were buried where we're standing?"

"People are probably always buried where we're standing," I said, nodding a hello to Bess Harding, who ran the gallery. Bess had the thin, bent shape of a lily, but she perked up when she saw Adam, even if she couldn't seem to make eye contact with either of us.

After the jailhouse, I directed Mik out to the highway, to the turnoff that led to the rolling green fields of Little's surrounding areas. I pointed out a few odd things along the way — rotting barns, an abandoned water tower, a rusting 1950s Ford truck embedded nose down in a field — before I had Mik pull onto an inlet of gravel along the road.

We slid out of the Range Rover, the heat coming off the dusty road hitting us. Our feet crunched over the gravel as I walked Adam toward the final stop before lunch.

"This one's my favorite." We stepped into a puddle of shade beneath a leafy oak. "The Fairy Tree."

Adam stared up into its messy branches. "What is it?"

I told him how Drake and I used to come to this tree as little kids, along with thousands of other children over the years. For as long as I could remember, Mr. Costa, the old man who had owned this property, would leave little treasures in the dimpled hollows of the tree, taking anything kids left him in return. I showed him the pockets and nooks of the tree, smoothed from years of little hands.

"When he passed away last year," I told Adam, "they found every available surface of his home covered with the treasures from dozens of years of Fairy Tree children — every surface thick with them, like snow."

I told him how last summer, a local artist took all of them — each bouncy ball, drawing, action figure, rubber band, pound of loose change, hair ribbon, smooth river rock, everything — and fashioned them all into an incredible replica of this tree. "It's in the main entrance of the County Library. Sometimes, I just go look at it, when I'm feeling sad, and I think about Mr. Costa. I almost took you to see that, but I thought maybe you'd rather just see the tree itself."

Adam remained silent, running his fingers over the lacquered wood sign at the base of the tree:

COSTA FAIRY TREE
"THERE NEVER WAS A MERRY WORLD
SINCE THE FAIRIES LEFT OFF DANCING . . ."
— JOHN SELDEN

He stepped back, his mouth a thin line. Across the street, a dusty sedan pulled over, idling in the hot sun. Adam didn't turn his head, but I knew he sensed it had stopped. He tensed only a little, the way Extra Pickles would if he heard a distant door slam.

I started to ask him about it, but he pulled me in close to him. "This is a good spot."

The sun through the leaves of the Fairy Tree covered us in dappled spots of light, and I almost laughed at how close I suddenly was to him, how abrupt he'd been. "Scene eight," he whispered into my ear, his breath tickling me. "First public kiss." I knew this was coming. I knew scene eight meant the first kiss. I knew it; I just hadn't expected it *right now.* The press of his lips against mine caught me unprepared. His lips were warm, but because I hadn't really had time to take a breath, they left me feeling like someone had just pushed me into a pool before I could inhale, leaving me swirling, eyes open, underwater. I was breathless for all the wrong reasons; still, there was the warmth of his mouth, that spicy smell of his.

Then he pulled back, just an inch or two, his lips hovering there, and I could tell he was watching the photographer, just on the periphery. He was waiting him out. Dazed, I waited, too, the suddenness of his kiss like a wave at the beach knocking me off balance, leaving me shivering in surprise.

The idling car sped away down the street.

As Adam took several steps back, I knew something had shifted in our day. I couldn't quite pinpoint it, but somewhere between the moment that car had pulled up and the space where he kissed me, the curtain had been drawn again, the distance between us thick. He gave me an almost businesslike nod. "That was a good shot. And the Fairy Tree thing was perfect. Nice work." Not meeting my eyes, he hopped back into the Range Rover.

I stared off down the road, at the swirling dust of the departing photographer, the simplicity of the day congealing, returning to the former, complicated space between us.

I slid into the backseat again. When I'd noticed the scene about the kiss in the script, I'd imagined something bigger, something perhaps with a sound track or at least better lighting. Not some out-of-the-blue face-smash for the quick camera click of a jerk in a Budget rental car.

I guess I needed to dial down my expectations. It might have a script, but this was no movie.

* ✳ *

After leaving the Fairy Tree, Adam's mouth a ghost print on me, we stood in the cool, canopied entry to Ander's Community Gardens. "Ready for lunch?" I said flatly, motioning to the entrance.

He walked with me under the wrought-iron trellis swollen with leafy jasmine and out onto a sprawling stone courtyard. Dozens of people sat at ten or so wood picnic tables. I waved at Dad, who was handing out sandwiches and chips at a table near a fountain on the far side of the courtyard. I could see Adam take in the scruffy nature of most of the picnickers.

I leaned into him, whispering, "This is Sandwich Saturday. One Saturday a month, Little Eats provides lunch to the families staying at the Welcome House. I always help out." When he continued to stare blankly, I added, "This was on your schedule today." Maybe Parker hadn't mentioned it to him?

"What's the Welcome House?" His eyes took in the rows of food, the people sitting at tables.

"A shelter that caters to transitioning families." I picked up a stray sandwich wrapper that had blown our direction, wadding it up as we walked.

"You mean homeless?" His eyes settled on a little girl in a red sundress at the nearest table.

"For now. But the Welcome House has successfully placed over two dozen families this year in affordable housing. Give up that trailer of yours and it could be one more."

Parker suddenly materialized out of the shadow of a nearby grove of slender maples, giving Adam a little nod. Adam's face darkened.

Parker was with a woman who screamed journalist with her notebook and crisp white sundress and sandals. The cameraman tailing her like a puppy also gave her away.

Adam tensed beside me, whispering, "That's Robin Hamilton from *Watch!* magazine. She's doing a story on me while I'm here. She seems sweet, but don't get sucked in — she's ruthless. Don't say too much to her."

"Okay."

As people started noticing Adam, the energy shifted. A woman in a Giants T-shirt grinned up at me from where she sat at a nearby picnic table. "Whoa, you're here with Adam Jakes? That's wild."

"It *is* wild," I agreed as Parker sauntered up, his hands stuffed into the pockets of his expensive linen pants.

He nodded at the group in front of us as if he were surveying a set. "We should get some lovely shots here."

A woman in a blue flowered dress joined us, nervously fiddling with the fabric of her skirt. I nodded to her. "Adam, this is Julie Meyers," I told him. "She's the director of the Welcome House."

Adam flashed his smile. "Hi, Julie." Julie turned pink and managed a breathy hello. "This is really great work," he told her.

She thanked him, glancing at me. I smiled encouragingly,

knowing how tongue-tied people got in front of Adam. "What can we do to help?"

"Good idea," Adam said, moving toward the table where Dad passed out sandwiches. "Can I help you with that?" He signed an autograph for a woman and her tween daughter, who stared up at Adam with a stunned sort of grin.

"I never turn down help." Dad motioned toward an ice-filled cooler. "Each person gets a sandwich, some chips, a cookie, and one of those sodas."

I joined them at the table, handing a sandwich to a man I'd seen last week. "How'd your job interview go, Bob?"

He smiled, accepting the sandwich and choosing a pack of Cheetos. "They're going to let me know by next week."

I patted his arm. "Fingers crossed."

Robin Hamilton sidled up to the table. "I didn't know that homelessness was one of your causes, Adam." Her voice dripped with a sugary sort of falseness, a candy corn voice.

Adam gave her his floodlit smile, the kind I'd noticed he could conjure up on cue. "I'm here with Carter and her family to support the work they do with Julie at the Welcome House." He held up his hands. "Just a pair of extra hands today."

Parker jumped in. "But Adam has a fabulous announcement. He's going to donate ten thousand dollars to the Welcome House fund so that Julie and the Moons have the money they need to keep Sandwich Saturdays going well past our departure from Little." He whipped out one of those dorky checks, the oversized ones that people held up at ribbon cuttings and lottery announcements. He'd clearly had it stashed and ready for this moment.

Adam did a good job hiding what was obviously news to him. "Right. These families all need our support." He posed as the cameraman grabbed a shot of him with the giant check.

Not as skilled at hiding sudden news, Dad cleared his throat, stunned. "Oh, Adam — that's, well, that's terrific. I know the Welcome House thanks you, too." Julie nodded enthusiastically, her face going pink again. "Thank you," Dad repeated. "It's too much."

"Nonsense!" Parker leaned in as the cameraman also shot a picture of him with Adam and the giant check. "It's the least we can do for such a great cause."

Robin pinched her lips together. "Did you know about this before today, Mr. Moon? Ms. Meyers?"

They both shook their heads. Dad said, "We didn't. But we're very grateful." Dad's discomfort rolled from him, shimmery sheets of unease. Julie stood by silently, gaping at the check.

More pictures. Adam with Julie, Dad and the check, Adam with the check and several families, including the starry-eyed tween who'd already gotten his autograph, Adam with Parker, Julie and the check. The check got its own mini–photo shoot by the spread of food. Parker wandered over to me as Adam signed autographs for a family with two small boys and nudged me, his face smug. "Well, they've just had the best day of their lives."

I tried to keep a smile fixed to my face. "I'm sure they had a good time." What I wanted to mention, but didn't, was that the best day of their lives happened two days ago, when they'd been green-lighted for community-supported housing.

I set about helping Dad and Julie clean up the garden.

* ✱ *

Mik pulled the Range Rover in front of my house. My hand paused on the door handle. "I hope you liked your tour — I had a few more things planned, but . . . well, you said you had to get back to work since we spent the afternoon at Sandwich Saturday."

Adam leaned toward me a bit and said quietly, "I'll tell you what . . . it beat those Hollywood tours by a mile." His eyes, dark and drawn, drifted over my shoulder. "We'll finish it, I promise. Can I keep this?" He held up the map.

"Of course." I hesitated. "About the check . . . that was really generous of you."

"I wish Parker hadn't sprung that on you guys." He watched the same kids who'd been clutching Super Soakers that morning as they squealed through a spinning sprinkler, their faces pink with too much sun. Turning back to me, he said, "I feel bad that it turned into a circus back there."

"It was fine." My voice betrayed my discomfort.

There was his hand again, just above my knee. "I could tell it bothered you."

I tried not to think about how all the energy in the world seemed concentrated in that warm space between his hand and my thigh. "We really appreciate your contribution, seriously. I hope I didn't seem ungrateful. I've just gotten to know these families, and I'm not too comfortable with them being, well —"

"Used?" He gave me a sad sort of smile, his hand slipping to the leather seat. "Look, Parker means well, he does. I'm sure he thought it was a win-win for everyone, you know?"

"I know." I fiddled with the door handle. "It's just hard for them, and I hate seeing it used as a publicity stunt. At their expense."

He gave me the sort of melty eyes I'd seen in some of his movies. "I'm sorry. He could have handled that better. I'll talk to him."

I shook my head. "No, don't."

"At least it's a publicity stunt that helps out at the end of the day, right?"

I opened the door slightly. "True. That money's going to help so much. We're really grateful."

His eyes softened. "You mentioned that." His phone buzzed. Frowning, he ignored it and sighed. "Look, next time we'll just hang out. Not as a job, but just as, you know, friends."

"Right, friends."

His phone buzzed again. Rolling his eyes, he snatched at it. "I'd better take this before Parker has an aneurysm." He clicked it on. "Hold on a minute," he said into it sharply. To me, his voice softer, he said, "I have to shoot tonight and tomorrow until, like, four but maybe we can hang out tomorrow afternoon? Maybe have a coffee or something?"

"I'd like that." And, as I said it, I realized it was true.

I slipped out of the car, giving him a little wave before closing the door. In seconds, the car disappeared down the street.

Across from me on the opposite sidewalk, a man in baggy jeans and a black Metallica shirt stood taking pictures of us.

I turned and fled into the house.

eleven

The next afternoon, Adam decided to wait in the kitchen until I was done with my shift. The café was crowded, and I could tell he didn't want to be mobbed. He was having the opposite problem in the kitchen. When I left him, he'd been trying to convince Jones he was at least worthy of a glance in his general direction, saying something like, "So, you've got some interesting tattoos." Poor Adam. I didn't tell him Jones was a lost cause. It took him six months to acknowledge Chloe when she started working here. And she made him cookies.

Out front, I retied my apron and started to clear some dishes when the entrance jingled. It was a bit after the rush, so we didn't have a line. A woman closed the door behind her. Tall and slim, she wore an expensive plum-and-black yoga ensemble and had wound her thick blond hair into a severe knot at her neck. Sunglasses the size of coasters perched on her head, and she let her violet eyes graze our café, barely hiding her disgust.

Arching a blond eyebrow, she surveyed our chalkboard menu hanging on the wall behind me with a look that suggested we had dead bodies on display. "An iced tea. Herbal if you have it. And" —

her eyes strayed over the pastries on the counter, the quiche and salads in the cold case — "ugh, that's it."

"For here?"

"I think not." She checked her phone and tucked a stray lock of hair behind her ear with a quick flick. If I were that lock of hair, I wouldn't try that move again.

"We have passion fruit or lemon tea."

"Lemon."

"Small or large?" My hands hovered over the stacks of cups.

"It doesn't matter." Her eyes didn't leave her phone.

I filled a large to-go cup with ice and poured the tea. Clipping some mint from a sprig, I started to dust the tea with some leaves.

"What are you doing?" I suddenly had her full attention.

I hesitated with the lid. "Um, getting your drink."

"Um," she exaggerated, "I didn't want . . . whatever that is." She motioned at the mint as if it were rat poison. "And for the record, I don't really want your germs *all over* my tea."

Without missing a beat, I set the cup aside and filled another cup. I handed her a mint-free tea and a napkin.

"A lid?"

I started to reach for the lid from her first cup, thought again, and grabbed a new one. Careful not to put my germy hands *all over* it, I placed it gently next to her cup.

She sniffed. "Is this the large?"

"Yes." I caught Mr. Michaels's eye across the room, suppressing a grin when he scrunched up his face at her.

The woman started to push a five across the counter, but her eyes caught on something behind me. "Oh!"

At some point, unnoticed, Adam had come through the door and was standing behind me. He'd seen the whole interchange between us. "Wow, Leila, you can be a real witch when you're not kissing my butt."

The woman's face went from pale to a flash of red. "Adam! What're you doing here?"

"Hanging with Carter." He crossed to me and put his arm around my shoulders. "My *girlfriend*."

The ice queen melted. She proceeded to bumble, explain, and apologize all at once, flashing me a toothpaste-commercial smile, a trained look that said, *I didn't know*.

"You can go, Leila," Adam interrupted, and she hurried from the café, leaving her tea on the counter.

My body hummed, either from the exchange with Leila or from Adam calling me his girlfriend. Probably both. "Who was that?" I dumped the tea in the sink, my hand shaking.

"That was my trainer. Who just arrived today and who will now also be leaving today." He waved in the direction of her exit. It was sweet how offended he looked. "Please accept my apology on behalf of my *ex*-trainer."

"Oh, she was nothing." I pulled out a new creamer for the self-serve counter and gave it a little shake before heading to the stainless server.

He followed me out from behind the counter, causing only a minor stir. Our regulars had already learned to ignore us. "She was a she-devil. Why didn't you say something to her?"

After refilling the creamer, I organized the little bowl full of sugar and Equal packets. "Because it's not about me. She's not mad at *me*. Dad says to just stare at them when they act like that and say, 'Okay,' and not take it personally."

Adam shook his head, following me back behind the counter again. "No way. You should've refused to serve her."

I didn't mention the dozens of people who couldn't refuse to serve *him* when he was being a jerk. "If we refused to serve everyone who acted like that, we wouldn't have a café to run. Plus, come here." I motioned him back into the kitchen. "We've made a sort of game out of it." I pulled a heap of aprons from a hook, revealing our secret clipboard. "We send them to U.R.E.P."

He frowned. "To Europe?"

I showed him the clipboard. "U.R.E.P. Unnecessarily Rude Entitled Person. That way, we can look at each other and simply say quietly, 'Send her to U.R.E.P.' It helps vent it out and not cost us customers."

Under the heading, *U.R.E.P.*, it read: *Reason for travel* and had blanks where Little Eats employees could vent. There were pages of reasons, written in different ink colors and in various handwritings. *No one loves me*, was a popular choice, as was, *Too many pesticides in my food*. "See, look." I clicked my pen, took the clipboard, and pointed to the blank spot for Reason #437. "Poor me. You put mint in my tea," I whined, and then Adam snatched the pen and said as he wrote, *Because my boyfriend just left me for a B-list TV actress with better implants.*

My eyes widened. "Whoa, that's a good one. Specific."

He shrugged. "It's true."

I replaced the clipboard on the hook and covered it with the aprons. "See, we all have our coping strategies. No harm done."

"She's still fired."

I pushed through the kitchen door. Turning, I smiled at him standing in the doorway, his long body casual, his arms crossed across his chest. "Thanks."

* ✴ *

Hunter Fisch wasn't happy.

And he'd been growing steadily unhappier for the past two days. I'd never seen a famous director in action, and Hunter was living up to everything I'd imagined about filmmakers — creative, passionate, slightly crazy. Hunter was thirty-seven (I'd looked him up on IMDb) and had made a name for himself directing family-friendly fare like *At the Park* and *It Takes Four*, two movies I'd liked a lot, actually. They were, as one critic said, "the right balance of sweet and quirky."

Right now, I was pretty sure he was feeling neither sweet nor quirky.

At five eleven, he appeared taller, even from the edge of his chair in Video Village where he was currently frowning at a monitor. His receding dark hair was buzzed short, and he hid large green eyes behind thick frames that seemed to shift from black to purple. He wore designer jeans and a T-shirt, and his signature move seemed to be swooping his beat-up Sundance cap and headset off his head and rubbing his hands manically across his stubbly hair while he said things like, "I wonder if you could try that again, but this time, *mean* it."

I had a little crush on him.

I kept as quiet as possible from my own chair in Video Village, where they'd given me a headset to hear action from the active set. They were shooting in the hospital, and sometimes I liked to sneak to the edge of the set and watch Adam while trying to keep out of the way. Once, yesterday, Hunter had noticed me. "Do you work for me?"

I'd pointed at Adam.

"She's with me," he'd said, giving his director a thumbs-up.

That was the last of Hunter's attentions I'd received.

Right now, he was rubbing his head again. He left his hat and headset on his chair and walked onto the set. "Um, great — Stephanie?" He frowned at the actress in the hospital bed. "I want you to try that again, and this time . . . I want you to be, well, *sick*." I tiptoed over to where I could watch him talk to the actors. The lens of his glasses reflected the scene: two actors and a hospital bed doubled and in miniature.

Adam, who had been crouched eye level with the tiny actress tucked into the hospital bed, stood and stretched his arms above his head, yawning.

Honey-haired Stephanie blinked bright eyes at Hunter from the bed. "Can you elaborate?"

Hunter's lips pinched. Carefully, he said, "You have cancer." His left leg shook slightly, like it always did on the rung of his chair, artistic ADD. *"Cancer,"* he emphasized. "Very late stage. You're extremely ill. You know, as in *not well*."

"Do I seem too healthy?" She glanced quickly at Adam, who shrugged and winked at her.

More head rubbing. "You seem *quite* well . . . which is a problem for this scene. Kelly!" Hunter called over his shoulder. Kelly, a petite makeup artist with cropped copper hair, appeared at his side. "Can we make her paler? More dark circles? Something?"

Kelly studied Stephanie, her nose ring flashing. "If you want it to be a zombie movie." She gave a quick shake of her copper head. "It's not the makeup."

Hunter sighed. "Right. Okay, let's try this again. And can we stop with whoever feels the need to sound like his own rendition of 'Jingle Bells'?"

One of the crew, an enormous, sweet-faced guy named Thomas, who had clearly gotten into the Christmas spirit, gave his head a little shake, the bells on his Rudolph antlers shivering. He quickly tucked them away in a bag. "Sorry, boss."

Hunter's expression snagged somewhere between bemused and annoyed. "We're going to have to start calling you Tiny Tom."

Everyone laughed dutifully and got back to work.

A half hour later, they broke for lunch.

* ✳ *

I joined Adam outside in the tent that had been set up for cast and crew so they could grab a quick bite. Adam found a card table off by himself at the edge of the tent, next to a cutout window, and I sat in the seat next to him. Parker brought Adam a sandwich and a Diet Coke. He never seemed to eat with the rest of the cast, always preferring a sandwich to the meals craft services provided. He sat at the table, staring out at the fringe of pines on the hills beyond the hospital. Quietly, so only I could hear him, he sighed and said, "God, I hope this movie isn't terrible." He took a bite of sandwich. Turkey Gorgonzola with a balsamic spread. I'd made a bunch earlier for our café cold case and brought one for Adam. Studying it, he said, "This is a good sandwich. I bet you this movie won't be as good as this sandwich."

I could see the parking lot from where we sat, rows of film trailers, people moving equipment in and out of trucks. It would be lucky if ambulances could actually get into the turnabout. Hopefully, no one needed the hospital today for its actual purpose. "Won't there always be people who will think a movie's terrible and people who'll love it? Believe me, there are people who don't like that sandwich. A couple of the mouthy ones are on the U.R.E.P. list."

He popped open the Diet Coke can. It hissed, releasing a sweet, chemical smell. "I need it to do well. I need this to be a good movie."

Something in his voice felt ragged, frayed, and I leaned in a little closer. "Doesn't it just matter what you think of it?"

He looked at me with a sort of pity. "That's never what matters."

"Why?" Out the window, white clouds drifted like feathers, the sky so pale the blue was more a faint tint than a color. When he didn't answer, I said, "I mean, you can't really control it. So why worry about it? I can't control what people think of that sandwich, but I'm going to keep making them because I think they're delicious."

He nodded, licking some balsamic from his fingertips. "It's a little different. This sandwich didn't cost twenty-five million dollars to make."

Hunter came over to our table. "You okay if we get rolling soon?"

"Sure." Adam crumpled up the paper, drained his Diet Coke. He rubbed his hands together, looking at me with tired eyes. "Let's do something fun tonight."

Tonight was definitely not in the script. Parker had told me that Adam would be busy getting ready for a big scene he was shooting tomorrow. "Parker said you have to prep for tomorrow."

He rolled his eyes. "It'll be fine. Besides, I'd rather do something fun with you."

His words lit in my belly like a low flame. "My dad's playing with his band at an old barn tonight. I don't know if you'd think that would be fun, but it'll be mellow. Loads of good food."

He perked up. "Your dad's in a band?"

"A Bruce Springsteen cover band. Glory Daze. D-a-z-e." I made an apologetic face. "He thinks he's very clever. But it's pretty out by the barn, you know, if you're in the mood for a little bit country, a little bit rock and roll. And Jones is making his famous chili."

"That guy doesn't like me." He pushed himself away from the table, leaving behind the crumple of sandwich paper and the empty can of Diet Coke.

Watching him, I wondered what it must be like to care what everyone thought of you all the time, to be so trained, your body some sort of social chromatic tuner. I gave him a quick smile. "Don't worry, Jones doesn't like most people. Oh, and, Adam?"

"Yeah?"

"You going to throw that out?"

twelve

The old barn belonged to Mr. Jensen, one of our regulars. He owned Blue Acre Farm, known for their apple juice, but I was more a fan of their pumpkin patch in the fall. Mr. Jenkins always had the best-dressed scarecrows, and his wife made a pumpkin pie that would make your mouth water from seven miles away. We served it at the café in the fall and it always sold out by midday. For years now, Mr. Jensen had been coming to Little Eats one or two mornings a week. He would wander in, still wearing his overalls and messy work boots, eat a bagel sandwich with egg and ched-dar, and read a book. Then, he left a dollar and a haiku as a tip. I kept one of his haikus taped to my bathroom mirror at home.

Always bright smiling,
her face lighting, shoulders bent
to listen. Carter.

He'd written dozens of them for us. But that one was my favorite.

When we got around back of the red barn, Dad was setting up with Glory Daze on a platform stage built on the far side of a sprawling, flat, open space ringed with trees. In the fading evening, the band members moved as shadows, the bobbing string bulbs above them stippling their faces with light. The Jensens' granddaughter, Lila, home from UC Santa Cruz for the summer, had turned the area into a fairyland. Lights looped through the fat oak that stood sentinel in the center of the space, then stretched like glowing wings across it. She'd placed bunches of wildflowers into dozens of metal vases and watering cans, setting them on any available surface. A long table sat against the barn wall, covered in faded floral tablecloths, and already piled with apple pies, salads, freshly baked breads, and clay pots of preserves. Nearby, over an open fire pit, Jones stirred a pot of chili the size of a wheelbarrow.

Adam's eyes widened. "What's the occasion?"

"Summer." I grabbed his hand to pull him toward the stage, and his fingers laced through mine, not letting go, sending tiny shocks up my arm.

When we got to the edge of the stage, Dad paused from the mic check he'd been doing and smiled down at us. "You two should grab some of that sourdough bread before it disappears."

Mrs. Jensen hurried by, trailing the scent of cinnamon, her white hair curled into a knot at her neck. "Oh, don't rush them. There's plenty more where that came from." She stopped to plant a kiss on my cheek; at only five feet, she had to stand on her tiptoes. "Hi, darlin'." She eyed Adam shyly. "Who's your friend?"

Adam let go of my hand to shake hers, his eyes sparkling under his Lakers cap. "Adam."

She gave his hand a quick shake. "Well, help yourself, Mr. Adam. That bread's especially tasty with those strawberry preserves."

"Will do." He smiled, watching her scurry away. "Okay, she's from central casting."

I frowned at him. "What's that?"

"You know, like if you were going to cast someone to play an old farmer's wife — you'd cast her. She's exactly what you'd imagine for the part." At my blank look, he said, "It's just an expression," and moved toward the food tables. Around us, people started to fill up the courtyard, holding beers or homemade ginger ale in glass jelly jars.

No one seemed to notice Adam.

I came alongside him to survey the spread of food. "Do you ever look at the world and not relate it to the movies somehow?"

Pausing, he plucked a slice of sourdough bread from a basket, tore off a piece, and chewed it. "Not really." He waved to someone behind me.

Turning, I saw Alien Drake and Chloe walk in through the open side of the barn.

"Hey!" Chloe called, running up to us. "Look at this!" She held up a copy of *People*. "It's you! You're famous!" The headline read: "Adam Jakes Finds a Little Love." Under it, there was a picture of us kissing beneath the Fairy Tree. For how lame that kiss had actually been, I had to admit it looked really romantic in the magazine, the fringe of leaves making a halo around our faces. I scanned the short article. It made several references to Little Eats but didn't mention me by name. I was just "small-town girl" or "Little local girl," which made me feel like I should wear braids and sell hot cocoa in the Alps.

Chloe smiled at Adam. "Do you want to see it?" She held up the magazine.

"Nope." He tugged at the brim of his hat, popping the rest of the bread into his mouth, his shadow shield spreading across his face.

Chloe frowned, tucking the folded magazine into her patchwork messenger bag. She smoothed the front of her haltered sundress and, laughing nervously, she scanned the festivities. "I know. This isn't very exciting. Everyone here is, like, a hundred."

"I like it." Alien Drake headed over to where Jones stirred the chili.

Chloe watched him, her eyes worried.

"You two okay?" I asked.

"He's so grumpy lately." She glanced shyly at Adam. "I think he's a little jealous of Adam."

Adam watched Drake's retreat. "Well, I'm a little jealous of you guys — this place is unreal." He sipped a jelly jar of ginger ale I'd handed him. "Seriously, this is the best ginger ale I've ever had." He made it sound like ginger ale was something grand, something important. "But that stupid article" — he pointed at her messenger bag — "I couldn't care less about." He drained his glass, then left in search of a refill.

Chloe tried to hide her hurt feelings under a wobbly smile.

"Sorry." I laced my arm around her. "He can be such a jerk sometimes."

She pulled out the magazine again and stared down at the cover. "Well, maybe he's used to being in *People* magazine, but we're used to the Jensens' ginger ale, so I guess it's all relative."

I squeezed her shoulder. "Thanks for showing me. He might be used to being in those silly things, but it's weird to think of *me* being in one."

"Right?" she managed. "That's why I wanted you to see it." Then, she rolled the magazine up and smacked me over the head with it.

"What!? Ow, Chloe!" It didn't hurt, not really, but I couldn't believe she'd just thwacked me with a magazine.

"How could you not tell me about the kiss! I could *strangle* you."

I rubbed the top of my head. "Next time, use your words. No *hitting*. We've been over this."

She narrowed her eyes at me. "And we've been over what sort of information you never, ever fail to mention to your best friend. Kissing a movie star. You call me, got it?"

"Okay, okay. It wasn't that big of a deal."

Her eyebrows peaked. "Whatever, Ms. Calm and Collected, but it's actually *incredible*," she breathed, watching Adam refill his ginger ale. "Every boy you ever kiss again will have to know he has to live up to Adam Jakes." She shook her head, her earrings swirling. "You have the proof." She held up the magazine. "What was it like?" She waited, clutching the magazine to her chest.

"Better than Tad and the Subway Date Disaster."

She let out a whoosh of air, annoyed that I'd dodged the question. "Well, I should hope so." She stared at Adam across the patio. "Seriously, you're the luckiest girl I know."

My stomach ached, not from being hungry or sorry, but from wishing I could pull Chloe into the shade of a maple tree and tell her *everything*. Like how I didn't really know how Adam made me

148

feel. Like how this was all supposed to be fake, but those stupid butterflies every time he was close to me felt disturbingly real. Besides Alien Drake, Chloe was my best friend. And I wanted to share this with her, ask her if this was how she felt when Alien Drake kissed her. But I couldn't. Maybe it was okay that I couldn't. Even friends couldn't tell each other every secret we had tucked away. Some things were meant to stay in their hidden places, right?

So instead, we stood in the quiet of the yard, the evening sky dimming, the dark patch of night overhead deepening. It was nice when the band began to play, slowly at first, softly. It gave us something to fasten our attention to as a way of ignoring how strange the silence had suddenly become.

Besides, I wasn't like Chloe. I didn't need to broadcast things all the time. And she could stand to do a little less broadcasting of her Adam obsession, especially while Alien Drake was in earshot. Over by the food, Alien Drake kept sneaking glances at Adam, his face long. Poor guy. It was one thing to pin pictures of a movie star to your wall, but it was something entirely different when he was standing two feet away from your boyfriend.

"Drake looks really good in that shirt," I whispered to Chloe.

"Yeah, he's adorable," she said distractedly, her fingers tapping along to the music.

People filled plates of food and bowls of chili, and began swaying to Dad's easy guitar. "Well, I'm going to get some food." I headed toward the chili line, joining Adam, who was already waiting.

As we scooped the steaming, spicy chili into our bowls, Adam leaned into me. "You need to tell Chloe to relax about the pictures and stuff. Cut a guy a break." He nodded in Alien Drake's direction.

Surprised he'd noticed, I nodded. "I agree, but Chloe's Chloe."

After we got our food, we found a spot to watch the band at an old picnic table under the oak tree. Alien Drake and Chloe plunked down next to us, enveloped in their awkward we're-obviously-mad-at-each-other-but-pretending-not-to-be bubble.

"You two need to make up," I said through a mouth of cheese and chili.

"We're fine." Chloe drank half her ginger ale and plopped the jar on the table.

"Yeah, fine," Alien Drake echoed, his voice not sounding in the same zip code as fine.

"Yeah, you seem fine." Glory Daze was playing something loud and fast, so I kind of had to shout it. Didn't matter. They ignored me.

Adam spooned a big bite of chili into his mouth and bobbed his head to the music. Squinting into the hazy light of the yard, I watched people flood the small dance area. My stomach still ached. Too much chili, I told myself, knowing that wasn't it at all.

Alien Drake studied me. "Go dance." He looked sideways at Adam. "Seriously, you should see this girl dance. She's the best dancer I've ever seen. The best dancer in this town."

"Easy, Footloose," I said, my face heating. "Let's not exaggerate things."

Adam stared at me, looking as if I'd lied about my age. "I didn't know you were a dancer."

Chloe nodded so hard her earrings jangled. "Don't let her whole fake-modesty act fool you," she told Adam. "She won a huge scholarship to a prestigious school in New York last summer and *turned it down*."

I glared at Chloe. "Thank you for reporting, Chloe. News at eleven."

Adam set his empty bowl on the table. "Why'd you turn it down?"

Chloe toyed with one of her earrings that had tangled from her vigorous nodding. "Are you serious? You don't know our Carter very well yet. She's a Hobbit. She'll never venture far from the Shire. She's tied here."

Adam swirled his spoon in his chili and turned to look at me. "Anything particular tying you here?"

Before I could respond, there was a commotion at the stage, someone trying to get Dad's attention. And Dad was trying to ignore him and finish the song.

Alien Drake mumbled into his food, "Speak of the devil."

My brother.

As if sensing my gaze, John turned, spotted me across the courtyard, and his face darkened. No brightness for me tonight. Just a tumble of unbrushed hair and a raggedy vintage AC/DC T-shirt. He stormed over to our table, his energy like an incoming wave of heat, and shoved a tabloid in my face, one of the trashier ones printed on thin, inky paper. "You want to explain this?"

Adam bristled next to me. "Whoa," he breathed, standing up just as Drake did, and out of the shadows behind us, I felt Mik materialize, too. I had a sudden mountain range around me.

"Wait." I tried to focus on the tabloid, on the grainy picture.

John's arm shook. "This came today. Where I work. I have to look at this crap where I work?"

The article blared, "Adam Jakes's Little Lover Has Loser Brother."

I cringed at the *lover* and the *loser*. Stupid and hurtful for the sake of alliteration. I put my hand on John's arm, trying to steady the article so I could read it, but he wouldn't hold still. This wasn't the first time I'd seen my brother's eyes cloud and whirl like this. "I didn't know anything about it, I swear." My stomach twisted, the chili sitting like cement. "I would never want something like this out there."

"Well, it's out there," John hissed. "It's definitely out there." His eyes darted to Adam. He seemed to notice Adam now, to absorb *who* he was standing near. "Did you have something to do with this?"

Adam shook his head, wary of John like one would be of a tiger suddenly out of its cage. "That's not really how it works."

Anger pulsed in me. How was this my fault? It was *out there*, as he said, because he kept making dangerous choices. "You know what, John? If you don't like the way your life looks in a headline, maybe that has less to do with me and more to do with you." My voice shook, but John reeled back like I'd slapped him.

John opened his mouth to respond, but, suddenly, Dad was at his side, his hand on his elbow. "John, you need to go. Your sister's here with friends. Now's not the time."

John shook him away. "Oh, right. Her *friends*." His eyes burned into me. "I don't know what you're doing with Mr. Hollywood here, but leave me out of it." He tossed the tabloid at me; it fluttered, then disappeared beneath the picnic table. "This is my *life*, Carter. I don't need you judging it."

"I wasn't," I said, meeting his flashing eyes. "But it seems like you are, or you wouldn't care so much about that stupid article."

With Dad not on stage, the music had already stilled, leaving a hush in the yard. People tried not to watch us — shuffled feet, picked at their food — but their silence gaped. We'd become the show. Adrenaline leaked from me, and I was grateful we didn't have photographers clicking away all around us. Or maybe we did, and I didn't even notice it anymore.

Above us, clouds moved across the moon, passing ghosts.

Dad walked John away, both of their shoulders slumping. Adam was trying to catch my eye, but I avoided his. Pushing myself away from the table, I asked Mik to take me home. Somehow, he was the safest mountain right now.

Later, Adam knocked on the rim of my tree house doorway, the curtain I used as a door silhouetting him.

"Come in." Surprised to see him, I scooted over a bit so he had room to sit next to me.

He poked his head in, smelling of cinnamon and nighttime. "Cool fort."

"Not as cool as yours."

He crawled into the tree house and sat cross-legged next to me. "Mik said he brought you here."

I went back to watching the emerging stars out the window. "I didn't think Mik spoke. That's one of the reasons I picked him to drive me."

"He speaks." Adam produced a plate of apple pie and a fork.

"Mrs. Jensen insisted. She said to give the fork back to Mr. Jensen when you see him next. You're lucky I didn't eat it on the way over." That explained the cinnamon.

We sat for a few minutes, listening to crickets, not touching the pie. It struck me that, like Parker had said, a million girls *would* kill to trade places with me right now, sitting in a tree house with Adam Jakes bringing them pie and smelling of cinnamon.

"What?" he asked, narrowing his eyes at me. "You're making a strange face."

"You're just, well . . ." I took a small bite of pie. "Being so *thoughtful.*"

He leaned against the wall, stretching his long legs out in front of him. "Don't sound so surprised."

I chewed my lip. "Well, you aren't always . . ." I searched for the right way to say it. "So . . . nice."

He got the same look as when Hunter gave him notes after a scene — interested, but wary. "How am I?"

I hurried to explain. "I mean, you have nice moments, but mostly you're aloof. Distracted."

He nodded. "Fair enough."

"Sometimes spoiled, selfish."

He held up a hand. "Feel free to keep the list short."

"Sorry." I fiddled with a piece of broken-off crust on my plate, not meeting his eyes.

His whole body sighed next to me, and after a moment, he said, "I'm not in the business of trusting people right away. Kind of the opposite."

154

I studied the curve of his chin. "Is that why you crash red Corvettes?"

His smile deepened the curve. "It was a Porsche."

"What's the difference?"

He pretended to search the ground around him. "I think I might have a brochure." His voice teasing, he leaned his shoulder into mine, sending a low hum of current between us. "Here's a shocking Hollywood secret. Tabloids lie."

"So you didn't crash a red Porsche and publicly humiliate a beloved Disney actress at a Lakers game?" I took a bite of pie, the buttery apple filling melting on my tongue.

Adam ran a hand through his hair, any stray bit of fun leaving his eyes. "Okay, sometimes they lie, and sometimes they just need a story, so they . . . embellish. Leave things out. Craft a version of it the public will respond to. Or we *give* them a version we know they'll respond to. It's entertainment." His voice split into that annoyed edge I was more used to hearing from him. "It's what I do. Entertain."

"In your job or your life?"

"What's the difference?"

"I might have a brochure." I peeked under the pie plate. Feeling him relax again next to me, I added, "It sounds awful."

"It's not so bad." He leaned over and popped the piece of broken crust into his mouth.

"Careful, movie star. I'm not afraid to use this." I wielded my fork.

Swallowing, he used his thumb and finger to wipe the corners of his mouth and then gave me a stare, sad at its edges. "Not all of us are fortunate enough to be born a Hobbit."

"Chloe is overly dramatic."

"Is she right?"

I studied the empty plate. "Yes."

"Because of your brother?"

I looked sharply at him.

"I know, your rules. But I'm a movie star. I'm used to getting my way. You know, spoiled, selfish." He shrugged and shot a Hollywood promotion smile my direction, which, despite knowing it was his Hollywood promotion smile, still landed its target.

"Maybe you're not so nice." Maybe not nice, but he had the charm thing down. There was a reason he was paid a lot for that smile.

"Sometimes it helps to talk about it." He cleared my plate to the side and took my hand, sending a flutter through me. Why, when he touched me, did I feel like I was standing on the narrowest of ledges?

"This," I said, gesturing to his hand, "is definitely not in the script."

I could tell he knew I was avoiding the subject because his eyes fixed on me, the weight of their interest coaxing me to talk. Tractor beam eyes. Another thing he was paid a lot of money for — that stare. A stare that said, *The whole world just vanished, and we're the only ones here.*

"You can stop looking at me like that."

"Like what?"

"Like you're interested in my problems."

"I am."

The weird thing was, he *seemed* interested. Without warning, I had one hundred percent of Adam Jakes's attention, and maybe he was an excellent actor, but suddenly, I *was* the only other person in the world with him. His spotlight eyes, just for me. Quietly, he said, "You know, with my drug stuff and your brother's addiction, it was just a matter of time before the tabloids made that link. You can't worry about it."

"I always worry about him."

"Lucky guy." My heart tripped. Who worried about Adam? Not his parents. Not his little sister.

I'd never told anyone how guilty I felt that John had so many problems and my life was so easy, but for some reason, I found myself telling Adam Jakes. "My mom says that we've both been exactly who we are since we were tiny," I said, the tree house its own tiny galaxy. "John was like a dog behind an electric fence who pushed through, shook the electric sizzle off his coat, and headed out into the neighborhood to see what sort of trouble he could get into. Me — I was happy to sit on the lawn inside of the electric fence, knowing it was there, never testing it, staring at dandelions."

Adam studied me. "What if there's no fence?"

"I always feel like there's a fence."

He squeezed my hand, leaving a tingling imprint. "You need to get out into the world. When you do that, the fences get wider and wider apart."

I grimaced, pulling my hand away. "I think maybe we've exhausted the fence metaphor."

He watched the sky shift through the window, the web of pale cloud across the star-filled purple. "It can be good to see what else is out there. If only just to see it."

I didn't answer, didn't tell him that I was tired of people telling me I should leave Little. That I should dance, that I should go off to New York. Should. Should. Should. What if I didn't want to go? Not because I was scared or intimidated but because it didn't sound like something I wanted to do? Why did being a teenager give you a sell-by date? People just assumed leaving was the best thing. What if I thought staying was the best thing? When I thought of my ideal life, it wasn't something out on some blurred distant horizon. It was here. Here with the café, teaching at Snow Ridge, taking care of my brother. Not that he'd let me.

I didn't harbor the big-city dreams so many of my friends seemed to have, and I guess that made me some sort of provincial freak or something.

"I have a question," I finally said.

"Shoot." His gaze slipped back to me.

"When something feels right, why, just because we're turning a certain age, do we have to toss it all out in the name of some sort of adult success, in the name of growing up? Why do we always have to want something else, something better? What if it doesn't actually get better? What if everyone out there is just lying to me and it really doesn't get better than this?"

Adam settled back against the wall, frowning, thinking, the crickets filling up the tree house with their singing.

He didn't answer me.

yesterday's sightings

Things Are Looking Up in Little, CA

Morning, sky watchers. No blog about space would be complete without talking once in a while about possible life on other planets. Yeah, UFOs, aliens, weird lights in the sky — that sort of stuff. We did some research (thank you, Google) and found out that every day almost two hundred people report some sort of UFO activity. Almost two hundred times a day, someone, somewhere in the world, sees something in the sky they can't explain. It got us thinking about how we, as human beings, always have a hard time with things we can't explain — UFOs, Bigfoot, the Bermuda Triangle. We're fascinated by the things we can't figure out, by the things that don't have a right or wrong answer. Even when we can't explain them, we need to make some sort of sense out of them — create lists, find connections, map it out. Maybe that's why, when we can't seem to figure out all sorts of other more commonplace mysteries (like why we all keep looking at the sky as if it might talk to us), we still need to try.

We think maybe it's a lot like love, that need to make sense of the sky. We don't know why we need it, we can't explain it when it happens or when it doesn't, but we need it like we need air or food.

So we keep looking for it.

See you tonight, under the sky.

thirteen

It was snowing again in downtown Little. True, two guys sprayed it out of hoses, but when I arrived on set this morning, I couldn't believe how real it looked. Drifts of snow lined the edges of the street, icicles hung from the eaves, and someone had fringed all the parking meters in the shot with pine wreaths and red bows. Probably Tiny Tom. That guy was *really* feeling the Christmas spirit. When I arrived, I saw him over by the crafty table, slathering a bagel with cream cheese, his head adorned with reindeer antlers.

I found my chair in Video Village, dumped my bag next to the chair, and sipped some ice water, watching the setup. The temperature was already in the low nineties, so the crew was in tank tops and cutoff jeans. It was disorienting, my town in Christmas mode and everyone in shorts.

Adam stood in front of Baby Face, a day spa. Its sign had been removed and its window display was now a charming kitchen store someone had cleverly named Marley's Host, with gleaming copper pots hanging in the windows, multicolored Christmas lights reflected in their shiny bodies.

Today, Adam was shooting the Ghost of Christmas Past scene. The one where he bumped into a former classmate on the street and started to realize he'd been a huge jerk way back when and that his life wasn't the ski-boat-parties-and-toilet-papering-the-nerd-kid's-house bliss he thought it was. Epiphany, Hunter had explained this morning, his face so close to Adam's that the brim of his Sundance hat almost touched him, wasn't an instantaneous thing. Epiphany, Hunter had explained, happened in tiny bits of realization that swirled around one's head until they formed into an *ah-ha* moment. Epiphany, he assured Adam (clearly enjoying saying the word *epiphany*), like all good stories, had an arc. This scene, he'd said, was "especially crucial to that arc of epiphany for Scott."

"You ready?" Hunter asked Adam, settling into his chair.

"Yep." Adam held still, frozen, something he always did right before a scene started, like he was transporting himself from one world to the next. Sometimes it seemed as if actors were time travelers or astronauts. Or both.

Hunter called for quiet on the set.

Unfortunately, he didn't have jurisdiction over the crowd of protesters who had formed by the roped-off section of the street behind us. They seemed to be multiplying, four times what they were that first day. Clearly, Nora had taken me seriously about organizing. A pack of people holding signs marched up and down the rope, hoisting bold, bright signs that read what they chanted:

Go Home, Hollywood!

No Big Hollywood in Little

We're *Not* Starstruck!

Hunter craned his head. "Oh, jeez — not again?" One of his A.D.s jumped out of her chair, rushing to the rope line. Tiny Tom, who'd strung silvery strands of garland around the roped-off sections, tried to reason with the slim woman at the barrier. Nora. Again. Tiny Tom and the A.D. were getting nowhere with her, Nora casting her gaze straight past them, her sign held high.

I slipped out of my chair. "Hey, Nora," I said, approaching the line.

She squinted at me. "Carter?" Her sign sagged a bit. "What are you doing with these people?"

"I'm, well, I'm sort of dating the lead." I pointed toward where Adam stood waiting outside the faux kitchen store. He gave her a charming wave.

"Carter, do you have any idea about the environmental impact of that foam they're spraying? It could be hazardous. And they just keep shutting down the streets with no respect for our daily lives!" Nora's voice rose in pitch like a windstorm.

I listened, nodding, and tried to make eye contact with some of the other protesters, giving them each a knowing smile. I recognized most of them from the town hall meetings and various city protests I'd gone to with Mom. One thing Mom always said a protester wanted was to be heard, so I made sure to listen. When Nora was finished, I told her, "They've done all the safety checks, and the city approved all the materials. They're not here long, and they're paying a lot of money for this space, which is good for Little, right? Can we just let them get on with it, so they can clear out of here on schedule?" I used the cool voice I'd seen Mom use with police or city councilmen.

Nora thought about it, her face darkening.

I bit my lip and added, "Besides, this isn't a long-term problem. They're out of here the beginning of July. You've organized such an amazing group. Don't you think it would be best to put them on something long-term?" I racked my brain for a list of

Mom's recent dinner topics. "The new housing development on Madison Hill? Or that company that's dumping stuff near the river?" I lowered my voice. "Think of the salmon."

She wiped at trickles of sweat on her face. "Yeah, I see what you're saying." She peered at the movie set. "They're really gone early July?"

I motioned behind me. "They're barely here; they're a blip on Little's radar."

"They're obnoxious." She glowered in the direction of Hunter, who sat up and gave her his best *We're all in this together* smile, but it melted quickly under her hot gaze. "Yesterday, one of them parked on Edna Barkley's front lawn. Her front lawn!" The protesters murmured behind her.

Edna Barkley was a crazy person about her lawn, which spilled dangerously close to the sidewalk on Pine. *Many* people had parked on Edna Barkley's front lawn. But I agreed, diplomatically. "That's terrible. I'll talk to them. But think of the salmon, Nora. . . ." I trailed off, gazing out in the direction of the river, as if I could hear their fishy cries for help.

She followed my gaze, listening. With a nod, she moved to huddle with several of the other protesters, whispering and slipping quick glances at me, motioning to the others with big sweeping hands. After a few minutes, they lowered their signs and headed back up the street.

Tiny Tom stared at me, his antlers sagging in the heat. "You ever think about a career in politics?"

"No, thanks." I returned to my seat and (no longer icy) water. Hunter gave me a thumbs-up and called for last looks, then quiet on the set.

Enter the former nerdy classmate.

The guy playing him, an actor named Ryan who'd given me a quick smile earlier, stubbed out a cigarette and pulled on a wool jacket. He got a pat of makeup from Kelly and meandered into the snowy street scene.

Adam came out of the kitchen store, wearing a red ski beanie and carrying a brightly wrapped present. After bumping into his Christmas Past, he started to move around him when Ryan said, *"Scott?"*

Adam squinted through the falling snow, clutching his package. *"Do I know you?"*

"It's Tommy. Tommy Winter-Smith from Washington Elementary?"

Everything looked dreamy, the falling snow, the green of the wreath on the door, the gleaming pots . . . until a scrub jay decided to land in the middle of the scene, twitching its blue head.

"Cut!" Hunter yelled. "Can someone get the stupid bird out of my shot?"

A crew member shooed it away. At least it wasn't carrying a picket sign.

They ran the scene about five times, each time dealing with something summery that decided to infiltrate the winter-scape. Finally, Hunter seemed happy with the result and they broke for a late lunch. I pulled my bag over my shoulder and walked over to Adam.

He swept off his hat, winter coat, and sweater. "Man. It's a hundred degrees." He seemed older with all the makeup. "We need to go swimming later."

"Chloe's uncle lives in a cabin on the river." I imagined the cold river water enveloping my sticky skin. "It's got a great swimming hole."

"Perfect." He gave me a tired smile, his eyes straying past me,

164

lighting on a pack of girls, maybe two dozen, gathered near the cordoned-off edge of the street where the protesters had been, clutching small notebooks. They took pictures of us with their phones and cameras. Mik stood there quietly, making sure they didn't cross the rope.

"Adam!" one of them screeched.

He gave them a wave and his turbocharged smile. "Hi, girls."

More screaming.

The girls had become their own sort of snowdrift, piling almost on top of one another to get as close to the rope line as possible. Behind them, like a layer of flotsam caught against the screaming blob of girls, paparazzi waited, smoking cigarettes in various phases of boredom.

Adam gave me an apologetic version of his smile. "I should go sign some autographs."

I waved him on. "Of course." He could try for apologetic, but he clearly loved it, and perked up as he neared them, the attention like an espresso shot.

He trotted over, making casual small talk as he signed their notebooks, their glossy head shots of him. One had the magazine cover Dad had shown me this morning — Adam and I sitting on a bench outside of Little Eats, Adam grinning at something fascinating I was saying (scene 9: look like I'm saying something fascinating). The headline read: "A Little Love." These magazines were getting redundant.

I wandered a bit closer to the line. Adam signed the magazine, and I heard the girl, an overdressed tween in plastic-heeled sandals, say loudly, "What do you see in *her*?"

Not really interested in the fake answer, I drifted toward the table set with coffee and tea service. My stomach rumbled, so I fished around in my bag for the sandwich I'd brought. I had it halfway unwrapped when Ghost of Christmas Past Ryan wandered over. He nodded at my sandwich. "Where'd you get that?"

"I brought it."

"Looks good."

I offered him half. Shaking his head, he told me, "They feed us great on the set. Yesterday, we had lobster salad."

"Cool."

He nodded distractedly. "Yeah, we get steak and all sorts of stuff. We had this killer chicken Caesar the other night."

A flush of pride went through me. "I made that."

"You did?"

"Well, it's my parents' café, actually, that made it. Little Eats." I pointed in the general direction of our café.

"Well, we can't *all* be the star of the show." He meant it as a joke, I could tell, but it sounded heavy in his mouth.

"Just the star of salad dressing, I guess." I glanced around the empty set, trying to manufacture a reason to escape this particular conversation. Something in this guy seemed sad, like he was wearing his own ghost of something past. I folded the wrapper back around my sandwich and jammed it into my bag.

Ryan made himself a cup of coffee. As he swirled some cream into his cup, he sighed. "I've been doing this ten years," he said, more to himself than to me.

"Acting?"

He laughed, the heaviness slipping into an edge. "Yeah, *acting.* I have a degree from CalArts, you know." He sipped the coffee.

I flashed him the kind of smile I'd seen Adam give fans, kind but distancing. "How would I know that?" I tried to sound like I was teasing him but, unlike Adam, I was a terrible actor.

His eyes fell on me, and he held up his hands as if in surrender. "Okay, you're right. Of course you wouldn't know that. Half the world knows what Adam Jakes had for breakfast, but four years of toil shouldn't be something people know." He took another short sip of coffee. "Of course, you would already know what Adam Jakes had for breakfast."

I squinted at him as if he were out of focus. "Are you being mean to me on purpose?"

Ryan's shoulders slumped. "I'm being a jerk, aren't I?"

Looking at him, I held up my thumb and forefinger in a pinch. "Little bit, yeah."

His face softened. "I'm sorry. I'm doing that so much lately. My girlfriend said if I don't knock it off, she won't care if I live in my car as long as I'm not living with her anymore." He watched Adam signing more autographs, his face slack.

I didn't know whether to flee or give him what was clearly a much-needed hug. "Are you sure you're okay?"

He peeled his eyes from Adam and gave me a smile that was more like a shrug. "Sure. It's just, all this time, and I've gotten a Sprint commercial, a bunch of TV walk-ons, a few bit parts in movies, a couple of plays. At least I have lines in this film. And I was in a play with Bart Jemson, you know, Matt Jones from that sitcom *Keeping Up*?"

I told him I'd never heard of it. He blinked a few times, deflating like a balloon. "You've never heard of *Keeping Up*? It won, like, six Emmys." At my shrug, Ryan shook his head. "See, I should just quit the business now and move back to Michigan."

I fiddled with the little packets of sweetener they had in a bowl on the coffee table, organizing them by color out of habit. "Please don't quit acting because I'm an idiot about random television shows. I mean, I live in Little, California." I tried to give him a self-deprecating smile.

"It was on for *eight* seasons. Oh well." He sighed and held up his coffee cup, a sad "cheers" of sorts. "At least they feed us."

Adam sidled up beside me. "Did you say something about a swimming hole?"

I looked at Ryan. "We're going swimming later if you want to come."

His eyes brightened, darted to Adam. "Seriously?"

Adam gave him a quick smile. "Hey, man, no offense, but I was sort of just hoping to hang out with Carter. You don't mind, right?"

The balloon deflated a second time, but he managed to sound breezy. "Totally. No problem. Great scene."

Maybe four years of CalArts did come in handy.

∗ ✳ ∗

After Adam finished shooting for the day, we stopped to grab our bathing suits and some food, and Chloe texted us the combination to the lock on her uncle's chained gate so we could go swimming. Her uncle was out of town attending some sort of survivalist training in the Oregon wilderness, so we'd have the swimming hole to ourselves. She signed off, *Jealous!* and I was hit with another sickening surge of guilt that I hoped the river would wash away.

When we arrived at the secluded property, Mik parked under the shade of a massive ponderosa pine. He waved off our invite, rolling down the window and opening a novel instead.

"Your bodyguard's reading a romance novel," I pointed out as we picked our way over the river rocks to the water's edge.

"*Spy* romance; more manly," Adam clarified, shooting me a teasing smile, and balanced a cooler on a flat rock. "Wow, this is great."

Nodding, I didn't tell him how relieved I was that Chloe's uncle was gone. I'd always thought he was crazy, with his darting eyes and constant need to be canning some fruit or vegetable and stockpiling supplies in his one-room cabin by the river. Alien Drake always joked that his place would make a great setting for a horror movie. Which was true.

But I loved his private stretch of the river, the sweep of the wide water into the swirl of the swimming hole, deep green and still, the trees secluding it from view, the granite boulders huge here, rounded elephant backs in the water. Somehow, even in the early evening heat, the air felt tinged with a damp coolness. We could be the only two people in the world.

I squeezed some sunscreen from a tube and rubbed it onto my face. "Chloe's uncle's kind of a recluse. He only leaves to go back-country camping or to survivalist workshops. He's lived here for over thirty years. He was a stockbroker who sort of just cracked one day. Moved here. We have a lot of people like that in Little, especially in the remote areas. Really off the grid."

"How very Henry David Thoreau of them all." Adam pulled any icy bottle of water out of the cooler.

I offered him the sunscreen. "Some of them. Some of them are more Unabomber than 'sucking the marrow out of life' sorts." I was about to go on, to say something about the different kinds of people who felt drawn to this river, to its flow, its gurgle and click over the rocks. It would have sounded really smart, too, except that Adam took off his shirt, and then I couldn't think of anything to say at all.

Movie stars really shouldn't be allowed to take off their shirts in front of normal people.

To say that the expanse of his smooth tanned skin struck me mute would be an understatement. It had some sort of paralyzing body-mind-soul reaction and I became a river rock statue: *Ordinary Girl Struck Dumb*. He must have seen my face because he hid a smile. "I'm going to jump in before we eat."

I wore a pale green bikini under my pair of cutoff Levi's and white tank. I loved this bikini mostly because it managed to cover enough of me while not pulling or puckering in any wrong place, but suddenly, standing next to The Body, I felt like keeping my clothes on. Which was probably the exact opposite of what most girls felt when they looked at Adam Jakes. Especially shirtless.

I plopped down on top of a rock half submerged in the river, wiggling my toes in the cool water. "Why didn't you want Ryan to come?"

He frowned. "Ryan?"

"That other actor."

Sighing, he turned and waded out into the river a bit, the water churning around his shins. For the record, the back of him was just as good a view as the front. "Would you believe that I just wanted to be with you?"

"Not really." Even so, when he said it, my stomach flipped.

He turned back to me. The light made the hairs of his arms glow, which only added a sort of superhuman element. "Well, it's true. I wanted to be with someone who didn't want something from me, you know? Who didn't see an afternoon with me as a potential career move."

"He says to the girl he's paying to hang out with him." I wanted to keep my voice a tease, playful, but it caught a bit, stumbling over the sound of the moving river. He must have only heard the tease because he laughed, then dove into the ring of water. I watched him splash around, a slick brown seal. Waiting for him to dive under again, I hurried out of my shorts and tank and dove in to join him, my body shocked by the cold water.

Gasping, I came to the surface, my toes trailing along the rocky bottom.

On the other side of the swimming hole, Adam pulled himself onto a flat rock, the sun dappling him through the trees. "You know," he said, rolling onto his back, "I wasn't very happy with our first kiss by that Fairy Tree."

I flattened myself, belly-down, to a nearby rock, my stomach and head both light. I told myself it was the shock of the water, but I knew it was more likely the shock of him, of being here in this place with him, everything green and moving water and light. "Oh right, well, you could have prepared me a little more. Give a girl a warning." The sun warmed my back. With my face resting in my overlapped hands, I closed my eyes, smelling the green scent of the rock beneath me, slipping into a sleepy river haze.

Adam sat up. "We have more kisses coming up in the script. Fourth of July. Big kiss there."

"Right. Kissing under the fireworks. Parker's not subtle." I felt dizzy with all this talk of kissing. "Where is he, anyway?" I mumbled into my hands. "I didn't see him today."

"He had to go back to L.A. for some business stuff. He'll be back tomorrow." I heard a splash, and suddenly, he was next to me on the rock, his skin wet, the cool water spreading out beneath him on the warm rock, spilling under my belly. "So, shall we rehearse?" I felt his breath on the side of my face.

Heart racing, I pushed up onto my forearms. I could see the curve of my body reflected in his sunglasses. "Rehearse?"

As an answer, he leaned into me, cool shoulder touching mine, and kissed me, his mouth warm. I couldn't be sure if the rushing sound was the water or in my head. Or both. Definitely both. This kiss was worlds away from the one at the Fairy Tree. Soft, slow.

When he pulled back, he smiled. "Well?"

"I'm not sure if you need to rehearse this sort of thing." I swallowed hard, my body tingling as I watched him slip back into the swirling water.

Besides, that hadn't felt like rehearsal.

That felt real.

Stop it, stop it, stop it, I told myself. I could not fall for this guy, not a guy who had approximately 16,437 individual fan clubs online.

I dropped my head back onto my folded hands, my heart hammering.

Pull it together, Carter. This was a job. It wasn't real. None of this was real. Of course, the more I told myself this, repeated it over and over into the warmth of the river rock, the more I realized what a big liar I was. Because it was feeling dangerously real to me.

fourteen

"What'd you do today?" Alien Drake shook the ice at the bottom of his drained mocha, his feet propped up on the railing. We sat in the shade of his porch, the afternoon heat leaking in around us.

I sipped my drink. "Worked. You?"

"River."

River. Flashes of yesterday's kiss pooled in my head.

Alien Drake gave me a strange look. "You have the dopiest look on your face right now."

"Do I?" I tried to wrangle my dopey expression into something resembling indifference.

Alien Drake narrowed his eyes at me. "You really like this guy, don't you?"

I lifted my hair off my neck, leaning into the fan we had propped on a lawn chair nearby that funneled cool air our way. "I don't know."

He grimaced like he'd swallowed something sour. "Ugh, you do, don't you?"

"Subject change!"

He shrugged. "Fine. You want to grab something to eat?"

I checked my watch. I had a couple of hours until I taught my dance class at Snow Ridge. "Sure."

"Unless you have to make out with your movie star." He folded his arms across his chest.

I sipped my iced tea, widening my eyes at him. "Well, that's a tone I don't love."

"Sorry. Where is he, anyway?"

"Working. He has a job." Adam was shooting a scene in an old house by the river, and they didn't really have room for me to just hang out there. I'd be stuffed in another room wearing a headset. He was scheduled to shoot for twelve hours, and I'd barely get to talk to him.

Alien Drake made another unpleasant face. "I didn't think movie stars actually worked. I thought they partied on yachts with supermodels."

"Only between shoots."

He pressed his plastic cup against his forehead. "What is *with* this heat? Satan's complaining. I hope it's not this hot for the Fourth."

He was so *pissy* today. It wasn't like him. "Do you hear that? It's your Hawaiian ancestors calling you a wuss." I spritzed him with the water bottle sitting next to us on the porch swing and gave up my spot in front of the fan. Like I had minutes ago, he was trying to change the subject. Our standard operating procedure when things got snappish between us. Change the subject before (not after) a fight erupted. Alien Drake didn't fight. He just wouldn't let it get that far. If it got close, he'd suggest going out for Taco Bell or frozen yogurt.

But for some reason, I found myself changing the rules. "You don't like him, do you?"

Alien Drake shook the ice again, clearly deciding whether or not to engage. Finally, he said, "Why do *you* like him?"

174

I'd known Alien Drake long enough to know this was a signature move, answering a question with a question. "I just do." And as I said it, I realized that yes, I liked Adam Jakes.

Too much.

I pulled the lid off my iced tea and fished out an ice cube. Aiming, I tossed it at the birdbath in the center of the patch of grass in Alien Drake's front yard. "You seem like you have a problem with that." No more questions for Alien Drake. I'd give him statements.

He fished around in his drink for some ice. "I'm just surprised." Following my lead, he tossed it at the birdbath, hitting it on the first try. A blue jay hopped back, taking a swipe at the cube of ice; startled, it squawked away. He tried again. Perfect shot. "To be honest, I'd expect this kind of behavior from Chloe and, well, most of the other girls in this town, but not you." The disappointment in his voice had a blade.

"I'm not allowed to have a crush on a movie star? Not practical, predictable Carter — is that it?" Something unknown began simmering in me, something deep that felt like lava thickening.

"That's not what I meant." Alien Drake did not look happy to be having this conversation. He looked like he was having nonelective surgery. His third cube missed the birdbath by about a foot.

"What did you mean, then?"

"Never mind."

"No, not never mind. Is it really so impossible to believe I might like him and he might like me?"

So I almost couldn't hear it, he said, "Actually, yes." Two words. Only two, but he might as well have heaved a stone house on top of me for the weight they held. "Sorry, Carter. It's weird. Chloe's got pictures of this guy tacked all over her wall and now you're *with* him."

I stood, leaving my iced tea on the white wicker table next to our chairs. "Are you mad at me or Chloe? Because she's the one drooling all over someone who isn't her boyfriend."

"Because he's a *movie star*." He kept shaking his head. "It just doesn't make any sense."

I took his porch steps two at a time. When I hit the landing, I turned. He sat miserably in his chair, his wide face flushed, no trace of his usual smile. I started to try to fix it, but for some reason, I wanted to stay mad, I didn't want to fix it. Not right now. I felt guilty for not telling him the truth about Adam, but it didn't matter what was true. "Look," I told him. "I don't know what's going to happen with Adam. It's all really new and strange. I can't explain it, but the thing is, with you, I shouldn't have to try."

Then I went home to get my teaching stuff for Snow Ridge.

✳ ✸ ✳

I dropped my bag on the chair by the stereo. Mr. Hines was already there, waiting in his wheelchair by the window, and I gave him a little wave. He frowned, which in Mr. Hines's world was as good as getting a hug.

I got the fan going and opened another window, and it helped move the still, warm air around the room. The room where I taught dance had pale hardwood floors and tall, wide windows that looked out onto the pool. Still shaken from my fight with Alien Drake earlier, I took a moment to just stare at the rectangular blue shimmer of it, at the two or three elderly women moving through its cool blue water.

A minute later, Adam poked his head in the door. "This where you teach?" He emerged into the room, trailed by what I thought at first was a film crew, but then realized were several members of the press, including Robin Hamilton and her cameraman from Sandwich Saturday.

"What are you doing here?" He'd brought press to my dance class? Wait. I scrolled through the texts from Parker on my phone. Oh, right. He'd texted me about it last night. I just couldn't seem to keep everything in my head. Hurrying to the stereo, I tried to look organized as I fed a CD I'd made yesterday into it.

Adam's smile faltered, but he turned to Robin. "See what I told you? So dedicated to Snow Ridge she forgets all about me. Gotta love her priorities." Robin scribbled something into her notebook. He gave me his lopsided megawatt smile. "But she's always glad to see me." His look said, *Fix this please; look happy to see me.*

I nodded lamely. "Sure am." I was a bad, bad actor.

Behind him, two of my regulars, Helen Brown and Elsa Pinter, stood in the doorway, their lined faces confused. They wore the sweats and light, summery shirts favored by the octogenarian women here at Snow Ridge. "Carter?" Helen patted her halo of white hair. "Are we having class?" Her eyes darted nervously to the cameraman standing behind Adam.

I waved them in. "We are. Sorry for all this. This is, um" — I bit my lip, looking at Adam — "Adam Jakes. He's here with me today." I felt dumb introducing him. It felt like pointing at a tree and saying, *This is a tree.*

Elsa squealed like a tween. "Oh, you're the movie star! We

read about you in the paper." She hurried over to him, fiddling with the loop of her too-big belt.

He made a show of kissing her hand, leaving her giggling and pink-cheeked. "Thought I'd join you today, if that's okay?" They nodded their white-haired heads.

A half dozen others drifted in, making introductions or eyeing Adam suspiciously, depending on the person. Two or three took one look at the camera, at the woman jotting down notes, and fled back to their rooms. "You're scaring off my regulars," I told Adam.

He grinned sheepishly, and I shot him the best ain't-we-cute? smile I could muster. Robin scribbled something on her pad.

I turned on the music, something light and peppy for warm-up. "Okay, all. Let's get in our places." Elsa wheeled Mr. Hines to the front row. Adam settled in a nearby chair, and I faced my nine students.

I worked them through a series of easy steps, the same ones we did each week but to different music. Whatever I could find on iTunes that sounded fun, sometimes classics, sometimes random indie stuff I could download for super cheap.

At the end of class, they always asked me to "do a dance" for them. That's how they always phrased it. "Are you going to do a dance?" As if there simply wasn't a verb for dance, just a noun. Usually, I didn't blink, but today I glanced at Adam, who sat in a chair by the window, staring out at the pool. I didn't need a journalism degree to notice he wasn't even really watching.

I started to pack up my bag.

"Wait!" Elsa squeaked. "Aren't you going to do a dance?"

Adam sat up, his eyes settling on me.

"I was thinking maybe I'd skip it today."

They protested.

Not politely.

"Well, so much for the idea that your generation has better manners." I laughed, skipping a few songs ahead on the CD until I hit an old favorite. It was deliciously languid and not too long, just acoustic guitar, and it let me move like water, lyrical and unhurried. Perfect for the end of a hot day. I tried not to imagine Adam watching me move, watching me spin in the slanting light of the evening, my body shifting to this slow, dreamy song.

When I finished, everyone clapped, including Adam, who was staring at me with distant, sad eyes. I hurried to take the CD from the player. Helen and Elsa scurried over to Adam so he could sign autographs for their grandchildren. After retrieving Mr. Hines, they gave me a final wave at the doorway. "Great class! That dance was beautiful," Elsa told me. Mr. Hines frowned his approval.

I wiped my forehead with the back of my hand, avoiding Adam's eyes. "Thanks, I love that song." I waved as Elsa wheeled Mr. Hines out of the room.

Mrs. Adler meandered toward me, a towel around her slender neck. I adored Mrs. Adler. At ninety-four years old, she simply oozed poise and grace, but wasn't afraid to tell you how she saw things. "Thanks, darling. Always the highlight of my week." She gave my hand the little pat she always gave me after class.

"I'm glad you liked the class." I popped the CD into its plastic cover.

She gave a dismissive wave. "Oh, the class, sure. Lets us shuffle our old bones. But the best part is always watching *you* dance."

I smiled, blushing, and stuffed the CD into my bag. She noticed my discomfort and put a cool hand on my arm. "Can you introduce me to your gentleman friend?" Her watery eyes gleamed as Adam came over to shake her papery hand.

"Adam," he said, almost shyly. Mrs. Adler could even make a movie star avert his eyes. She was that classy.

She introduced herself. "Well, I'll be. Ninety-four years old and I'm shaking the hand of a movie star. You're no Paul Newman, but you'll do."

Adam let out a genuine laugh. "Well, thank you, Mrs. Adler. Ninety-four years old is impressive."

She waved him off, the towel slipping from her neck. "It's not impressive, young man. Nothing impressive about something I have no control over. Just get up each day."

I bent to retrieve her towel. "It seems impressive to us."

She hooked it once again around her neck, somehow making it elegant. "You're young. Always getting impressed with the wrong sorts of things. Give it some time." She gave a little wave before shuffling from the room.

"She's a riot." Adam watched her go. "That was fun. You're a good teacher." His eyes fell on me. "And dancer," he added softly.

I turned away. "Oh, that wasn't really much of anything." I moved around the room, repositioning the chairs that were pushed up against the wall back into rows so they'd be ready for the book club I knew they held at night.

Before he could respond, the reporter sidled up. "So, it's Carter, right?"

I blew a strand of hair from my eyes. "Yes."

"Nice to see you again. Robin Hamilton with *Watch!* magazine."

You could even *hear* the exclamation point in the way she said the magazine's name. "I was wondering if I could chat with you for a minute for my story?"

Adam's face darkened. "Hey, Robin, I don't want Carter feeling pressured. She's a private citizen."

Like he was some sort of general in an army.

"It's okay." I waited for her question, my hands hovering over the back of one of the chairs.

Robin's eyes lit up. She asked about my job at Little Eats, about the way we met, about our time together so far, all questions Parker had prepped for me. Then, she had a final question, touching her pen to her lip conspiratorially. "So, girl to girl, Carter. Does it bother you that he's shooting a *kissing* scene with another local girl?" She flipped through her notes. "Someone from your grade, if I'm not mistaken. Beckett Ray? Do you worry he'll stray?" She giggled at her rhyme. My head clouded. Beckett Ray? What was she talking about? I clearly couldn't hide my surprise because she looked positively gleeful. "Oh, didn't you know? She was just cast. He was shooting with her all day at a house by the river!"

I squeezed the back of the chair. "Adam's a professional. If he's working, he's working." I didn't really know where that came from, but I thought it actually sounded pretty good.

The cameraman snapped a picture.

Adam put his arm around me, his eyes guarded. He had my bag slung over his shoulder. "We should really be going. Let Parker know if you need anything else." As he ushered me out of the room, and out of their sight, his arm dropped away from my shoulders and he handed me back my bag.

fifteen

Outside, the evening darkened the trees. We crossed the parking lot where Mik had the Range Rover tucked in the shadows. Before we could reach it, Adam caught my arm, turning me toward him. "Why didn't you take that scholarship?"

I watched over his shoulder as Robin Hamilton and her cameraman pushed through the doors of Snow Ridge. Seeing us, she stopped, nudging her camera guy. He snapped a few pictures. Adam turned, saw them, too, and knowing they would mistake this for a fight (not in the script), he hurried me into the Range Rover. "My car's here," I started, but Adam assured me he'd have someone drive me back to it later.

"Okay." Soon the cool air of the Range Rover enveloped us.

Mik pulled the car out of the lot.

With Snow Ridge fading into the distance behind us, Adam asked me his question again.

"It's kind of hard to explain." I studied the houses passing us outside, each yard familiar to me yet foreign — little universes of their own. On one lawn, a family sat in folding chairs, their yard threaded with colored lanterns, the kids playing with sparklers, the Fourth starting early.

Mik turned the car toward town. *We must be heading back to base camp.* I closed my eyes, leaning my body into the soft leather of the Range Rover, my muscles limber from dancing. The car hummed over the road.

I heard myself talking before realizing I'd started. "Remember when you were little and you were just supposed to love something? No one asked you why. You could spend hours and hours on it, and nobody worried about whether you were going to turn it into anything. It didn't have to be about anything . . . *productive.* You could just paint or dance or collect bugs or sea glass and it was just a lovely thing, remember?"

Adam shifted in the seat next to me. "I never really had that."

I hadn't thought about that. He'd had the show, always the show, so he'd been creating something for that bigger world all along, the world that wanted products. He sighed, his head turned toward his own window. With the purple sky behind him, he looked like he should be the prince in one of those fairy-tale retellings Hollywood kept churning out. Which, now that I thought about it, he had been a year or two ago in a remake of *Sleeping Beauty.*

Finally, his head still turned away, he said, "I used to collect baseball cards. I remember there was a store in this funky part of L.A. that my dad would take me to, rare cards and that sort of thing. We'd spend hours in there. Then people found out I collected, and they just started sending me all these really hard-to-get ones, so I stopped. I mean, it was nice of them and all, but it just took the fun out of it."

I nodded. In so many ways that was what had happened to my

dancing, that slow melting of fun. "That's like dance. I don't know when it happened, but somewhere, all the fun just *evaporated*."

Mik pulled the car up to the gate.

I took a breath, knowing I was about to tell Adam something I'd never told anyone else. Why did I feel like I could talk to him? Maybe because I knew he was leaving soon. In a week, he'd be gone and could take my secret with him, but even as I thought it, I knew it was more than that. "You know that audition, the one that got me the scholarship?"

He nodded, tractor beam eyes fully locked in.

"Well, it was part of this summer camp, right after my sopho-more year. All these dancers in San Francisco. We'd applied to get in and were all just a bit too proud of ourselves for being there." My throat felt dry, and somehow, Mik knew to hand me an icy bottle of water from the front seat. I thanked him, sipping it, as he pulled up to Adam's trailer. Mik slipped silently from the car, leaving us there.

I told Adam about that summer afternoon in San Francisco. If there was a moment when I really began to doubt dancing, it hinged on that afternoon.

There had been a dancer, a guy who was probably in his late twenties, and he came to talk to us. We'd been sitting on the floor of a studio, the mirrors all around us, just chatting and laughing. We'd just finished an especially hard day of classes, so we were tired, but happy.

When he came into the room, something about him made us all just shut up. Instantly. He was dressed in a tight black tank top and jeans, his arms muscular and tan. He had dark hair and a severe

184

hairline and, without much intro, he launched into a speech about how hard this profession was, telling us he "didn't want to lie to us" and that we needed to know "what we were in for" if we expected to dance professionally. He used that word a lot, in all its forms: *profession, professional, professionally*. Each time he said it, it felt like someone was punching me in the stomach.

Then he told us to close our eyes.

Sitting there in the backseat of the Range Rover, the heat of summer seeping into the closed car, I described it to Adam: all of us in our beat-up jazz shoes, our slouching leg warmers, our faded leotards, all these outfits we'd worked so hard to make look like we'd just thrown them on haphazardly. We sat there in that too-hot studio that reeked of sweat, and we listened, our eyes closed.

Then he told us: If you could imagine doing anything else in the world besides dancing, anything at all, you should do that. Do *that* instead of this. Because dancing was competitive, exhausting, ruthless, and it was a very, very short career. He told us: Unless you can *only* imagine dancing, with all its pain and heartbreak and constant drive to prove yourself, you should go home, get good grades, and go to a regular college, because you're not cut out to be a dancer.

"Then he walked out of the studio. He didn't take questions or anything. That was it." I finished, not sure if it was Adam's face darkening or the light leaving the sky outside.

Adam shook his head, his eyes wide. "And you listened to him?"

I licked my lips. "He was very convincing."

Adam made a sound like he had something caught in his throat, a sound of disgust. "He was some jerk that camp paid a hundred bucks to come scare a bunch of kids." Adam took a deep breath and leaned back against the car seat. "Oh, Carter — if you listen to every idiot who claims to be a professional in this world, every so-called expert who makes you feel like crap, you'll never try anything. That guy probably went home to his junk apartment and fed his cat and got Chinese takeout and resented all of you — all the possibility you stood for. What a jerk. He was just trying to sound important. Don't listen to guys like that."

I hurried to explain, my cheeks reddening. "It wasn't just that guy; it wasn't just what he said. He just got me thinking about the whole world of it, the whole dancing world. It's when I realized it had stopped being fun and started being, I don't know, *forced*."

"You can't have fun all the time. Sometimes it's hard. Sometimes it's frustrating and miserable, sometimes people are mean, but you have to push through that. You're talented. Sometimes being talented is just hard." His voice caught on this last sentence, and something suddenly connected us, a ribbon of understanding twisted out and tied me to him.

I drank more water, my head spinning. "*That* was the problem. I was sick of being talented. I didn't want to be talented. At some point along the way, talent started screwing everything up. It started dictating things. It started saying yes, I could do that, or no, I couldn't do that. It stopped being about the love and started being about how good I was. That summer, I *hated* dancing."

"So you turned down the scholarship."

"Yes."

"And proved that jerk right."

Tears started to spill down my cheeks, blurring his face.

"Oh, don't do that. Don't cry." He hurried to brush them from my face.

His sweetness startled me enough to slow my tears. "I'm sorry. It's just . . ." I fished for the words that clouded my brain. "I just, mostly, don't think I'm right for that sort of world. For that world of winners and losers and *pushing through*. I'm not sure I'm built for that, don't even know if I *believe* in that sort of world. Not when I think about that family last Saturday who was just trying to find a home, think about Bob who just wanted to get a job — *any* job— and how hard that is for him. And I have so much already: my family, my home, my job. I like my life here. It might seem boring and small, but I like it. I have so much, so who am I to spend time pushing for more? It's just greedy."

Adam leaned into the front seat, dug around in the glove box, and returned with a tissue. "Listen, if you're happy teaching dance to those old people, if that's enough for you, and you don't want to go to New York and be some big-shot dancer, that's fine; it's sweet, actually. So you want to make the world better, devote yourself to those families on Saturdays — that's a beautiful thing. I just don't understand why you can't do both. Why didn't you just keep dancing here? Don't let some jerk with a spray-on tan be the reason you gave up the thing you used to love the most."

I dabbed my eyes with the tissue, watching the night sky bloom into violet. "What frustrates me is that there was so much weight given to one choice over the other. If I had taken the scholarship, left Little, then I'm brave or amazing or whatever. But people didn't want to just let me stay here. Wouldn't stop telling me what a mistake I'd made. They said I was scared or letting myself down or not expanding my horizons. I hate that expression, by the way. What if I like my horizons? What if staying means I'm loyal and care about my life here? But people didn't see it like that. So I quit. It was just easier than listening to them."

"People always have advice when it has no impact on their own lives," Adam said quietly.

"Yeah, true." I wiped at my eyes, embarrassed. I wanted to roll down the window, to escape the heat starting to build, to put an end to this conversation. I didn't really want to be having this talk. It felt like scraping my heart on a cheese grater. "I just feel like other people are always encouraging me to take all these big risks or whatever because they mostly never did. They were hanging out at the river or taking a nap. But, hey, they want *me* to go make something of myself."

"Having talent has its own sort of responsibility." Adam pushed open the door, letting the cooling pine air into the car.

I studied him. "I don't want to sound like a quitter or a whiner or whatever, but the truth is that I don't like to compete. I don't like it when people up the stakes on me. It's like the higher up you go, the crazier the people get who show up alongside you. Anytime the stakes are too high, I just don't like the company around me. It's like there's some sort of fast pass for narcissists that exists when there's a winner on the line."

When he took my hand, he was chuckling.

My stomach twisted. "Don't laugh at me. Not all of us are cut out to be superstars like you."

He shook his head. "It's not that. I'm not laughing at you. You're just bringing up all these things that came up in rehab for me. It's kind of scary, actually, how you just sounded like me two months ago."

My heart squeezed. Was it possible that our worlds might not be on separate sides of the galaxy after all?

His hand let go of mine, and its absence felt like the dark parts of space. He took a low, quiet breath. "Sometimes, I regret not having a regular life. A regular childhood. You know, baseball teams and pizza parties. People think it's so amazing to be in the movies. And it is. It's great, but it's hard not to wonder what it would be like to be . . . normal. To have just chosen my own path rather than had it all decided already."

I opened my car door, too, so we could catch a cross breeze. The sky darkened even more and I thought of all those little stars, all the ones we couldn't see, hidden out there in the dark, sparkling without anyone seeing them at all. I didn't mind being that sort of star, the kind no one saw but still held its own small part of the sky.

Watching him, I wanted to say something to him about regret, about how I didn't really believe in the idea of regret because it was always based on what *might* have happened. People always held up the now, the concrete now, and compared it to what might have been, and that wasn't a fair comparison.

Instead, I told him, "I'm just trying to make the best choice I can, with all the information I have at the time, and then, if it doesn't work out, I'll figure out something else. That's the best I can do."

"I get that. More than you know." He smiled at me, but his face was already retreating behind its curtain and, before I could respond, he was out of the car, leaning in. "I'm sorry to do this, but I've got to run. I'll get Mik to drive you back to your car, okay? I have an epic shoot tomorrow, but the Fourth is going to be great, I promise." He gave me a sort of half smile, not really meeting my eyes, and then disappeared into his trailer.

I just emptied my heart and he's *got to run*?!

What just happened?

Feeling foolish as Mik drove me back to Snow Ridge, I realized that after all of that, we hadn't even talked about Beckett Ray or reporters or the script or anything else. I was getting distracted and trusting him. I needed to stick to the plan.

No more improvising.

yesterday's sightings

Things Are Looking Up in Little, CA

Morning, sky watchers. Well, tomorrow is the Fourth of July. All hail the Stars and Stripes. We've been wondering why the flag used stars to represent the fifty states. So, after poking around a bit with our pal Google, we found mostly that they are representative of the heavens, of the human need to look up and feel inspired by all that dark, all that scattered light. To aspire. One blogger we came across said he felt like the stars give people a chance to imagine their own possibilities; they provide a reminder that each of us has the capacity to make our best future, to find our purpose. That sounded pretty good to us. So, while you're kicked back tomorrow night, looking up at the fireworks, take a minute to consider the stars, the ones always up there reminding us of what might be.

See you tonight, under the sky.

sixteen

Parker was dressed for the river. I knew the look well. Between the months of April and October, it came into the café *a lot*. He hadn't shaved and wore a pair of raggedy Bermuda shorts with his T-shirt and flip-flops. He appeared almost normal, like some of the Hollywood shine had dulled. As he perused the script, he tugged at the bill of his faded blue ball cap; it was inscribed with the name of a movie studio I'd seen pop up on movies usually featured at the Dream, a theater that showcased artier films than the Vista. He hurried through our schedule for the day. I'd been in dozens of dance shows over the years, starting with my first satin-drenched, Bambi-eyed Bon Bon in *The Nutcracker* when I was four, but nothing compared to the production Parker had just outlined for me leading up to my fireworks kiss with Adam.

Sitting again at the iron table tucked away in the backyard of The Hotel on Main, he must have recognized a certain look on my face, a certain glazed overload, because he sat back in his chair, the garden already warm at seven a.m. "You all right? You look a bit peaked." He took a sip of the orange juice Bonnie had brought us fifteen minutes ago when we'd started. She'd looked a bit less chipper than she had for our first meeting in her garden, the skin beneath her eyes bruised with fatigue. I knew firsthand that after a while, Hollywood or not, work was work.

"What time do we report for the parade?" I asked.

"Ten thirty. You're in the first car. A vintage Mustang." He held up a picture of a car, slick and shiny like a candy apple. I thought of the pink scarf Chloe had given me, wondered if they'd let me wear it. Parker tucked the picture back into a folder. "Fabulous, yeah? But no lingering. We're going to rush you in and rush you out. For security reasons." His phone buzzed. He eyed it, then texted a quick reply. "Oh, and here's your dress." He handed me a white eyelet sundress in a clear plastic bag. I noticed the label. "Oh, wow. Um, I'm pretty sure I'll get that dirty. And that I can't afford it."

He blinked his river-green eyes at me and rubbed at his scruff of beard. "You don't have to pay for it, love. The designer sent it."

"Sent it to me?" I held the dress as if it were made of glass.

He was checking his phone again. "You'll look gorgeous in it. With some sandals. Nothing tarty, yeah?"

"Um, have we met? I'm not even one of those girls who can pull off 'tarty' kitty at Halloween. I always go as a baby. Or a pirate." I hooked the dress onto the back of my chair, careful not to let it drag on the ground.

A smile softening his face, he reminded me to change out of the dress for the lunchtime barbecue at the fairgrounds and then put it back on for the afternoon barbecue at Snow Ridge Senior Living.

Nodding, I said, "Thanks for letting me go to that. It means a lot."

"It's a great publicity stop." He scanned his phone, frowned at something, and then added, "A shot of you with those geriatrics you teach to dance. Priceless."

Not amused, I sipped my orange juice.

He flipped through a few more pages of the script. "We want you to arrive at the private party for tonight's Fourth of July gathering no later than six." He paused to make sure I was keeping up. "I'll be there at four to make sure things are going smoothly, and the guests will begin arriving at five. We want shots of you two strolling the vineyard. It will be a perfect build for the fireworks kiss shot."

"So romantic," I mumbled.

He flipped the script shut. "We *sell* romance, love. We don't necessarily live it."

"We're watching fireworks there?"

"You and Adam. And invited guests. And three hundred lucky Little locals."

There had been a contest running all week on our local radio station to win tickets to the exclusive private Fourth of July party being hosted in honor of Adam's Little film shoot. I'd scored some tickets for Dad, Chloe, and Alien Drake, but when they'd announced yesterday that they'd given away the last ticket, I'd suddenly had quite a few people trying to contact me. One more reason I was glad I didn't have a Facebook page.

I watched Parker start to rearrange things in a red backpack that still had its tags. Inside, I noticed a thick book, a bottle of water, and a white-paper-wrapped sandwich of some sort. Not one of ours. "You're not going to the parade?"

He shot me an almost apologetic look. "I'll be back for the party, but I have a rare day off, and you guys are so snotty about your river I thought I'd see what the fuss was all about."

"Here." I pulled the script across the table and wrote out a series of directions on the back of it. "Go here. You'll avoid some of the people up from Sacramento for the day. This spot's pretty much locals only. When you get to the sign where it says 'no river access' keep going. A resident just put that up to try to keep people out."

"Cheers." He stuffed the script into the backpack. As he swung it over his shoulder, he opened his mouth to say something, but then closed it again, his eyes settling on me. His look felt heavy, searching.

I squirmed a bit. "What?"

"Nothing. See you tonight."

* ✳ *

I'd been to every Little Fourth of July parade since I was a kid but never in a featured car. And, of course, never with a movie star.

It changed things.

Not only did Mik run alongside of us, but three other Mik look-alikes joined him to ward off the masses. They sweated in the heavy sun as they ran, their huge arms bulging in matching black T-shirts and slacks. When they first joined us, I couldn't imagine needing four Miks. Now, I wondered if four would be enough. People pressed in on all sides of the bubble of space the Miks kept around the car, but otherwise people shouted, whistled, tried for close-ups. One group of tween girls all wore red, white, and blue shirts reading: *The United*

States of Adam. The collective scream they emitted when we passed caused several of the dogs in the crowd to start howling.

Never more grateful for Chloe's giant sunglasses, I searched the crowd for familiar faces. I'd tried for the scarf, too, but Jewel had vetoed it, saying it didn't match the car. As we cruised through the town, waving at the clumps of people in chairs hunched together in any bit of shade they could find, my stomach sank.

I recognized almost no one.

I'd always loved events like the Fourth of July parade in Little mostly because it was the same group of faces year after year. You could go to things like Summer Nights or Victorian Christmas and basically see the same people you saw at the grocery store or the post office — only in better moods. More relaxed, enjoying themselves. We lived a mellow life in Little, but it was still *life*. Events like these reminded us all to take a step back, turn off our phones, smile at one another a bit more. Even if you didn't know each name, you knew the faces belonged here.

Today, the parade had record turnout. Maybe double or even triple its normal size.

As we neared the end of the street, the curve that would take us to the point where Mik would load us into the Range Rover, I'd only seen a smattering of familiar faces, and I wondered if everyone in Little had skipped the parade this year, tired of Hollywood taking center stage in our normally peaceful world.

The sun hot on my back, I wished I could join them. Wherever they were.

* ✳ *

After the parade, we quickly ate hamburgers at the fairgrounds while Adam signed autographs for the kids not taking advantage of the huge bouncy world they'd set up just inside the main entrance. I found myself staring out over the periphery of pine trees, my smile fixed, cement-like. I'd changed into some white shorts and a tank top so I could try out the bounce house, but mostly I stood by Adam, smiling like a zombie on Prozac.

Every half hour or so, Adam would chug some sort of electrolyte drink that Mik would hand him. He offered me one, but I shook my head. "Make sure you stay hydrated," he insisted, tossing an empty bottle into a nearby recycling bin. He seemed energized by the constant stream of attention, each signature zapping more life into his eyes.

Maybe this was why so many celebrities became politicians. They were the ones who could keep up with this sort of pace, their bodies naturally porous things ready to soak up all the adoration.

* ✳ *

It was fifteen minutes after four when we stopped by Snow Ridge for the barbecue. It was being held in a sort of atrium by the pool, and someone had hung festive red, white, and blue bunting on all the patio tables. I had changed back into the white sundress (a little worse for its wear from the Mustang ride), but had ditched the heeled sandals for some blue flip-flops I'd borrowed from Chloe. After ten minutes, I started to ignore the cameras, angling my body away from them or making sure I was standing in shadow. After a half hour, I wandered away from Adam (and the cameras) and found myself accepting a cool drink from Mrs. Adler, who wore a chic chambray tunic and flowing white pants.

She clinked her glass against mine. "You look lovely, dear."

"Hollywood's rubbing off on me." I took a sip of the sparkly punch.

"Let's hope not." She squinted at me. "Though you do look a bit like a glazed ham."

"Been a long day already." I tried to brighten my smile. How did Adam do this, always be so available to people? At the café, what they wanted was clear: their food, their coffee, a quick smile. It was a simple equation. What they wanted from Adam, well, that was something else entirely.

Mrs. Adler and I watched Adam play a lighthearted game of Ping-Pong with Mr. Lively, who wasn't all that lively but had sharp blue eyes and a crisp left-handed swing that seemed to come out of his otherwise lifeless body.

"This guy's got some skills!" Adam called to us. He had his sunglasses pushed into his hair and wore a linen shirt the color of blue sea glass. If you didn't know this was work to him, you'd guess he was having a pretty good time. Or, maybe he *was* having a good time and it wasn't just all for show? It was impossible to tell.

"How's your movie star?" Mrs. Adler sipped her drink through a slender straw. No doubt she'd noticed I was wilting like lettuce left overnight on the counter.

I watched Adam, the combination of the day's heat and too much sugar and starch lulling me into a haze. "Not at all what I thought," I heard myself telling her.

"None of the good ones are, dear." She plucked a deviled egg from the platter on the snacks table and managed to eat it in three dainty bites. "Of course," she paused, dabbing at the corners of her mouth with a star-spangled napkin, "none of the rotten ones are, either." Then, she refilled my punch.

At least people wouldn't let me dehydrate.

* ✳ *

I asked Mik to make an unscheduled stop.

Adam followed me out of the car. "Why're we stopping here?"

I pushed through the creaky iron gate of the Little Cemetery and walked him through a row of gravestones. The summer heat had settled among them like fog, but every few seconds a breeze ruffled the few flags or flowers people had left, some dry and withering, others fresh and new.

"One of the places on our tour we never made it to." I veered from the main path, through a row where the graves were marked with flat slabs pressed into the ground. Toward the back of the cemetery stood a wide stone marker, etched with a crescent moon. It marked the entrance to my family's plot. Five generations of Moons.

I crouched down next to one the color of smooth, creamy milk, my grandmother's grave. Dad had been here already. He'd left a blue bucket dotted with stars and filled with red, white, and blue flowers.

I touched it briefly, the smell of the red roses ripe in the air. "My grandmother loved the Fourth. Well, she loved all holidays — any reason to have people over for enormous amounts of food — but she especially loved this one. The parade, the picnics, swimming, fireworks. When you stood on her deck at night, you could see the fireworks over the fairgrounds off in the distance." I pulled open my bag and extracted some sparklers. I pushed them into the ground and lit them, their sizzle and spark mostly lost in the bright daylight. "She loved a day that ended with fireworks."

Adam stood beside me. "I didn't know you'd lost your grandmother."

"The month after I went to dance camp. She was actually why I started teaching the dance class at Snow Ridge in the first place. She'd just started living there my sophomore year. Had felt like her house was too much." I felt tears pricking my eyes. "She came to every dance show I had from the time I was a Bon Bon in *The Nutcracker*."

Adam knelt and read the inscription on her headstone. *ALICE MOON, mother, grandmother, lover of life.* Then he stood and wrapped an arm around me, and I found myself curving into him. "How soon after she passed did you stop dancing?"

A bubble of annoyance popped in my belly, and I eased out from under his arm. "I didn't quit dancing because she died." I glanced at him, trying to un-barb my voice. "You know, Mom thought that, too."

Adam shook his head. "Maybe you didn't quit. Maybe you just needed a break, time to sort it all out. I mean, between Dance-Guy-the-Dream-Killer and your grandmother dying, you might still be sorting it all out." He pushed his hands into his pockets, the sparklers reflecting in his sunglasses, almost brighter in reflection.

A hot wind came across the cemetery, and the sky held the lazy drone of an airplane. Why hadn't I ever considered that I was just taking a rest? "I guess I always just thought of it as quitting." When you stop doing things, people have a way of assigning a sort of finality to them.

Adam tucked his hands into the pockets of his shorts. "I'm not sure we ever truly quit the things we love. We might not be practicing them, but that doesn't mean we've quit them. I think, sometimes, things we love need to go dormant or come out in a different form for a while."

The thoughtful Adam was back. Not the one who'd dashed out of the car. Here was the attentive, bring-some-pie-to-my-tree-house Adam. And he had a point. I tried to put up a wall, to shrug off his words, but the truth was, until now, I'd never thought about my dancing as anything other than something I just stopped doing. Even the classes I taught at Snow Ridge felt like something totally separate from dancing, something secondary or lesser, like I'd failed myself in some way, failed the expectations people had set up for me.

I studied my reflections in Adam's glasses. Then I reached out and pushed his sunglasses up onto his head, wanting to see his eyes. "Did you need a break from acting? When you went . . . wherever you went?" He hadn't talked much about his rehab, about his months dealing with his drug charges, the reckless driving, the smashed-up car, only hinted at them. It was hard to believe the guy standing here surrounded by pines and headstones was *that* guy. The tabloid guy.

Will the real Adam Jakes please stand up? I wanted to scream.

He stretched his arms up over his head and turned a slow circle, taking in the green-and-stone sweep of the cemetery. "Yeah," he finally said, lowering his sunglasses back down. "I did." His phone buzzed. Looking at it, he groaned. "That's Parker. He wants our ETA. But we can stay here as long as you need to."

The spell was broken, Adam already scrolling through his phone, disappearing, fading to black.

I made sure the sparklers had gone out and dribbled a bit of my water bottle on them just to be sure. "It's fine. We can go."

✶ ✴ ✶

I'd only been to Gemstone Winery once before, for a wedding. It had been a small wedding, sleek white linen and sage green, the endless lawns stretching out to a view of Little far below and pine forests beyond.

Today, hundreds of people packed the lawns and dozens of red-white-and-blue-striped tents gave the grounds the look of a circus. As we drove up the winding graveled road to a private parking spot, I could hear a band playing even through the closed windows of the car.

The main house of the winery was stone, wide and tall, ivy snaking its sides. We parked in a smaller version of the stone house next to a few classic cars and what looked like a white horse carriage. I had a vague memory of the bride and groom arriving in it.

Parker met us at the car. "We need you to go around the back through the vineyard. We have photographers there." He seemed a bit less tense than he had this morning, his face bronzed from his day at the river.

"Did you find that spot I told you about?" I took his offered hand as he helped me out of the Range Rover.

"I did. It was aces." He shut my door.

Adam and I took a stroll through the vineyards, the photographers a harmless distance away, though I could hear the cameras snapping. I pointed out the view of Little. He chatted about baseball. Parker had reminded us to only talk about safe things in case any of the reporters overheard us. From a distance, I'm sure we looked casual, happy, but I was aware of how detached I was from myself as we meandered along, like viewing my own life through a crack in a fence.

At a small turn of the path, we came to a fountain under a trellis flowering with fuchsia blooms. Adam laced his fingers with mine, sending a warm jolt through me. I tried to listen to what he was saying, something about a trip he took to Indonesia for a futuristic film he'd shot last summer. The sweet smell of the vineyards wafted around us; the trellis bloomed brightly; I could hear the band playing on the other side of the stone house; and suddenly I felt soaked in sadness.

Adam noticed, leaned into me a bit, and whispered, "You okay?" I could hear cameras behind us, like tiny dogs nipping at our heels.

I nodded, hoping to shed this feeling so foreign to me. "I'm fine. Just tired."

"We should get you something cool to drink." He signaled to Mik, who'd been walking a few paces behind us.

Hydration therapy again.

I didn't need something cool to drink. Truth was, I was sad because none of this was real. And that was suddenly a huge problem.

Because I really liked this guy, the version of him that broke through his cloud cover once in a while. I had expected to tolerate the tantrums of a brash, selfish movie star for a few weeks — smile, grit my teeth, and quietly count my cash, help my brother out, ease my parents' stress. Adam wasn't supposed to have flashes of cute and smart and interesting. He wasn't supposed to make me feel like this. Like I could float away into the sky.

Only in the movies, right?

Except, I knew this wasn't going to end well.

Sipping the tall iced glasses of lemonade that had magically appeared, we passed under the trellis and out to the edge of the vineyard.

"Look!" Adam pointed out across the valley. "The cemetery."

He was right. You could see the cemetery from here like it was a child's model. Next to it, the funeral home looked like a match-box. "Thanks again for stopping with me."

"You really know how to impress a date." He gave my hand a squeeze. "Ghosts. Fairy Trees and dead guys. Cemeteries. Super sexy, by the way."

I took a breath of air. "I really love going there."

He gave me a funny look. "Okay, now you're just freaking me out."

I laughed, feeling some of the haze lift. "To see my grandma!" I gave him a playful shove and he moved his arm around my waist. I imagined away the cameras, focused only on the way his arm felt around me. "Actually, there's something really calming about a graveyard."

"If you say so, Crazy."

I sipped my lemonade, chewing a stray piece of ice. "Seriously, I go there and all of the stupid stuff from my life seems, well, *stupid*. Pointless. I mean, sooner or later, we all end up right there. So, we need to not stress out all the time. We need to know that we have a life and that is a good thing."

"Yes, being alive is better than being dead."

"You know what I mean." Somehow, I knew he did. We stared out over the valley, and I thought about how the feeling I got at a graveyard was similar to the one I got watching the sky at night, drinking in all those stars. There were many things in this world to feel small — stars, cemeteries, oceans. They relaxed me. I liked being reminded of being small, mostly because it took the pressure off when people pushed you to be big.

"Mr. Jakes?" One of the Mik look-alikes appeared next to us.

"You can call me Adam." He dropped his hand from around my waist.

"Parker needs you both at the front of the house. We got the pictures we wanted."

Adam glanced down at me. "You ready?"

And just like that, the haze returned. "Sure."

seventeen

by nine, the sky had grown the deep color of grape juice with an illuminated rim of pale still edging the horizon. Chloe and Alien Drake had joined us for dinner. Pulled-pork sandwiches, coleslaw, plate-sized wedges of seedless watermelon, huge vats of homemade ginger ale, root beer, lemonade — all spread out on red-white-and-blue-checked tablecloths. As we loaded our plates in line, Alien Drake and I managed to joke a bit, the tension between us thawing.

Now, he and Chloe snuggled next to each other on our blanket, eating, listening to the band play covers of songs whose only connection was that they had some derivation of the word *America* in them.

As night beckoned the crowds to their blankets, the band's singer announced one last song before the fireworks show. Into the mic, he said, "This song was a request from our special guest, Adam Jakes. It's an original song that we wrote, and it goes out to Carter Moon. It's called 'Stargazer.'" His guitar hit the opening notes, the drummer keeping an even rhythm, and he belted out:

> *Every night, she watches the sky.*
> *Every night, she wishes on a star.*

Did she know she was looking for me?
Did she know she didn't need to look so far?

I squirmed a little on the blanket. He had them write a song for me? Parker hadn't mentioned a song. I felt eyes on me from the other blankets as the song filled the air around us.

After a minute, Adam whispered into my ear, "Do you like it?"

I nodded, my throat closing.

As I looked around at the people listening, believing this song was meant for me, that it was true, I was struck with how much we needed to know we were loved. We needed people to tell us, show us, remind us. I studied the stars wide above me, realizing it was because we knew how small we were that love mattered so much. Even when everything in the world pointed to the contrary, love carved out its own vast galaxy for us, made us the most important thing in it, at least to somebody. But I also knew as I listened that I didn't want a fake song from Adam.

I wanted a real one.

The crowd listened around me, their heads bobbing along to the easy beat. People sneaked glances in our direction, trying not to look like they were staring. When the band finished playing, Adam gave my hand a squeeze, jumped up, and crossed the darkening lawn to the stage.

Chloe studied me from across the blanket, her eyes wide. "You are in so much trouble."

"Why?"

"You *love* him."

My chest lurched. "I don't love him. I've known him for, like, five minutes. It's taken me longer to love a sandwich. We're not *in love*. We just started dating." Chloe and Alien Drake exchanged a concerned look; they knew overacting when they saw it.

Chloe motioned toward the bandstand. "He had a song written for you and played in front of, like, four hundred people. Who does that?"

Alien Drake nodded, clearly impressed. "I've never done that."

Chloe gave his face a pat. "We know, sweetie."

I watched Adam laughing with the lead singer, and I chose my words carefully. "Don't get me wrong; that was amazing, the song was amazing, he's amazing."

Alien Drake, bemused, interrupted, "Just so we're clear — everything's amazing."

I licked my lips, wanting to start preparing my friends, letting them know this wasn't going to last, even though I couldn't really tell them that. "Yeah, I like him. But I'm trying not to get too attached, okay? I mean, where can this possibly go? He's a *movie star*. We'll all be seniors at Little High next year, but Adam will probably be filming a movie in France or something. What's he going to do — fly home to meet me for study hall? Come to prom? I can't get attached." As the words spilled out, I realized I wasn't preparing my friends — I was preparing myself. Even wrapped in lies, I couldn't have shared any truer words.

But, of course, it was too late.

Chloe's eyes found Adam up by the band. He was checking out the lead singer's guitar, noticed us watching him, and gave a small wave. Chloe let out a sigh and shot me a worried look. "If you say so."

A few minutes later, Adam settled back down next to us on the blanket. The night had darkened enough for the fireworks to start launching. "Thanks for the song," I whispered, my throat tight.

Before he could respond, light burst open in the night sky above us.

I jumped a little, mostly from the noise, and Adam put his arm around me. "Okay there, Jumpy?"

I nodded, but inside I was miserable.

When he leaned in to kiss me, I tried to ignore the sound of cameras. Instead, I imagined them as part of the cannon-thump of the fireworks launching, as part of the necessary space between that thump and the blooming of scattered light above us. Mostly, though, I needed to pretend all the noise — all the clicking of cameras around me and the popping of fireworks in the sky above me — was simply outside of me. When, really, I knew the noise was no match for the pounding in my chest, for the way he made me feel when he was near me.

* ✳ *

After the fireworks left the sky smoking and dark, we walked alone toward the Range Rover, Mik having run back to the house for some of our things that we'd stashed in the entryway.

As we neared the garage, I saw the lit end of a cigarette before I saw him emerge from the shadows.

T.J. Shay.

"You've got yourself some rich friends, Carter," he drawled, his face falling into the light of the motion sensor we'd set off with our approach.

A familiar current of unease moved through me. "What are you doing here, T.J.?"

Adam drew closer to me, his hand taking mine. "This is a private party."

T.J. flashed a ticket stub. "Yeah, I know. Big winner!" He gave a practiced leer. T.J. had spent years cultivating his gangster image, and he almost had it mastered. In a few more years, it would cement itself into place, but I still remembered when he used to wander our house in a Batman costume and, for me, parts of that boy lingered beneath the leer.

I let go of Adam's hand, crossing my arms across my chest. "You called into a radio station contest?"

Shrugging, he stuffed the ticket into the pocket of his baggy shorts. The shorts looked more like they used to be pants, pants that had met with an unfortunate exchange with a chain saw. The hems sagged in varied lengths, frayed at their edges, and a long chain looped at his waist. I knew it was attached to a knife. T.J.'s beloved knife. He bragged about it the way a new parent would a small child who'd just started walking. How many times had he shown me that knife when he used to hang out at our house? I used to find it sort of boring and sad, little boy with his grown-up blade, but here, in the shadows, it served its purpose.

"What do you want, T.J.?" My voice wobbled a little; this guy was a long way from Batman costumes.

"Where's your brother?" He dropped his leer, and without it, his face just looked slack and mean. "We can't seem to find him, and he owes us some money."

"I already gave you money." I thought of the stack of hundreds in the white envelope I'd passed him through his open car window in the Taco Bell parking lot back when things first started with Adam.

T.J. shrugged. "It wasn't enough."

"How much now?" Adam asked.

T.J. eyed Adam the way one observes their options at a meat counter. "You going to pay me, Hollywood?"

"How much does he owe you?" Adam asked again.

"Adam, this really isn't —" I began.

T.J. cut me off. "He owes me fifteen thousand dollars."

That number weighted my feet to the ground: *$15,000*. The last time I'd asked John he'd said it was three grand, four tops. "There's no way he owes you that much."

He lit another cigarette. "Interest." Blowing the smoke away, he added, "And I don't think you know your brother like I do. Fifteen is generous. That's after what you gave me. Your boy's got a problem."

I shook my head, anger melting away any lingering waves of fear. "John's not here, T.J., and I think you should go."

T.J. laughed a quick puff of air. "Right, like you're going to make me."

A blur passed us, quick and dark, and suddenly T.J. was face-down on the ground, Mik's hulking form pinning him like a bug.

Adam walked over to T.J. "This is Mik. He doesn't like it when people don't leave when I want them to."

"Get. Him. Off," T.J. wheezed.

"Didn't I meet a sheriff earlier at the parade? Nice guy. Redheaded. Is he here?" Adam asked Mik. Mik nodded, motioning

211

back down toward the lawn. People had mostly cleared out, and the catering company was moving tables, stacking plates. Someone had turned on some floodlights.

"That's Luke O'Casey. I'll get him." I started to turn toward the lawn.

T.J.'s eyes bulged, but he still tried for tough guy. "Tattling is not in your brother's best interest." His breath came in ragged gasps.

I waited, half turned toward where I'd last seen Sheriff O'Casey.

Adam took slow steps toward T.J., waiting until his feet were at T.J.'s eye level, and then he crouched down next to him. "*Tattling? Seriously? What are we, five?*" His voice came out low and graveled. "This isn't about tattling. . . . This is about reporting you to the proper authorities."

"Wait!" T.J. rasped, his eyelids beating like hummingbird wings. I had a flash of him darting through the late evening of our yard, his Batman cape streaming behind him. "Carter, don't get the sheriff. I'm leaving." His eyes looked upward. "Er, I mean, I'll leave."

Adam stood and gave Mik a quick nod. Mik released T.J., who, like a small animal that'd been trapped beneath the paw of a suddenly generous Rottweiler, dashed off down the driveway.

* * *

That night at home, I texted John:

T.J.'s looking for you.

When I woke up the next morning for my shift at the café, he still hadn't answered, and it occurred to me that I hadn't seen him or heard from him since that night outside the Jensens' barn.

I texted him again:

Where did you go, John?

∗ ✳ ∗

"Jones?" I poked my head into the kitchen. "Did you clean the bathroom already?"

He didn't glance up from his morning prep, small piles of chopped red bell pepper, onion, and tomatoes. Ready for the breakfast rush. "Sure did."

I leaned on the door frame, watching him chop. "You didn't have to do that; it was my turn."

He gave his tattooed shoulders the smallest of shrugs, more of a wink. "Seems to me, you've got enough on your plate this morning."

He meant the reporters outside. They seemed to be multiplying, filling up our café tables, perched on curbsides, hanging out on the back of their rented cars. A plague of press. I'd been approached by individual members before, but this morning a pack of them crowded the gates of Little Eats.

"That was some kiss last night at the fireworks — are you two serious?"

"Did you know about the song?"

"What will you do when he goes back to L.A.?"

"Is Adam helping with your brother's gambling problem?"

Parker's words echoed in my ears. *Don't talk to the press.* I had tried smiling in a friendly-but-distant sort of way, and hurried inside to the ever-present snapping of cameras.

"I can still clean a bathroom," I said to Jones, but crossed and gave his arm a squeeze under the auspices of reaching for a roll of paper towels.

He stopped chopping a red pepper and let his eyes fall on me, those gray eyes that looked like sheet metal. "I know you can clean a bathroom. You can do a lot of things. But other people can also help you."

I wasn't used to Jones stringing that many words together. It struck me as the only sort of advice he'd ever given me. "Thanks."

I flipped the sign from CLOSED to OPEN, my gaze falling on a clump of men with cameras leaning against the outside of the waist-level white fence that separated our patio from the main sidewalk. One of them, his straw bowler hat pulled low, perked up when he saw me through the window.

I moved out of sight before he could raise his camera.

* ✳ *

The next couple days of shooting were at the Little Club, Little's only tennis and golf (nine holes) club. I sat in my chair in Video Village, watching Adam shoot a scene with the actor who played his father, one of the pivotal scenes where Scott realizes he's been wasting his life and needs to make a change. *Building an epiphany arc.*

The actor playing the father, someone I recognized from television but couldn't quite place, sat across from Adam at a table by the window, staring out over the golf course. Hunter crouched beside him, one arm resting on the white linen tablecloth. He gave him some whispery direction, his other hand moving in big gestures, his Sundance cap bobbing as he spoke.

Someone slipped into the seat next to me, a flash of dark and light out of the corner of my eye.

Beckett Ray.

I had sort of forgotten about Beckett Ray. Until now.

Catching my eye, she waved in an overdramatized way considering how close we were sitting, a wide smile on her pale face. "Hi!" she whispered.

I nodded, trying to find the sort of smile that wouldn't seem like I'd tasted something awful. She stared intently at the actors, her lake-blue eyes searching the scene as one would the surface of an ocean where someone had gone under.

Why was she here? She wasn't in this scene.

Hunter called for a short break, still huddled at the table with Adam and the TV actor.

"Isn't this incredible, Carter!?" Beckett chirped. "Well, I don't know how incredible it is for you. You're not an *actor*. But as an *actor*, this is just thrilling." Beckett held the word *actor* in her mouth as if she were having it bronzed.

"Are you in this scene?" I licked my lips, my mouth suddenly dry.

She tossed her dark mane of hair. "Oh no, I'm done shooting my scene. But Adam suggested I watch some of the shoot. You know, get some guidance, make connections. Acting's really all about connections. It's not what you know, it's who you know, you know?"

I didn't know.

I shrugged, pretending to search my bag for something, anything to avoid eye contact. Gum. I found gum.

"This has been such an incredible opportunity for me." Beckett

215

swelled like an overfilled balloon, waving away my offer of minty gum.

Adam finished talking to Hunter, spotted us, and sauntered over. "Well, if it isn't Little's two most beautiful women." His eyes darted to the crew members nearby, making sure they'd noticed. This was one of my least favorite versions of Adam, the one who played to the whole room, who saw every person as a potential audience member. I even preferred obsessed-with-his-iPhone Adam over this guy.

Beckett's laugh trilled throughout the room. Probably because his comment was just so *incredible*. At least to an *actor*.

Adam narrowed his eyes a bit at me. "Did you like the scene?"

Before I could answer, Beckett jumped in, her voice almost squeaky. "Adam, you are so at *ease* in that scene. I just love what you're doing when your father asks you about your lunch — how the way you describe your hamburger is this huge metaphor for what's wrong in your own life. You never noticed the pickles before. Brilliant."

"It's not too overt?" He tilted his head, his arms crossed on his chest.

I actually did think it was too overt, that he lingered too long on the pickles comment, as if the audience would miss it if he didn't punctuate it for us, but I didn't tell him that. He didn't want to hear that; I could tell by his face he wanted praise and only praise.

"It's perfectly in balance," Beckett gushed. "You never noticed the *pickles* before. But you do *now*, right? Brilliant."

"Brilliant pickles," I added.

They both stared at me.

I buried the pack of gum in my bag. "You know, I should really go help my dad with the lunch rush."

Beckett gave me an overly sympathetic nod. "It's so cute that you work for your parents. Carter's such a small-town poster girl."

Why couldn't something heavy fall on Beckett Ray? Just this once. A pulsing started behind my eyes. I didn't seem to know about acting and pickle metaphors, but I did know I seriously had to get out of this room. The air-conditioning felt too chill, the corner where we sat too dark, everything shoved aside at odd angles to make room for the film equipment.

"You okay, Carter?" Adam's brow furrowed. "You look kind of weird."

"I think it's just the air-conditioning." I scooped up my bag, gave a short wave, and hurried from the room, but still in time to see Beckett stand and curl up next to Adam like a dark-haired cat.

* ✳ *

I ended up working the rest of the day at Little Eats, a welcome distraction so I didn't have to think too much about Adam and Beckett. I was just about to switch off the lights for the night when I heard a light tap at the back door of the café. Jones had gone home, but I thought I'd wait out the last few reporters still hanging out near the front fence, the night darkening their faces. Opening the door a crack, I found John standing there, hands shoved into the front pockets of his jeans. His face was sallow, but his eyes flickered with relief when he saw me. "Hey, little sis. I was hoping you'd be here."

Dad would be furious at me for letting him in, but I held the door wider. "Hey." I ushered him in, locking the door behind him, and he followed me out through the kitchen to the front. "You hungry? We have some sandwiches left."

He slid into a chair at one of the blond tables. "That'd be great."

I hurried to put a plate together for John, pour some tea over ice. I sat across from him while he ate for a few minutes, his eyes downcast, his face dimly lit by the low glow of the drink cases.

"Did you get my texts?" I toyed with the pile of paper napkins I'd set out in front of him.

He shook his head. "I don't have my phone anymore."

"I didn't know that."

Without warning, he broke down, dropping the rest of the sandwich onto its plate, tears streaking his face. I froze. The only time I'd ever seen my brother cry was when he'd fractured his arm falling out of my tree house when he was twelve. "Oh, oh, John," was all I could manage. Chewing my lip, I scooted my chair closer to his, not sure if I should hug him or punch him or call my parents. I opted for sitting and watching him cry.

After a few moments, he took a ragged breath. "I never meant for T.J. to come after you." I started to explain that he hadn't really come after me, but he rushed on. "I heard he was bothering you at Fourth of July, threatening you. I never meant for any of this . . ." He trailed off, his red-rimmed eyes blinking. "I never meant any of it."

"I know." We sat quietly, listening to the hum of the drink

218

cases, the passing of cars on the street outside. "I just want you to be okay."

He took a long drink from his sweating iced-tea glass, emptying it, then mopped his damp hand off on his jeans. "I can fix it," he said.

Listening to him, my heart hurt. I'd heard him make that promise to my parents so many times before. Needing a minute to myself, I said, "Hang on a second, okay? I'm going to get you more tea." I grabbed his glass and headed toward the kitchen where I was brewing a fresh batch. Even before I'd reached the jar of tea, still warm from its earlier soak in the sun, I heard the click of a lock and the bell on the front door jingle. I dashed back out to the front.

John was gone.

At the table, surrounding his empty plate, he'd left a spray of shiny green glass drops, the dragon tears he used to scatter under the trees in our yard, back when he told me about the fairies who lived there and I'd believed him.

eighteen

"**H**ave you seen this?" Chloe slapped a copy of *Entertainment Now!* on the counter. It was folded to an inside page, something called "Caught!" What would these entertainment magazines do if the world suddenly lost the exclamation point? I squinted at the picture. I was in a little cutout window shaped like a jagged heart, looking bereft (probably because I'd just cleaned the espresso machine), and the main picture showed Adam with Beckett, both laughing on the set. I'd spent today helping Dad, ignoring Adam's texts, and avoiding the Little Club, but the picture must have been taken back when they were in a scene together because Beckett was wearing an apron.

The caption read: *Adam Jakes Breaks a Little Heart.*

Seriously, what if my town had been called Pineville or something?

I pushed it out of the way. "She's in the movie with him. I already knew this." I turned back to the decaf latte I'd been making for the very patient gentleman in the tan khakis and polo shirt who Chloe had just stormed in front of at the counter.

"Look where his hand is!" Chloe widened her eyes at me.

I handed the man his latte and a free cookie for being so patient. The heat was making people cranky and demanding, and he hadn't even blinked an eye when Chloe cut in front of him. "Thanks for your patience." Smiling his response, he settled into a seat by the window and flipped open a copy of the *Sacramento Bee*.

Upon closer inspection of Chloe's magazine, I could see that, yes, Adam's hand appeared to be on Beckett's hindquarters. Pushing aside the thick rope of dread coiling in my stomach, I said, "They're just working together."

Chloe snorted and circled the offensive hand with one of the many Sharpies she kept in her pockets. I wanted to tell Chloe that it really wasn't any of my business where Adam Jakes put his hand. He wasn't paying me to monitor his extracurricular habits . . . or his taste in girls. Of course, I couldn't tell her this, but even if I could, it wasn't true. When I glanced at the picture again, my belly-knot of rope twisted and yanked. I tried to sound unconcerned. "Thanks for being outraged on my behalf."

She glared at the photo. "You need to tell him this is unacceptable boyfriend behavior. I don't care if he is a movie star." She shoved the article at me until I picked it up, folded it, and set it beneath the counter. I'd bury it in the recycling later when she wasn't looking.

"Okay, okay. I haven't seen him today; he's working. I'll talk to him tomorrow. I'm sure it's nothing." I wiped the counter down and started to prep for closing. "Now, if you're looking for something to do, you could wipe down the drink cases."

* ✳ *

The next morning, I sat on the shaded front steps of Chloe's house, waiting for the Range Rover to pick me up, the early air still stained with leftover yesterday heat. The paparazzi outside my house had multiplied, so I suggested to Parker they pick me up at Chloe's this morning. I'd set my alarm for five and slipped out the back of my house hopefully unseen. Now, even at six a.m., morning buzzed around me. Sprinklers shushed, a lawnmower hummed, a low-playing talk radio whispered from the roofers working across the street. One of them sat on the open tailgate of his truck, sipping from a silver thermos, checking his phone. When he glanced my way, I gave him a little wave. He held up his cup in salute.

I surveyed the street for gawkers, one of those funny long cameras looped around their necks, sitting in a tree or watching me from across the street in a car. At least here, I couldn't see anyone. How did Adam live under constant surveillance? I hadn't even gone three weeks and my nerves felt shredded. I had taken to wearing my huge sunglasses even when I didn't need them just to have an extra layer between the gawkers and me.

No matter, in a few days, this would all be over.

The last couple of days — the Little Club, that stupid photo of Adam and Beckett, John's breakdown in the café — had let the fatigue I'd been fighting settle firmly into my limbs. When Dad came home from practicing with Glory Daze last night, he'd narrowed his eyes at me. "You okay?" I didn't tell him about John; instead, I'd shown him the magazine. As he studied it, I'd told him it was part of their scene and the tabloids were making it up, but my stomach flickered with doubt. "Shocking," he'd said, pulling a cold beer from the fridge. "The tabloids got something *wrong*." I'd tried to laugh along with him, but it came out flat.

And this morning, it was still bugging me. Even though I knew I didn't have any grounds to be feeling this way (I was essentially an employee), it felt like Adam had broken my trust somehow, like he'd lied to me. Chloe was right. It was unacceptable boyfriend behavior, even from a fake boyfriend. I needed this whole thing to be over. It was too much, and I was sick of feeling like every moment of my life was one lie patched to another. I just wanted to go back to being me, my life before Adam came to town.

I made a terrible liar.

Because, honestly, the whole thing had stopped feeling like a job sometime around our river kiss. At that point, my heart had become a murky, foreign thing in my chest. And it was Adam's fault. He was supposed to be a jerk, a reckless Hollywood creep, and he had been, he *was* at first, but then he wasn't. At some point he'd become funny and smart and I liked being with him. Now this stupid magazine picture said, Nope, in fact he *is* a huge jerk. This was the problem; it was right there on the page grabbing Beckett's butt.

The Range Rover pulled up to the curb, engine purring. Adam scrambled out of the passenger seat. "You ready?" He held the door open for me. He had bed head and no shirt, just a pair of jeans, and the sight of him, his bare skin, sent shock waves through me. He was doing it again, breaking my movie-stars-going-shirtless-around-regular-people rule. I should be allowed to ticket him. I thought of the magazine picture, tried to push it from my mind, but I imagined having to sit there on the set today and watch Beckett flipping her lovely dark hair.

I pushed my sunglasses to the top of my head, fingering the skin beneath my eyes. "I think I'll skip the shoot today, if that's okay."

"What's wrong? You sick?" He frowned, reaching into the backseat and pulling out a T-shirt. He slipped it on as if he just hadn't had time to get dressed before picking me up. He reached out to feel my forehead. Even if it was cool before, I was sure it went hot at his touch.

That stupid picture.

Even though I'd sworn to Chloe I didn't care, I'd grabbed the magazine out of the café recycle bin before heading home. Last night, curled on the familiar pale pink quilt in my room, I'd stared at the offending picture for much longer than I cared to admit.

Why *was* his hand *there*?

"I'm just tired." I hitched my bag up on my shoulder and tried to look casual.

He shifted uncomfortably. "I'd like you to be there today. You should be there. You left early the other day, and I didn't see you yesterday. The script says you're at the shoot today. It'll look like we're having problems if you skip."

Was he going to get contractual on me? "I think it already looks like that, don't you? I mean, according to *Entertainment Now!* you've been 'Caught' — exclamation point!" Even whispering, my voice was razor-edged.

His brow furrowed with confusion. "What are you talking about?"

"I'm referencing a little move I like to call the Beckett Butt Grab!"

"The what? Who's Beckett?" He shot a nervous look around the neighborhood. This particular fight was *not* in the script, but he didn't need to worry; the construction guy wasn't sitting on his tailgate anymore, and miraculously there was no one around.

"Beckett Ray!"

His face clouded even more. "I'm going to need more than that."

"How about a visual aid?" I dug into my bag and pulled out the inky magazine, folded to the article. I held it up for him to see. "Look, here's you — grabbing Beckett on what can only be described as her rear region. And me, sad local girl, licking my wounds — only I think they caught me having just cleaned the espresso machine. It's not an easy job. I can't really help clean up your image if you're going to run around messing it up."

Adam gave the photo a once-over, his brow furrowing again, then relaxing. "We're not worried about that one. Last week, they reported on Steven Spielberg's alien alliances. No one believes *Entertainment Now!* It's garbage."

I didn't get angry very often. In fact, I prided myself on being a calm person who could really hold it together, but at that exact moment, I wanted to punch Adam Jakes in his movie-star face. That would be just what Hunter Fisch needed — protesters *and* a leading man with a black eye.

I shook the magazine at him. "I don't think you should be blowing this off. No matter what magazine it is, it looks bad. Robin Hamilton warned me about the kissing scene with you and Beckett and then this?"

"Robin Hamilton *warned* you? Because you two are BFFs now?" He tossed the magazine onto the sidewalk. "Don't look at that." His somber expression stilled my anger. His voice came out quiet but clear. "She played a waitress in a scene we shot. She had one line. I believe it was, 'More water?' There was definitely not *any* kissing happening. Robin Hamilton was just trying to get a reaction out of you. And obviously it worked."

It didn't match up. Why did so many things with this guy not match up? "You invited her to the shoot at the club. You said, 'How are Little's two most beautiful women?' or something gross and fake like that." Hot tears welled behind my eyes. I was embarrassed to be acting like this, falling apart in front of him *again*, but I couldn't stop myself.

Adam's look could only be described as confused pity. "She *asked* if she could come. And the whole beautiful women thing, that's just something to say. It doesn't mean anything. I didn't mean to be gross or fake." He thought about it for a second. "Okay, no — yes, I did mean it to be fake. It's just like 'How's the wife?'"

"No one says, 'How's the wife?'" I mumbled, my anger ebbing. I couldn't help adding, "Unless they're in an episode of *Leave It to Beaver*."

Sensing a thaw, he cupped my face in his hands. "Why are you so mad about this?" His expression shifted to amusement. "Wait, are you jealous?"

I flared again. "No. I'm embarrassed. It makes me look bad. It makes you look like a bad boyfriend — again. It ruins what we're trying to do here."

"Seriously, we're doing great." He dropped his hands from my face, but my cheeks felt branded with them. He studied me, probably noticing the dark circles beneath my eyes. "Did something else happen?"

I pulled my sunglasses back down, not telling him about John, about the spray of dragon tears he'd left on the café table. "No."

"You can't read this stuff, okay? I *never* do." His voice softened. "Even the legitimate magazines. They use stuff out of context. Like you'd just cleaned the espresso machine, it's the same thing with that shot of me and that girl. It was probably in passing, during a scene or a botched take, and the angle worked out. It's nothing. I don't have any interest in her rear region or any other region of her, okay?"

"Okay." I felt silly. "I'm sorry. I'm not jealous."

It was hard to hear him over the mower that started up again in the neighbor's yard, but I could have sworn he said, "It'd be okay if you were."

* ✳ *

I joined Adam for his shoot at the graveyard. The crew worked carefully around the graves, creating snowdrifts, hanging pine wreaths with red velvet bows. It seemed to me, they made an extra effort to be cautious and respectful as they winterized the slim strip of cemetery they'd been permitted to use for shooting the Ghost of Christmas Present scene.

"Hunter?" Adam stood in a green path, out of the scene, frowning, dressed in winter running gear. Kelly, the makeup artist, worked on his face.

Hunter stopped talking with one of the A.D.s and raised his eyebrows at Adam. "Yeah?"

"I'm not too clear about why I follow my teacher into the graveyard." He motioned at the actress standing by a grave, holding a fake poinsettia Tiny Tom had given her. Kelly waited, a makeup sponge poised by Adam's face.

Hunter rubbed his head. "You see her go in and you wonder about her. She's your teacher, you're on a run to clear your head, you see her go into a graveyard, and you follow her in."

"Why?"

Hunter's mouth twitched. "Curiosity. It's been a weird day for you so far, and you feel drawn to her." He turned back to the A.D.

Adam sighed as he ran a hand through his hair. "Okay."

He seemed distracted, his eyes moving over the assembled crew, over the graves, until his gaze landed on me, sitting on the stone bench just outside Video Village.

He trotted over. "Does it make sense to you?"

I shook my head. "I'm not an actor. I don't really know why your character does things." Flashes of his conversation with Beckett crept, like smoke, into my brain. Maybe I should mention something about brilliant pickle metaphors.

Adam didn't notice. "But you're a dancer. You understand motivation." He plopped down on the bench next to me. "This is the Ghost of Christmas Present. I have this history teacher who, without meaning to, actually teaches me something — not about history, but about the present." He was doing it again. That whole referring to himself as the character, saying "me" when he really meant Scott.

I thought about his scene. "Okay, she's visiting her mother who died, right?"

"Right."

"Well, death makes us think of life, makes us think about what's happening right now. It forces Scott, er, *you* — to see your

228

teacher as vulnerable. She forces you to actually see another person in pain. It makes you think of Cheryl, that she might die. It's" — I struggled to find the right word — "it's *immediate*. That's the whole point of this particular ghost in the story. To force you to look at what's happening *right now*."

He nodded, fiddling with the zipper on his tracksuit. "Yeah, right. That's good."

He squeezed my knee before hurrying over to the actress with the poinsettia. She nodded, the poinsettia bobbing up and down. I hadn't told Adam, but I'd read *A Christmas Carol* over the last week. I'd actually never read Dickens's novella, only seen it at Christmastime as a play. I didn't usually go for Victorian novels, so bleak and dreary. But this one got to me. And the Ghost of Christmas Present was my favorite of the spirits, how he could change his shape to fit any space, how he could only live in that one present moment.

The now.

Living in the now was a popular sort of notion in Northern California, especially around here. Live for now. *Carpe diem*. Over the years, our customers at the café had worn T-shirts bearing versions of this particular concept. *Live Now. Present Moment Only, Please. Goddess of the Now*. I'd often wondered about people's need to constantly remind themselves to be aware of living right now. It seemed sort of obvious to me. Of course we lived right now. When else would we be living?

Watching Adam work through his scene, though, I started to think I'd missed a bit of what that whole living *now* really meant to other people. Probably because I lived far too much in the now. I'd never had to wrestle with it the way some of our customers clearly had.

My trouble wasn't with now. My trouble was with the future.

I did *now* really well.

Dad always told me I was good at noticing moments, at appreciating the little things in life. It struck me as an odd thing, being good at noticing moments. Moments, in and of themselves, were actually pretty boring little bits of time. For most people, they were like confetti or snowflakes; they didn't amount to much until they were in groups. I think I was the opposite. I avoided the groups, the mounds of confetti or snow that had built up in my life, because I was more frightened of what those mounds might tell me to do.

I lived in the now so I didn't have to move forward.

Sitting on the bench, the warm wind blowing across the graveyard, I wondered if I'd been choosing the now so I didn't have to think about the point when the ghost of my future came along and poked me with his crooked, bossy stick.

* ✳ *

But like it or not, like Scrooge, I would have to think about it. When I got home that evening, my Ghost of Christmas Future was sitting at the kitchen table reading the newspaper.

Two of them.

"Hi, parents." I leaned down to kiss Mom. "When did you get home?"

She reached up to give me a hug. "About an hour ago." Her dark hair had lightened in the summer sun, and her face looked tan in the yellow light of the overhead lamp. "Join us." Something in her voice told me this wasn't a casual invitation.

I pulled a pitcher of herbal iced tea from the fridge. "Want some?" I offered, pouring myself a glass over some ice.

"We're good," Dad answered, taking off his reading glasses and resting them on the folded newspaper in front of him. He pushed out the chair next to him with his foot.

I settled into it. "What's up?"

They exchanged a look across the table. Uh-oh. That look was usually reserved for conversations about my brother. I sat up straighter. "Is everything okay? Is John okay?" Had they seen the dragon tears I'd scattered by the maple tree in the yard?

"Actually . . ." Dad cleared his throat. "This isn't about John."

"Oh."

Mom folded her hands in front of her on the table. I could see her working something over in her mind; it moved across her face like cloud cover. "We have something we'd like to talk about with you."

I waited, my eyes darting between them. "Okay."

Dad cleared his throat again. "We're, here's the thing . . . we're concerned about you."

"About me?" I'd never had a conversation like this with my parents. I wasn't the sort of kid who caused concerns for parents. "Is this about Adam?"

"Not really." Mom folded and unfolded the nearest corner edge of the newspaper. "We've been meaning to talk to you about this for a while."

"It's about graduation." Dad toyed with his glasses. "About

what's going to happen after you graduate next year." He glanced again at Mom.

At least now I knew which conversation we were having. We'd all been having it for years with our parents. Of course, now it was becoming less theoretical and more — *tell us exactly what will happen next*. Next. The Future. Chloe's and Alien Drake's parents had already asked for the lists. College lists. Life-after-high-school lists. *Life* lists. The Future with its crooked stick was big on lists.

So much for living in the now.

I breathed out a sigh. "Right, okay." I launched into my plan. I'd stay here after graduation and work at the café. Teach at Snow Ridge. Life as usual. "Only, I'll be able to pick up more shifts once school's off my plate."

My parents exchanged another look. Mom nodded slowly, her eyes on her folded hands. "Yeah, that's sort of what we thought you might say."

Outside, the evening darkened, yellowing the lamplight even more. Dad picked up the pen lying next to his glasses, clicked and unclicked the top. "Thing is," Dad said, taking a breath, "we're not okay with that plan."

My neck cooled. What did he mean they weren't okay with my plan? "You don't want me to work at Eats?"

Mom reached for my hand. "Honey, we're worried you're not thinking broadly enough. We'd love for you to work with us at the café. But we were hoping you'd go get an education first. Then, come back to us if you want, after college, in the summers, after having another life out in the bigger world. Some experiences that will be your own, that aren't tied to Little."

Not them, too. The hum of the fridge, the clicking of Dad's pen, filled my ears with a buzzing. Mom's hand smothered mine and I made a fist. "Dad didn't go to college. He's always had the café."

Letting go, she glanced at Dad, who sighed. "Yes, but we always thought you'd go off to dance somewhere. And now . . ." His voice trailed off. *Click. Click.*

"It's been a year," Mom finished.

"I know how long it's been," I snapped, slumping in my chair, aware that I'd just pulled a classic teenager pose. I sat up a bit. No need to give them any ammunition.

"Please don't get defensive, Carter." Dad tilted his head, studying me. "We're allowed to have this conversation with you. We're your parents." Dad wasn't one to discipline me, didn't need to use a dad voice very often, and he hadn't used it at all for quite some time. It sounded heavy-edged in the small space of the kitchen. His big shoulders sighed with him. "We want you to know that we're honored you would choose this life, this town, our family business. It makes us feel like we've done a pretty bang-up job."

Tears bit at the edges of my eyes. "But I'm fired."

Mom laughed in surprise, sitting back in her chair. "Oh, Carter. You're not one to be dramatic."

She was right. I hated drama, opted for peace and ease. Which is why I didn't want any grand plans. I just wanted my life, the life I already liked. "I think I should stay." I looked straight at Mom. "Don't you always say that life should be about serving those not as fortunate? I want to stay here and do that."

Her shoulders sagged. "I do say that. But I think there is value in building yourself first. I went to college and figured out who I was *first*."

"I know who I am." Another glance. There was something else they weren't telling me. "What?"

Dad bit his lip. "We're also afraid you're staying because you think you can help your brother."

Mom leaned toward me, resting her weight on her forearms. "He needs to get his own help, Carter. You know that, right? We can't help him when he won't help himself."

I stared at her. "How can you say that? We're his *family*."

Mom sighed. "Honey, he has a serious problem. A gambling addiction." She paused, those words floating and strange. "He keeps making bad, addictive choices. I've . . ." She pushed some hair behind her ears. "Well, I've been seeing someone who specializes in helping families with a member who has a gambling problem. She's been able to give me some incredible resources."

My heart raced. "For John? Somewhere he can get help?"

"Yes."

"And he's agreed to go?"

Dad's eyes darkened. "No, not yet."

"I'll talk to him." I tried to look at both of them at once, catch their eyes. I'd rather talk about John than talk about me.

Mom started to say something but bit her lip. "That'd be great." She splayed out her fingers on the table. "But let's not get sidetracked. We want you to put a list together for yourself." I flinched at the word *list*. She hurried to say, "Just some options. Dad and I aren't saying absolutely college, though we think you would love it, especially a program in dance therapy or something.

234

But it could also be culinary school or a true gap year." She smiled at my face. "Come on, this isn't a prison sentence. You're lucky to have these sorts of options. You should see some of what I've seen." She stopped her own lecture. "Okay, no lessons, sorry. We just want you to plan for something that will teach you about what you can love and learn from beyond Little."

Dad put his hand on my arm. "Even Hobbits have to take adventures. That's how they bring stories back to the Shire."

My parents were so wonderful. I knew I should feel lucky and grateful and excited. But I didn't. I felt kicked out of my own house.

Mom stood up, arching her back. She hadn't even showered since she got home, and she always liked a good shower after her trips. Her fingers resting on the back of my chair, she asked, "Deal?"

"Deal." I avoided her eyes.

yesterday's sightings

Things Are Looking Up in Little, CA

Morning, sky watchers. The other day, we overheard someone refer to a lonely period in his life as feeling like "a black hole." Obviously, it's a bummer to feel like that and we felt bad for the guy, but it got us thinking that he probably doesn't really know what a black hole is. Because black holes are filled with so much stuff, so much dense stuff, that it's not really about emptiness or loneliness at all. It's about too much stuff in too little a space so there's not even room for light to squeeze out. (At least, that's what it seems like to us from the description on NASA's site.) But what grabbed our attention most was that black holes often happen when a star is dying. And even cooler, we thought, was that even though scientists can't see them, they know where they are because of the way certain stars and gases act around the black hole. They act weird. Different.

And it made us think about how sometimes we all end up orbiting a strange, dense black hole. A dying star. And it makes us act weird and different.

What do you think?

See you tonight, under the sky.

nineteen

I tapped at the glass of Alien Drake's window. It was too late to ring the doorbell, and he wasn't answering my texts. After a few seconds, his round face appeared in the window, his eyebrows standing at attention. "Hey," he said, sliding the window open. "You going old-school tonight?"

I could barely hear him over the hum of the air conditioner. "You weren't answering your texts."

He scrambled away from the window, returning with his phone. "Dead." He held it up as evidence. Behind him, his walls were covered with star maps, pictures of planets, and a wall-sized diagram of Area 51.

I felt a deep ache for the days when we used to just lie on the floor and look at the glow of the peel-and-stick stars on the ceiling of his room, the rain falling outside. "Can you come out?"

"Roof or walk?"

"Roof."

"I'll get provisions." He slid the window shut again.

In five minutes, we were sitting on an old quilt, the night a gleaming sheet above us. "So spending too much time around dying stars makes some of us act weird, huh?"

He popped open a bag of cheddar popcorn. "Glad to see you're still reading our blog."

I looked sideways at him. "I deserved that. I'm so sorry I've checked out on you. The last few weeks have been bizarre."

He brushed some cheddar dust from his fingers. "Don't worry, I won't hold this against you, promise, but yeah, black holes. You. I was talking about you and your movie star."

"I got that." I grabbed a handful of popcorn.

"Still, you aside, it's interesting that they used to be stars, right? Stars that essentially collapsed under their own weight."

I chewed my popcorn. "Especially now that I've had a front-row seat to a star collapsing."

Alien Drake wiped his hands on his jeans. "Your guy doing okay?"

"Right, *my* guy." A streetlight kept blinking on and off, the motion sensor tripped by some neighborhood cats.

"He's not your guy?" He opened a Diet Coke and it hissed into the night.

I shrugged, lying on my back, staring up at the dense sky. Now. Now could be the moment I told him everything, the deal with Adam to pay for John's rehab. I could come clean and stop acting so weird.

But I chickened out. I just couldn't handle another person's disappointment tonight. "Show me some stars. Real ones. I don't really want to talk about the other one right now."

He paused, his stare covering me, knowing I'd just skipped over something he couldn't see. Then, he recapped his drink and followed my lead, tucking his arms behind his head. "I wish I could show you Sirius right now."

"The Dog Star?"

"Yeah. But you can't see it now." Around us, crickets sang, and a car passed on the road below.

Alien Drake's voice felt like part of the night air. "It has this little companion star, a white dwarf. Its name is Sirius B, but some people call it the Pup."

I knew that, but I humored him. "Cute."

"Even though Sirius is this dynamic, bright star, even though it's multicolored and spangled, it always needs its Pup. Doesn't go anywhere without it." He sat up again, pulling his knees to his chest. "See what I just did there."

"Subtle."

"More star metaphors."

"You're on a roll." I sat up, too, pulling my own knees close. The thing about the Pup was he didn't have a choice. Besides, no one ever asked him how he felt about all that glare.

I changed the subject. Again. "My parents just told me I have to leave Little after graduation, do something productive, expansive — I don't know. Something else." The Smiths' dog started barking, a beagle's long, painful bark-howl, like he was howling for me.

"They're throwing you out of Little?"

"That about sums it up."

"Right out on your butt?"

"Pretty much."

He put his arm around me. "I'm so proud of your parents."

Scowling, I shrank against his arm. "How can you be on their side?"

In that moment, the crickets seemed to take a break, and the beagle stopped its howl, leaving behind an inky sort of silence. Alien Drake sighed into it. "Oh, Carter, don't be such a Hobbit. We're *all* on your side." I was going to punch the next person who called me a Hobbit.

* ✳ *

"You ready for this?" Adam asked me the next day, leaning into me, whispering into my hair.

We stood on the sidewalk outside Little Eats. Four o'clock. Time for our big public fight, the first sign of trouble. Exactly three weeks after I first saw him, a few days earlier than the original script. The picture of Adam and Beckett didn't get much traction, but Parker didn't want to take any chances. He needed this fight to be about my issues, my distaste for Hollywood, and not about the Butt Grab. We needed to change the story. I could see the headline already: "Big Trouble in Little Paradise" — exclamation point.

"Ready." So I didn't have to look at him, I surveyed the scene, spotting at least a dozen cameras waiting. The photo should be out in hours somewhere on the greedy eating machine of the Internet.

He cupped my elbow, his face serious. "You've been amazing through all this, by the way. I know my world's not easy."

My throat tightened, but I gave a casual wave of my hand. "A million *birds* would love this opportunity."

He frowned. "Parker?"

"Yeah."

"What a bunch of crap."

But Parker was right. A million girls would have loved this

opportunity. Even if half the time I felt like an overpaid, over-exposed prop. But the other half had felt special. Like I was someone special.

My body tense, we walked a bit down the street, just far enough to make sure we'd collected the photographers hanging out in the Little Eats patio, letting them trail behind us like toilet paper on our shoes. When Adam felt certain we had enough of an audience, he spun around. "Could you guys leave us alone for five seconds? We're just trying to take a walk here."

They perked up, the collective calamity police.

I said my lines to the photographers the way Parker and Adam had coached me. "I hate this! You need to stop following us." Adam made a show of trying to calm me down until it was my turn to lose it on him. "And *you're* not helping. I can't even talk to you without someone butting in, needing you, distracting you. I'm not cut out for all this! I just want my life back." I personally thought this last bit was over the top, but Parker had insisted. They'd need sound bites, he'd assured me.

Adam pretended to look hurt, shocked, even. "We should talk about this later." He tossed an apologetic grin at the photographers. They were drinking us up like lemonade.

It was too easy.

Adam called Mik, who was on standby the next street over, and within a minute, the Range Rover pulled alongside us. "Just go," I told Adam, tossing my words to the photographers like a beach ball. "I'm walking home." I turned away.

"Carter, wait —" Adam called after me, his voice the perfect blend of pleading and hurt.

And, just like we'd practiced, I pushed my way through the pack of cameras, wiping at tears they would think they saw, tears that weren't really there, but that would make it into all the copy they wrote later about our fight.

* ✳ *

I walked through the dull heat up the hill until I found myself in front of Alien Drake's house. He wasn't home. I leaned my head onto the stained glass window on his front door, my legs wobbly. The fight had been only minutes and a complete invention, but my insides still felt hollowed out. I wasn't a fighter, fake or otherwise. Turning, I saw the fan still propped there from the day I'd argued with Alien Drake, its white plastic blades dusty, and the whirl of my life hit me.

Sitting down on the first step of Alien Drake's porch, I cried. For real this time.

And it wasn't for Adam, for our fight, or for the beginning of us ending things. Everything with Adam was too new to cry like this. I had too many other things I'd tucked away, shelved in some sort of dark-hearted bookshelf. My grandmother, my brother, my dancing, my future somewhere unknown, somewhere that wasn't Little. A future that had always loomed, even in the easy years of being a kid, because people imagined things for me outside of here.

Why weren't we whole until we'd left ourselves behind?

"Carter?" Chloe stood holding Alien Drake's hand on the walk. "Are you okay?"

I held up my phone. "I was just about to text you, I swear." The path blurred with my tears, but soon, they were both sitting on either side of me on the steps.

"What happened?" Alien Drake asked, setting down the bag of Burger Town he'd been holding. I could smell the grease and salt and warmth from it.

I sniffed. "Did you get fries?"

He fished out the fries and some ketchup packets, and I dragged a fry through the puddle of ketchup Chloe hurriedly made on some folded napkins.

"What's going on?" she asked.

I shrugged, sipping the root beer Drake handed me through its straw. I watched the brown liquid move up and down. "Adam and I had a fight."

Alien Drake unwrapped a burger and bit into it. Chloe shot him a withering glare. "What? *She's* eating."

It made me laugh, how regular and expected their exchange was, how familiar. "I'm okay, I am. I just thought . . ." I searched for what wouldn't feel like a lie. "I thought I might know him, but I don't think I do. His world's just too different."

"People from different worlds can work out," Chloe insisted, sweeping another fry through the ketchup. "I mean, what if you're star-crossed lovers and meant to be?"

I glanced sideways at Alien Drake, who hid a smile. Chloe's Shakespearean knowledge could be sadly lacking at times. "Yeah, the whole star-crossed-lover thing doesn't usually work out. It more often ends with stabbing and poison."

Chloe rolled her eyes. "I meant *fated*. Don't be such a book snob."

Alien Drake finished his burger. "What happened?"

As the neighbor's sprinklers came on next door, as a woman jogged by with a baby stroller, as all the ordinary neighborhood movements sighed around me, it struck me that I wouldn't have to lie to them. What was wrong with me and Adam had nothing to do with our arrangement. It had to do with *us*.

"I don't ever know what's real," I told them. "It's too much, all the cameras in my face. His whole image . . . he's being constantly built. He doesn't just live a life — he invents a life. Every day. For millions of people to wonder about. He walks around as his own reality show. And sometimes, it's just too hard to separate the different versions he puts out there. Like, what I knew about him from tabloids and stuff — for the most part that doesn't match up with how he's been with me. Then, sometimes it does, and it's so confusing."

Alien Drake watched a pack of teenagers drive by in a green Jeep, each dressed in some version of river clothes. "I don't think anyone ever knows what's real."

I pulled my eyes from the Jeep. "What do you mean?"

"Facebook's the perfect example."

"You know I don't have a Facebook page." Parker had said that my *not* having a Facebook page had been one reason they thought I'd be a good fit for their plan. Other than our blog, I spent basically no time online.

Alien Drake ran a hand through his hair. "Okay, but *think* about it. Not just Facebook. Everything. We're all trying to post our best features. Pictures, texting, just standing in line at the post office, we only give people the bits we want them to see. We walk around updating our status so people only get a version of us. Online, people have their own image-controlled environment. When I'm online, I talk about our blog, or a restaurant I liked, or share a book I've read or a movie I've seen. It's all a part of me, but it's not the whole story. Adam Jakes plays that game as an extreme sport. He's like an Ultimate Fighter of the social media world."

I chewed a fry. "But people get a sense of you. The real you. Even if it's just little bits."

He fished around in the bag for some more fries. "Maybe. But I only let them see certain things. Planned things. Controlled things. The tabloids are all controlled. Reality TV is controlled. Even if it's not scripted, the producers make choices. They edit things together to create whatever image they're going for. To create a story. Maybe you've only read someone else's Adam story and now you're getting to know him. You're getting to write your own story."

"But I'm *not* getting to know him. I don't know what's him and what's his act — his actor face or his real face." As I said it, I thought about my brother, and how he had a face just for me. Being two-faced was usually an insult, but maybe we all had two faces or three or a dozen? Were there different versions of me out in the world depending on the parts I shared at certain times? It was weird to think one person might see me one way and another person might have a totally different impression of me based on a separate list of experiences.

"I just want to know the truth," I said finally, watching a family walk by on the sidewalk. The little girl with them, maybe three, straggled behind, tugging at the end of a yellow balloon, watching it dance above her head.

245

Alien Drake watched them, too. "I'm not sure there's such a thing as a single truth. Just a whole bunch of different renderings."

A sprinkler came on across the street, dotting the asphalt of the road with tiny black specks. "That's scary," I told them.

Chloe tucked her dark hair behind her ears, watching me with her cool eyes. "I know."

I glanced between the two of them. "Do you guys ever think about all of this just ending?"

"Like the end of the world?" Chloe's eyes widened.

"No, like the end of *our* world."

They each wound an arm around me and squeezed, a friend sandwich. They didn't have to say it for me to know the answer.

Across the street, a man leveled his camera at us from a parked car the color of sand. He took a few shots and then pulled away.

Chloe clapped her hands together. "Oh, do you think that will be in *People*? Will I get to be the friend whose shoulder you cry on?" She stood, trying to catch sight of the beige sedan before it turned the corner.

I tugged at the back of her shirt. "You're always that friend, dummy."

Turning, she smiled sweetly. "I know . . . but this time it might be in *People*."

I caught Alien Drake's eye. "Slow learning curve, that one."

He pulled Chloe onto his lap.

* ✳ *

An hour later, I was sitting cross-legged on my bed with Extra Pickles when someone tapped on my door. "Come in."

246

Dad poked his head in the room. He held a small white box in his hand tied with a gold bow. "Hey, this came for you. Today was the big fight, right?"

"Yeah." I patted Extra Pickles's head. The box was from Morning Glory, my favorite bakery. Dad brought it to me on the bed, and I opened it. Nestled inside was a single, perfect vanilla cupcake with pink icing and star sprinkles. There was no note.

"From Adam?" Dad settled on the cedar chest where I kept things like yearbooks, old dance programs, a shoe box of elementary school pictures.

I shrugged. "Probably Parker."

Dad scanned my walls. "I haven't sat in here in a while. You still loving this green?"

When I was ten, I'd begged my parents to paint my room Kermit green with white trim. I had been obsessed with the Muppets, the old ones from the seventies, and I wanted my room to match Kermit, my favorite character.

"I'm still digging the Kermit."

Dad smiled. "He's a classic."

We both noticed the awkward pause. Dad wasn't much for small talk, and he was being sort of fidgety, clearly trying to work up the nerve to say something to me. "What's up, Dad?"

He gave me a steady look, his eyes searching my face. "Why aren't you dancing anymore?"

"Did Mom put you up to this?" I set the cupcake box on my side table.

"No!" He flushed. "Okay, yes. We've been having a lot of talks about you lately."

I pulled my ivory pillow onto my lap like a shield. "So it seems. What does Mom think?"

"That you freaked out."

I narrowed my eyes at him. "I didn't freak out."

"Sure you did. It's okay, Carter. People freak out. It's not always a bad thing. Sometimes it's a response that reminds you that you're alive with choices. You were handed this huge thing, this massive piece of praise, and you freaked out. It's okay."

"It never happened to you. You went from high school to Little Eats. Point A to Point B. Simple."

He licked his lips. "Is that what you think I did?"

"Didn't you?"

"Actually, I tried pretty hard to do the musician thing for a few years before I came back to Little." He explained he'd been with a band that had bopped around Northern California, getting gigs here and there, hoping to be picked up by a label. "But it didn't happen, and we landed in Santa Cruz, where I met your mom."

My stomach hurt. "Why haven't you ever told me?"

"You never asked."

"I'm not asking now and you're telling me."

He sighed, his face freckled with the light coming in through the blinds. "You might be an old soul, Carter, but you're still seventeen."

My stomach churned, and the air-conditioning in our house felt wrong, too cold, too dry. "You think I should have taken that scholarship." Extra Pickles stared up at me with big eyes, whining at the increased pitch of my voice.

"I don't, actually." Dad fiddled with a stack of my laundry I

248

hadn't yet put away. "Personally, I don't think you would like New York, which is why I didn't say anything at the time. I don't think you need to want New York or all it stands for. But I think you made a mistake just stopping."

"What do you mean?"

"You don't have to go to New York or college or wherever to be a dancer. I played in a lot of cool venues. It was great, until it wasn't, and then I came home, and I have the café now and I love it. That was my journey. That was my choice. But you just stopped. All those years of love just ceased to be. And I think that was a mistake." He folded and unfolded a sweatshirt that kept falling off the stack. "Mom and I both think that."

I leaned into the wall behind my bed, the light changing the room, shifting to evening. "But you didn't say anything before."

"We weren't sure you were ready to hear it."

I thought back to the day I told the school no, the sound of dead air on the other end of the phone. "Other people wanted me to go."

He laughed, a funny short breath of air. "This isn't about *other* people. This is about you." Leaning forward, his wide shoulders shifting, he said, "Carter, I love how much you help other people. You're so much like your mom. But what you don't get is that you have to work out your own self first. You have to decide what you want from your own life. Then you have to be accountable to it. And just so you know, people criticized me for throwing in the towel too early. My former bandmates never spoke to me again, and I spent some years feeling like a failure."

"You did? *You?*"

"Listen to me, Carter, because you know me and I don't like to give speeches. That's been hard with John, and I've never really had to with you, but I'm going to try one, okay?"

"Okay." Touched by how hard this was for him, I sat up a little.

He cleared his throat. "Here's the thing you need to know. Here's a hint from Grown-up World. There's no right way. Not really. Just perspective. We *choose* whether we succeed or fail. *We* do. It's all our own spin on it. We create our own definition of success or failure. You can't hold yourself up to other people's versions of things. Not society's idea of things, and not other people's. Your own. But regret . . . well, that's a real thing. Take it from me. You should try things on, see if they fit you. If they don't, it's not failure. It's a choice. But always let yourself have a choice, let yourself have possibilities. People say, 'Follow your dreams, blah blah blah,' but no one's checking up on that, no one's out there with a clipboard saying, 'Yes, Carter Moon. Dream followed!' You're accountable to yourself. So if you don't ever take the chances, if you don't ever at least try, you're going to be sitting in that café when you're forty wondering about them."

"You don't know that for sure." My voice wavered.

"Sure I do. Why do you think I started Glory Daze? There's no irony lost in that name. Besides, you're already wondering or you wouldn't still be teaching that Snow Ridge class, you wouldn't be finding a way to keep it in your life."

"I like that class because it's just fun. It's not about me." Even as I said it, though, I knew that it was about me. I could tell myself it was about the old people there, and somehow it seemed less selfish of a pursuit if it was about helping them, but I kept doing it because they asked me to "do a dance" each week without wanting anything from it, without suggesting that it be some sort of future goal. "I just don't want to be selfish. Mom's always saying how I was already born on third base, so I shouldn't act like I've hit a triple."

Dad laughed then, familiar with one of Mom's favorite expressions. "You have never been an entitled kid, Carter. Even when you were nine, you donated all your birthday money to a wildlife foundation." He leaned back against the wall, studying me, his eyes glossy. "We think it's great, but Mom and I never meant to teach you to give up yourself entirely. That's not what we meant at all. It's not selfish to love something, to put something beautiful out in the world. If you can keep it about that, and not turn it into a bunch of narcissistic mega-crap, well, that's its own sort of service. You've got to figure out what makes the world beautiful for you, so you can help make it beautiful for other people."

Around me, my room breathed with its familiar sounds, Extra Pickles's breathing, the slow spin of the ceiling fan. "I just like it here."

Dad stood. "Honey, you're one of those lucky people who will like a lot of places. And you will always have *here*." He bent to kiss my head, and Extra Pickles followed him out of the room, leaving me alone.

yesterday's sightings
Things Are Looking Up in Little, CA

Morning, sky watchers. Last night, we sat on the roof and thought about constellations. Constellations are these patterns that human beings stitched into the sky starting, like, 4,000 years ago (probably longer) to make sense of it, to be able to point at a group of stars and say, That's Orion, or That's the Big Dipper. But they are just groupings of stars. They exist only because humans invented them, made them up to create order out of the crazy, wide sky, a sky that would exist without humans ever naming it. It's a human need — that order — because it gives us a sense that we have control. But we don't. Not really. At any point, you could make up your own patterns — point out three or four stars and call them the Donut. As long as you know what star you're looking at, the patterns already there don't necessarily matter at all.

It got us thinking about all the patterns in our own lives that we assume we must follow — graduation, college, work, marriage. Who stitched those patterns together and decided they were the only way to look at life?

We were just wondering.

See you tonight, under the sky.

twenty

I worked the next couple of days at the café. Adam's shooting schedule was insane, and Parker thought it would make our fight more believable if we didn't have much contact. I tried to lose myself in the busy buzz of the café, tried to let the rhythm of the summer crowd clear him from my mind, but every time the door pushed open, I found myself wishing he would be coming through it.

After work, I walked home. Evening fell in Little in that summer sort of way, where the sky melts into sherbet colors at the horizon over the pines, and the air starts to carry small pricks of cool mountain nights within its heat. This was my favorite time of day in the summer, that easy melting. It loosened the knots of my busy mind.

No one was home, so I poured a glass of iced tea, grabbed the box of frozen Junior Mints I'd been saving, and crawled into the childhood space of my tree house to watch the sun set through the wide window.

My parents wanted a list of my options — something that would help grow me outside of Little. But I only seemed to want to watch Little melt into nighttime. I wasn't sure I wanted more than this — the sweet glow of twilight, nothing beyond the way the ease of it seeped under my skin, the way the frozen Junior Mints tasted in my mouth.

Somehow, that made me wrong. I should want more than Junior Mints on a summer evening.

I read once somewhere that dancers must have passion, talent, and ambition to succeed in the professional world. A trifecta of skills. For years, I'd confused ambition with hard work, with that energetic pulse that pushed me to class each day, that made me ice my aching muscles and get back up again to dance. Hard work. Dancing was hard work. But hard work was not ambition.

Ambition was something else.

And I didn't have it.

Adam had it. It drove him to endure the crowds, the tabloids, the constant stream of attention, both bad and good. It buoyed him. Beckett Ray had it — it sent her head spinning with big-city dreams.

But not Country Mouse me.

Why didn't I seem to want more than this town?

I popped another mint into my mouth, staring out at the gloaming, thinking about the day I turned down that scholarship last summer. Would I ever regret not choosing New York? I didn't think I would, but Dad wasn't talking about New York. He was talking about dancing, the simple act of it. Not what I could parlay it into, but just doing it. Because it made the world more beautiful to me to be dancing in it. He'd said I would regret leaving it behind, that I was already building my regret.

Why had I felt there were only two options?

1. Hardcore professional-track dancing, the path all my teachers had wanted for me, expected of me.
2. Nothing.

When I thought about it, it seemed so immature. Like a child who, because she couldn't stomach a massive sixteen-scoop sundae, suddenly refused all ice cream. I'd turned down New York, but I didn't have to turn it *all* down. Why hadn't I considered the wide expanse of middle ground, of other possibilities?

There was a knock on the door frame, and Adam poked his head into the tree house. "Let's make up," he said with a smile.

Seeing him was like sinking into a hot bath.

I motioned him in. "I forgive you."

"Um, you mean I forgive *you*."

"If you say so." I thought of our fight. Yesterday, Chloe had sent me a text: *I'm that shoulder!* — with links to several of the online celebrity sites documenting our fight, a picture of me actually crying on their shoulders afterward, and a few other articles about the fight. They had headlines like, "Big Trouble in Little Paradise?"

I'd deleted the text.

Adam settled against the wall next to me, staring out the slat of window. "Wow, look at that sunset." I noticed the faint traces of makeup at his temples. He must have just come from shooting.

I offered him a Junior Mint. "Beautiful, huh? I love this time of day."

He popped it into his mouth. "You love whatever time of day it is." He brushed some hair away from the side of my face, his touch, as always, leaving an electric glaze on my skin. He dropped his hand back into his lap. "I don't know how you do it."

"Do what?"

"Just always love being right where you are." He breathed in deeply. "It's like you were born without any restlessness at all. You don't seem to need anything other than what you have."

I shot him a wary look. "I'm warning you, if you make any Hobbit references at all, I will punch you in the face." But I thought about what Dad had said earlier, about being the sort of person who just loved things. Somehow, I felt like I should apologize for it, for being fine right here.

He held up his hands in mock defense. "No, seriously, I would give anything for that. To be able to — how did you describe it when I first met you? Not venture outside the fence. It's very grounded and sweet."

I gave a sort of snort. "Yeah, lots of good it's doing me. People don't trust it."

Adam thought about it. "I think people tend to confuse your sweetness with being naïve or sheltered, and I don't think that's you. You know there are bad things in the world. You're even try-ing to make them better. Just like your parents."

"My parents are kicking me out." He looked at me quizzically, and I told him about my list, about the talk with my parents about life after Little.

Adam helped himself to a few more Junior Mints. "I think they worry you'll have regrets." At my dark look, he hurriedly added, "I know, I know . . . you probably don't believe in regret."

Sighing, I said, "I think my theory might be faulty. Apparently, you can't have regrets until you're too old to do anything about them." I shook the last of the mints from the box. "I'm sure they're worried that the regret won't be about what might have happened, but more about never trying in the first place." A breeze came in through the window, cooling my face, and sending the wind chimes in our neighbor's yard singing.

Adam contemplated the evening light sneaking into the tree house. Outside, the sherbet colors had faded, leaving the sky bruised and pale. "You know, you can love a place and still leave it. It's always here. It's not going anywhere."

"I know. It's just that I like it here already. I have roots here."

Outside, the crickets started an early chirping. Adam said, "I'm not sure I like the whole roots thing."

"Why not?"

"It's so limiting. It's like, well, you have roots here, so you have to rip them up if you want to go anywhere else. It's so . . . botanical. Like we're a bunch of semi-transplantable shrubs or something." He gave a little shudder.

I studied the shadows moving along the walls of the tree house. "Having roots is a real thing. You don't get it because you're, well, because you're famous. Your world is too big."

He winced. "Judge much? I can't have roots because I'm from Hollywood? Small towns have the market cornered on roots? It's not true, you know. I know I can always be in L.A., but it doesn't mean I can't go other places, be other places."

"But that's your job."

"I guess. But I like to think of L.A. as my home port. I can sail around wherever, but it's always a place to put down my anchor. Yeah, I like the anchor metaphor better than the root one. More room to move with the anchor metaphor."

My mind reeled with anchor and shrub imagery. I saw his point, but I was sticking with my roots. "I think small towns get such a bad reputation. No one ever criticizes kids who want to stay living in L.A. or New York. They're allowed to stay in their home-towns without people thinking they're closing off their options."

Adam shrugged. "Maybe, but I think the point is to try new things."

"I try new things! Yesterday, I ate a white beet."

"Yes, that's an adventure, all right."

"Have *you* tried a white beet?"

"I doubt it."

The room had darkened around us, cocooning us in the upcoming night. I wanted to tell him that I thought there were anchor people and there were root people and those were different sorts of people. I wanted to say that not everyone had to have adventure for their lives to feel full, but I heard the back door slam shut. Hurried footsteps crossed our deck, then Dad stuck his head through the tree house door, his face twisted with worry.

"What is it?" My body tensed.

Dad nodded quickly to Adam. "It's your brother. He's in the hospital. We have to go."

Adam's gaze slipped between us. "Mik's out front. He can drive us."

* ✳ *

This was not the Christmas hospital of Adam's movie shoot. No festive decorations, no nurses wearing holiday-themed scrubs. It was empty and white. The woman working the front desk gave us a wan smile before handing Dad a clipboard, dark circles beneath her eyes, no Kelly to dab on some concealer at last look. After Dad filled out the necessary information, he'd gone off in search of the doctor while Mom and I sat in the waiting room on a couple of cracked blue chairs. Adam stood near the vending machines, avoiding the stacks of magazines strewn about. Two had his picture somewhere on the cover. The only other person in the waiting room was an old man in a flannel shirt and running shorts reading a hunting magazine. He sat with his fish-belly-white legs splayed out like opened scissors. He hadn't recognized Adam or, if he had, he didn't care. Above us, two of the fluorescent lights buzzed, shuddering off, then on, every few minutes.

Mom watched Adam in what she thought was a sly way, but I noticed. "Stop staring at him," I whispered.

"I'm not." She kept staring. "He's so good-looking."

Adam's phone buzzed. Annoyed, he texted something. "Adam, if you have to go, you can go," I told him. "We'll be fine."

He tucked his phone into the pocket of his lemon-colored shorts. "They need to reshoot something. Hunter's imploding. You sure you're okay?"

"We're *fine*," I assured him. "The doctor said he's not in critical condition."

Adam glanced first at me and then at Mom, his face creased with concern. "You can call if you need anything." He crossed the room in big strides and gave me a sloppy bear hug, my body enveloped; before I could hug him back, he stepped away, engulfing Mom next.

Surprised, Mom gaped at me over his shoulder. Pulling back, he nodded once more at me before disappearing through the glass doors of the hospital into the purpled light. I could see Mik idling the Range Rover through the window, his brake lights glowing. Several hospital employees standing outside perked up as they watched Adam climb into the back. They watched the Range Rover disappear.

"What was that?" Mom adjusted her shirt.

"Turns out, the jerk's a pretty nice guy." I studied the spot where the Range Rover had been parked. I would miss Adam Jakes when he left Little in a few days. That, at least, was the truth. I wasn't sure about all that had happened between us, about our blurry line between what was real and what was scripted, but I knew when he left, he would leave behind an Adam-shaped space in my life.

Dad emerged into the room, his face pale. He twisted his baseball cap in his hands. "We can go see him." He motioned for us, his face sad. "He's in pretty bad shape."

* ✳ *

Pretty bad shape didn't really cover it. I hovered in the doorway, my breath caught somewhere in my chest. John was like wadded-up Kleenex, a crumple in the bed under pale sheets. His body seemed like one tie-dyed bruise, swirls of yellow, blue, purple, and rust covering his skin. His left eye was swollen, like a halved apple had been fastened to his face, and his mouth had a gash bisecting it perpendicularly, dividing it into quadrants. He was bandaged, wrapped, taped, stapled, essentially held together like a rag toy.

My brother, the patchwork quilt.

Mom made a sound like a wounded animal, a whimper. Slowly, she went to his side, touched his arm. He stirred, one eye opening only a slit, the other not opening at all.

"Mom?" He tried to sit up.

"Don't," she breathed, her voice shaking. "Don't try to move."

They whispered a bit to each other. Finally, Dad motioned for Mom to follow him into the hall. They brushed past me in the doorway, and I went to sit with my brother.

"You don't look so hot." I smoothed some hair out of his eyes.

"Take pictures," he managed through his cracked lips.

We sat in silence for a couple minutes.

"Carter?"

"Yeah."

"Don't —" He tried to lick his lips, but he couldn't even manage that. "Don't give T.J. any money."

"I won't." I held his hand. "Mom has help for you. She has a place you can go."

He blinked one eye at me. "Yeah, she mentioned." Even under the mounds of blankets and pain medication, I could sense his body resisting.

"You have to go. It's best for you." I squeezed his hand.

"I know."

We listened to the hum of the hospital room, the whirl of the air-conditioning. Someone flushed a toilet in the next room.

I wanted to ask him where T.J. was, if we could do anything, but my brother had fallen asleep again.

✳ ✳ ✳

Outside, I texted Mik so he could give me a ride home. My parents were staying with John for now, and I would drive my car back to get them. The night had cooled, but compared to the icebox temperature of the hospital, it felt warm. My body shuddered a bit in the sudden freshness of air. It wasn't too late, maybe ten, but a spray of stars freckled the night sky. I tilted my head up, scanning it, and didn't see the man until he was standing next to me.

"Oh!" I started.

He held up his hands in apology. "Sorry, didn't mean to scare you." It was the man from the café, the one with the decaf latte who Chloe had powered in front of the other day to show me Adam's hand on Beckett's backside. This time, he was dressed in khaki pants and a green polo shirt, and wore a badge on his belt. "I'm Clint Meadows, Senior Investigator." He gave a nod toward his badge. "Sorry about your brother in there."

"Oh, right, thanks." Investigator? John must have done something pretty bad this time.

"Did Adam mention he'd given me a call?" I shook my head. Investigator Meadows nodded, his closely cut hair gray in the faint outside lights of the hospital. "Probably best. Adam shadowed with me a while back for a movie he was working on. A week or so ago, he called me about some of the stuff going on with your brother." He gazed out over the parking lot, narrowing his eyes at a couple of guys leaning against a Honda. He let his eyes slip back to me. "I looked into it. Small stuff, mostly."

My mouth went dry. "Not small to us."

"Right. No, of course. Listen, I'm heading back to Sac tonight. Got another case I need to get back to, and I already spoke to your parents, but I wanted to let you know you don't need to worry about T.J. Shay, okay? That kid's not going to bother your brother anymore." He rested a cool hand on my shoulder.

"Really?" This felt too simple, too easy, that Adam could just make a call and — *poof!* — the bad guy's gone. Of course, T.J. wasn't the real problem; he was just feeding on the real problem. And the world had plenty of T.J.s.

Investigator Meadows let his hand drop away from my shoulder. "What happened to your brother in there, well, that looks bad right now, but it was the sort of thing we needed to grab T.J. and his brother. They messed around in waters they weren't prepared to swim in, if you know what I mean. Been watching too many Mafia movies, in my opinion, and got a bit big for their britches. What a couple of idiots."

I didn't know the details, but if Investigator Meadows had bought my brother some time to figure himself out, I had no way to repay him. "Thank you."

He pulled out a phone, frowned at the screen. "You're welcome," he said, tucking it back into his pocket. "And tell Adam I said hello. Hope he doesn't have to hold a gun in this movie. That kid couldn't hold a gun to save his life." Laughing, he walked toward a silver sedan, got inside, and drove off down the curve of driveway.

twenty-one

"Wake up, Sleeping Beauty." Adam sat on the edge of my bed, holding a coffee and some sort of Danish.

I pulled the covers to my nose, peering into the dim light of my bedroom. "What time is it?" I mumbled. "What kind of Danish is that?"

"Apple. And get dressed. We're going on a little trip." He poked at me through the covers. "Get. Up."

I pulled the sheet over my head. "I work at eleven."

He pulled the sheet back off my face. "Today you're not working at all. I'm not long for Little, and I want to take you on a trip."

·I peered at him. For a guy who'd shot a movie all night, he didn't even look tired. "My brother's in the hospital."

"Okay, this is ridiculous." He stood up and whipped the covers from my bed.

I leaped up. "What if I'd been naked?"

"Then it would have been my lucky day." He held up a sundress. "Get dressed."

"Another dress?" This one was pale pink with tiny parrots in lime green and white all over it. "It has parrots on it."

He tossed it at my head. "There's a good chance you'll have your picture taken in that today."

"Will they ask me if Polly wants a cracker?" I held the dress up against me.

"Oh, and you'll need a swimsuit and a hat and something warm to change into." With that, he left the Danish and coffee on my nightstand, and went to wait outside my door.

* ✳ *

We drove to Tahoe. The trip started out in an ordinary enough way. Once we got to Tahoe City, we veered right, stopped at Tahoe House for sandwiches, more coffee, and a half dozen of their amazing raspberry pockets. A few photographers had managed to follow us up there, snapping pictures as Adam smiled at the woman at the counter. After giving a brief wave to the photographers in the parking lot, we drove the pine-lined edge of the lake past Sunnyside, blue flashes of lake breaking through the trees, and, at some point, pulled into a private lakeside home.

I'd lived near Tahoe my whole life and never once set foot in a house like this one. Mik punched in a code at the gate, and we entered a shady circular driveway. The gate closed behind us, shutting out the world. We got out of the car, and I just stared. The house was massive. Whoever designed the house had clearly decided on a theme of Mountain Extravagance. Seriously, a small forest must have given its life for all the wood constructed in front of me.

We entered through two polished wood doors into a great room with sweeping ceilings, angled wood beams, gleaming hardwood floors, and smooth granite counters. Adam had said we'd be going to his friend's "mountain cabin," but this was the biggest house I'd ever seen. Floor-to-ceiling windows showcased a stretch of green lawn, a private beach, and a wide blue yawn of Lake Tahoe. I moved toward the window to take in the view of the lake.

When I was little, I'd thought Tahoe was the ocean. Once in a while, my parents would drive us up for the day, and we'd play at the park at Commons Beach. I would stand at the edge of the blue water, looking out at the waves, the color changing in stripes of blue and green and gray. It always seemed like the lake spread out forever, the far mountains blurry.

"Some view, huh? Sweet cabin." Adam came to stand beside me at the window. He turned, dropping his bag onto the suede couch in the center of the great room.

"And by cabin, you mean castle?" I couldn't pull my eyes from the view. At the end of a gray dock, a sleek speedboat bobbed lazily.

Adam followed my gaze. "Want to go for a ride?"

* ✳ *

We cut the engine far out in the lake's blue center, the air swirling around us. The sudden silence crushed against my ears but was soon replaced with the waves lapping the sides of the boat. We'd left Mik on the dock, sprawled in a lawn chair, another romantic spy novel half-finished in his big hands. Watching him stuffed into his chair, his face serene, he became one more piece of all of this I would miss.

Adam turned from the wheel. He had flipped his hat backward, and he seemed younger somehow, like a small boy playing with his father's tools. He must have noticed me watching him. "What?"

"Do you ever feel guilty about all you have?" I motioned to the boat, but also back in the general direction of the house, a gesture meant to imply — *all of it*. I kicked my legs onto the white cushioned cover of the engine, the boat's rocking making me sleepy. Everything that had happened with my brother last night felt so far away, like the patchy memory of a dream. In a few weeks, that might be what Adam felt like, too.

Adam pulled off his shirt, tossing it onto the seat next to him. "Sure, sometimes."

I tilted my head, tugging the brim of my hat lower, struck by the way his skin gleamed in the sun. It was like he had no freckles or imperfections or anything, just miles of bronzed skin. It wasn't fair. Turning my eyes to the water, I said, "I would feel guilty."

"Do you feel guilty now?"

"A little." I thought about all the magazines devoted to documenting this life Adam led. Celebrity. Wealth. The amount of energy people spent tracking it, wanting it, wishing for it. Mostly, it was harmless. A distraction. For most people, celebrity was a sort of pageant, and peeking in on that world gave them a visible fantasy, a grown-up version of dressing up like a princess or a superhero. Celebrities were like exotic zoo animals, and most of us just watched them through the glass, munching on popcorn.

But for people like my brother, people with darker, addictive natures, that visible fantasy tipped too far into jealousy, into restlessness, into trying to make something bigger out of something small. He'd started gambling to win something, to be larger than us in some way. And it ate him up.

"Thanks for what you did for John," I told him. At his look of surprise, I told him about Investigator Meadows coming to see me last night at the hospital. "He's hoping you don't have to hold a gun in this movie."

Adam laughed. "Hey, I got pretty good."

"I'm sure." The shadow of a bird passed over the water. "But, seriously, thanks."

"Celebrity has its privileges."

"Obviously."

We were quiet for a minute. "To answer your question, I prefer to feel lucky," Adam said finally over the sound of the waves. He unwrapped a sandwich, chewed it thoughtfully, his sunglasses full of reflected light and water. "I'll admit it's not fair. That I have this life and other people don't. Absolutely, it's not fair. But we can only live the life we've got." He shrugged. "If I spend too much time worrying that it's better than someone else's or not as good as someone else's, well, what a miserable way to spend my allotted time on this planet. I don't want to live like that." He took another bite of sandwich, staring out over the water.

I followed his lead, unwrapping my own sandwich. "Who could possibly have a better life than you do?"

"George Clooney."

I laughed. Wasn't that a funny thing? Even Adam thought someone had it better.

"But he's old."

Adam smiled at me, plucking a raspberry pocket out of the white bag. "Good point. You're right. No one has a better life than I do." But even as he said it, I saw the dark flicker I'd seen that night stargazing when I'd teased him about his arrest, when the light from a passing car had let me see the mask come off, even for a moment.

We'd come to Tahoe partly because Adam's friend was throwing a party. I had yet to meet the friend, didn't even know if he was actually on site, but it wouldn't be a small party. I could tell by the setup. Adam told me it would be a press-free party, though, so I didn't need to worry about reporters. Still, he warned me, even specially invited guests and catering staff couldn't help but tweet things, post things on Facebook, take pictures, so I should consider it a public event. My stomach bubbled with nerves. So far, I hadn't had to play too much in his world. I had a sense that was about to shift. The house glowed with lights, the energy building as a catering company set up café tables and brought in mounds of food from white vans parked in the circular driveway. A bartender spread out glittering glassware and bottles.

Around seven thirty, people started buzzing at the gate. Within a half hour, dozens of people milled through the house, stood out on the deck or the lawn, holding cool drinks, chatting with one another. Everyone seemed twenty-one, not a day older or younger. Like life-sized models for the Forever 21 stores. Most of the girls wore sundresses similar to what I had on, their hair in various summery updos, and the guys wore collared shirts and Bermuda shorts, but they all seemed partly gilded, diamond studs glittering in earlobes, expensive watches on tanned wrists. They seemed straight from the pages of *The Great Gatsby*, walking Instagram photos, bronzed people, who played tennis and golf, darted down ski slopes in the winter — all slightly bored, but still, each stealing glances at Adam over the glimmering rims of their cocktails.

I hedged closer to the guy passing out the crab cakes.

Later, as I stood with Adam, who was sampling the shrimp tower, an electric sizzle moved through the room, and I could tell someone important had just arrived. I craned my neck, making out a glossy, dark ponytail. The ponytailed girl turned toward us, her smile flashing, and I heard Adam mutter, "Oh, man, what is she doing here?"

Ashayla Wimm, her beauty like a tidal wave.

Adam vanished from my side. I scanned the room, trying to see where he'd gone, but there was no sign of him.

Everyone watched Ashayla, this sudden, consuming center of light. Everything else, everyone else became reflections, extras. She worked the room, nodding to people, stopping to chat, her body seemingly made of liquid.

Then Adam reappeared, like a seal diving then emerging again in a separate space of ocean. Across the room, his back purposefully to Ashayla, he spoke animatedly to a couple dressed in almost identical striped polos. I drifted closer. He was telling them a story from the set, something about Hunter flipping out over the protesters returning, his gestures wide, his voice silvered, the story captivating everyone near him, drawing them to him like moths. They laughed exactly where he wanted them to laugh, eyes widening at all the right places. As he acted out the protester's retreat, their laughter buoying him, it was clear how much he needed them to be watching *him* and not Ashayla.

As his story came to a close, Adam grabbed a cocktail from a passing tray. He swallowed it in two gulps before the waiter had even moved on. I wasn't an expert, but I was pretty sure someone right out of rehab wasn't supposed to be sucking down martinis.

I set my half-eaten shrimp on the edge of the table. Watching him, I couldn't believe I'd ever, even for a moment, worried about something as small as that picture with Beckett Ray, couldn't believe I thought Adam and I had begun building a sort of something that could exist as part of the same world, the same sky. I thought of the article Chloe had brought to the café the other day: "The Star and the Moon." The first headline I'd seen that hadn't made some sort of reference to Little. It was Robin Hamilton's story, which had been, despite Adam's warning, funny and sweet. Chloe had tacked it to the message board in the back, circling it with her green Sharpie. "'The Star and the Moon' — so stinkin' cute!" Cute, but a complete fantasy, conjured up because my last name just happened to fit so perfectly in the title. *The Star and the Moon.* Cute words with no meaning. Everyone saw the moon, that unofficial ringleader of the sky. And it was pretty clear, especially tonight, that in the orbit of this particular star, no one could see me at all.

My world couldn't be farther away from his if I lived on Neptune. Too bad my last name wasn't Space Particle No One Notices. That would have been much closer to the truth.

I slipped out the side door of the kitchen, the cool air of the darkening Tahoe evening hitting my face, and followed the side stairs down to the lawn. Someone had lit lanterns, and they had just started to dot the velvety grass like stars, glimmering in the approaching twilight. I made my way down to the lake, my bare feet moving gingerly over the pebbles of the beach.

A lone figure stood at the dock.

Parker.

He smoked a cigarette, one hand holding the neck of a Corona, and gazed out over where the moon was just beginning to rise beyond the distant mountains.

He turned when he heard my creaky steps on the dock, flicked his cigarette guiltily into the lake.

"You know, some fish is going to die now because of that," I said, only half joking.

"I'll add that to my list of moral offenses."

I motioned toward the house. "You don't like the party?" The air chilled my arms, rippling them with gooseflesh. I should have brought my sweater out here.

He took a swallow of beer. "It's Adam's thing. I'm getting a bit old for all of that. I'm like a grandfather in there." He wore a simple pale linen jacket over his T-shirt and jeans, and suddenly, he slipped it off and wrapped it around my shoulders, all the while navigating the half-empty beer bottle.

I huddled into its softness, its smell something like cut grass, green, but with the lingering cling of cigarettes. "Thanks, Gramps."

A smile twitched his mouth. "You all right, love?"

I sighed, studying the water glowing in the evening light. The lake shimmered with ripples of indigo that matched the sky. Everything was darkening, shifting with twilight's rosy glaze. If I owned this house, I'd never leave. I'd sit here every day and watch the different shades of light tinge the lake all its kaleidoscopic colors. Adam's friend, the guy who owned this, probably spent a couple of weeks a year here, tops. I frowned at the thought, and Parker mistook it for annoyance.

"Don't pay too much attention to Adam in these sorts of environments. He's got his own role to play." He drained his beer, seemed like he might toss the bottle, glanced at me, and set it on the dock.

"Obviously, I don't know him at all." Sending those words into the cool of the night air freed something in me, and I felt myself smiling. Of course I didn't know Adam Jakes. He was a *movie star*. Our time together was nothing.

I was such an idiot.

Parker rocked back and forth on his heels and toes, following the natural movement of the dock. He gave me a smile almost apologetic in its edges. "Don't take it personally. Adam is whoever he needs to be for the room he's in. He's an actor. He wears a lot of masks."

"That's hard for me, I guess." I pushed some wind-tossed hair from my eyes. "I'm kind of what-you-see-is-what-you-get."

Parker grinned. "Yes, yes, you are."

It felt like a compliment. I pointed up toward the house. "You know, Ashayla Wimm's here."

Parker's smile vanished. "Here now?"

"Yeah."

Swearing, he lit another cigarette, keeping the flame of his lighter protected from the wind off the lake. "That's just what I need. Ashayla and her free publicity advice talking Adam into another stunt like the one he pulled in January."

I shivered, only this time it wasn't because of the wind. "Stunt?"

Parker caught his mistake too late. "Oh bugger. That . . . that's not . . . I shouldn't have said that." He blew smoke into the wind.

His words rolled through me like thunder, low, distant, but changing the air. "The car, the drugs, that redhead — that was a stunt? His rehab, too?" I swallowed hard. "None of that was true?"

"True?" Parker rolled the word around his mouth like a too-large wad of gum. Then his face softened, and he gave me a faint smile.

"You're such a sweet kid — sorry if that sounds condescending, love." He tapped ash over the lake. "But the truth is kind of relative."

"Is it?" Why wasn't I surprised? It was like what Alien Drake said about the way we controlled the image we projected to the world. Adam had an image he needed to control. The last year was clearly part of a manufactured plan, some sort of crafting of a bad boy who would later repent. Like Scrooge, like Scott. Even the movie was part of it. *None of this can be accidental*, he'd said that day in the garden.

I was part of that dumb public they jerked around like puppets. Feeling sick, I asked, "Did he actually go to rehab? Just tell me that. I mean, isn't that why the movie got pushed back?" All that talk about rehab, about his need for a break, how much he related it to what I was going through with my dancing, with my brother. Was that just for show?

Parker rubbed a hand through his hair. "It's not what you think; it's not completely fabricated. He was a right mess. Utterly exhausted."

"So he thought it would be better for people to see him as a drug-riddled bad boy than as *tired*?" The dock gave a bigger rock beneath our feet, and we both leaned to steady ourselves. His beer bottle tipped, rolled into the lake. Sorry, fish.

Parker seemed to shrink beside me, and it struck me that he didn't have as much control as he pretended that he did. He crafted his own sort of reality out of the fantastical world of Adam Jakes. He tried to explain. "When he crashed that car, well, people just assumed things. And we let them. And we added on. That was Ashayla's brilliant suggestion." When he saw the disappointment

274

ripple across my face, he sighed. "Hey, I work for the guy. I'm in the Adam Jakes business. He's a brand, Carter. He needed some time off, to clear his head, and it was the only thing that wouldn't get him sued by the studio for screwing up the shooting schedule."

"Rehab?"

"Yeah. Have to protect the brand."

"Wow." I thought about all those people who had delayed their schedules, the hassle of turning summer into Christmas, all so Adam could craft some sort of comeback story. My head throbbed.

"Come on, don't look at me like that." Parker stubbed his cigarette out on his loafer. "He's a good kid, Carter, but he's a kid. A kid with too many people worshipping him and too much money, and he didn't even know if he wanted to do this anymore. It's a total cliché, but it's just the way it is." I noticed, this time, he didn't flick the butt into the lake.

"You're such liars," I whispered, looking up toward the house. "I'm going to find Adam." A chill moved through me, separate from the wind off the lake. "I can't do this anymore, either."

Parker shook his head. "Not now, Carter. Talk to him later."

"I want to talk to him now." The periwinkle light of the lake, the sky, the pale stars emerging, became elastic, like the world was a deck of cards reshuffling. I moved toward the small ramp leading off the dock and onto the beach.

"Wait!" Parker called after me. "Let's talk about next steps, how to best play this. You're just reacting right now."

"No," I said, shaking my head. "I'm done. I'm out."

* ✳ *

I found Adam leaning against a window frame, laughing at something a red-haired guy was saying, the party reflected in the glass behind them. Ashayla Wimm was nowhere in sight.

"Hey, stranger, where you been?" He flashed me an easy smile, lazy, pliable.

It was like I was finally seeing him for real, like someone had scrubbed off his flashy shine and left him dull. "I'm leaving," I told him. "Could we please find someone to take me home?" The party droned around me, churning. Dizzy, I put a hand on a nearby chair to steady myself.

His smile faltered. "Hey, don't leave. Are you okay?" He squinted at me through bleary eyes. "You don't look okay."

The crowd around us stilled a bit; I could feel them lean in, listening, waiting. I wasn't interested in giving them a show. I'd had enough shows to last me a lifetime. "I'll be outside waiting for a car." I hurried through the room, the music pressing in on me, the crush of people parting against me like waves.

Adam followed me outside onto the wide front porch. No one was out there. Why would they be, when Adam Jakes, movie star, was inside where they could pretend to be a part of his spectacular world?

He grabbed my arm. "Wait, what just happened?"

I whirled on him, yanking my arm away. "Do you ever just get sick of lying to people?"

"What?"

"I know about you, okay? I know you didn't go to rehab, that you didn't do any of those horrible things. You're not some bad boy on the path of recovery — you're just a liar who uses people."

Genuine fear seized his features, seemed to sober him up. "Wait, what? Who told you that? Did Ashayla say something to you?"

"Not that you'd notice, but I wasn't exactly hanging out with Ashayla Wimm."

"Then who?"

"It doesn't matter. Is it true?"

His expression, even shadowed, answered for him. He reached out for me again, but I moved away down the short steps and onto the curve of the circular driveway. It was warmer out here than by the lake, but I still shivered in my shirt, my bare feet cool on the cement. I'd left my shoes somewhere back at the party. "I'd like Mik to take me home. I already told Parker, but I'll tell you, too. I'm done, Adam. I'll do whatever press release or whatever, but I'm out. We're finished with whatever this is we've been doing."

He took a couple of steps toward me. "Give me a chance to explain."

I couldn't look at him. "I just want to go home."

"Please don't go," he pleaded, sounding young and scared. "You have to understand, I'm just playing the part the world wants me to play. All of this, it's just what people expect. It's part of the game."

I stared out at the gates to this incredible house, the gates that kept everyone out, granting only a select few, a *lucky* few, the chance at whatever it was the world inside promised them. And here I was, inside them, and all I wanted was to leave. I forced myself to look at him, the movie star, standing in a dark driveway, asking me to stay.

It wasn't enough. I took a step closer and said quietly, "I have a brother who is ruining his life because of his addiction. And it's just

277

a plot point for you, a game, as you say, some sort of show so you can eventually look a certain way to a bunch of strangers. Why do you think you don't have to play by the same rules as everyone else?"

He ran a hand through that great hair of his and somehow it managed to look even better than it had before. He thought about it for a second, then shrugged. "Because I don't."

He was right. He didn't. When the world was in constant orbit around you, you got to make all the rules. "Must be nice."

His eyes, tired and sad, caught the light of the nearby porch lamp. "It's my job, Carter. I need things to *look* a certain way. I don't have a choice."

I shook my head. "I don't care who you are, you always have a choice. And you don't need it. You *love* it. You crave all the attention, and you go after it even if it means creating huge lies. I mean, come on, Adam, is there anything in your life that's actually real?"

His eyes were like individual moons as he took a step toward me. "How I feel about you is real. I know I feel real when I'm with you."

His words seemed genuine and I wanted to believe him, but I pulled from somewhere deep that let me fight them, that fought wanting to wrap myself in the warm curve of his arms. This guy sold lies to millions of people. What stopped him from lying to one girl in the shadowed curve of a driveway? Especially if it meant protecting his image. "If this were one of your movies, that might work. I guess it might be enough. It might even be true. But this is my life, not some final scene, and the thing is — I don't believe you."

Deflated, Adam looked up at the night sky, the stars dull tonight and shrouded in cloud cover. Finally, he said, "I'll have Mik take you home."

twenty-two

It was late when Mik dropped me off in front of my house after our silent ride home from Tahoe. As he drove away, I could see the shadow figures of Chloe and Alien Drake sitting on the roof of Drake's house. My stomach seized, realizing I was supposed to be there with them tonight. I hadn't even texted them to tell them I was in Tahoe.

Climbing the ladder, I called up to them. "You have room for one more up there?"

Chloe's head appeared over the side. "We're mad at you."

I stopped my ascent. "I know, I'm sorry."

She offered me her hand, her face softening as she helped me up onto the roof. "You look terrible. Cute dress, though. Nice parrots."

"You can have it."

Her eyes widened. "Seriously? Thanks!"

Alien Drake frowned at me from where he sat, eating peanuts. "Chlo's right. What happened to you? Why does your face look so blotchy?"

I had cried most of the way home, Mik stealthily handing me tissues, as I stared out into the dark at the passing trees. "Adam and I just broke up."

"You broke up?" Chloe's face paled in the moonlight. "How is that possible?! You're in *People* this week! Look at you two! You're adorable." She held up a magazine, a shot of Adam and me sitting outside Little Eats eating a grilled cheese sandwich on its cover. The caption read:

CITY MOUSE,
COUNTRY MOUSE
Adam Jakes dines
with small-town love.

Seeing Chloe's face, my body flooded with guilt. What a hypocrite I was. An hour ago, I'd stood there outside the Tahoe house and called Adam a liar when, throughout all of this, I'd constructed my own spectacular prism of lies.

Alien Drake stood and moved to take down the telescope. "I think it's for the best."

Chloe sat down, tossing the magazine onto the quilt beside her. "Of course you do."

"You did the right thing, Carter," he assured me.

Chloe groaned. "You're just saying that because you're sick of her picking him over us. But it's Adam Jakes. And he picked Carter. He picked *her*."

I couldn't do it anymore. Collapsing onto the quilt, the sky heavy with stars above me, I knew I couldn't lie to them anymore. "He didn't pick me at all; his manager did."

Chloe's head tilted in confusion. "What do you mean?"

I pulled my legs into my chest. "It wasn't real. None of it was real."

Alien Drake zipped a pocket closed on the telescope bag, then took a seat next to me. "Wait, what are you talking about?"

They listened intently while I told them, Chloe holding my hand, Alien Drake asking questions. I told them everything, sending my story out into the night, the crickets and stars providing a sort of force field around us. I was scared of how angry they'd be. That maybe they'd never speak to me again. My heart broke all over again seeing their faces darken as I talked. But then their looks softened as they heard me out. "The dumb thing," I said, not crying anymore, feeling numb, the moment dreamlike, "is that I really started to think we could have something real. How stupid is that?"

I waited for them to yell at me, to tell me that I was a horrible person, that I'd betrayed them, knowing I deserved whatever they tossed my way.

Instead, Chloe squeezed my hand, her eyes glossy. "The whole thing sounds awful, Carter. I can't believe you tried to do this without us."

Her understanding washed over me. "I'm so sorry. But I promised them I wouldn't tell anyone."

"And you were trying to help John, as always," Alien Drake said softly.

Chloe's eyes lit up. "Maybe Adam feels as bad as you do. Maybe you should try talking to him."

Alien Drake rolled his eyes. "Geez, Chloe, did you not just hear what she said? The guy's a total fraud."

Chloe's face crumbled. "I can't believe this whole thing wasn't real. I mean, Adam Jakes picking you, it just made it seem like, well, he could have picked any of us."

Alien Drake let out a snort. "Hello! I'm actually sitting right here."

She shook her head, biting her lip. "That's not what I meant. I didn't mean me. I didn't mean he could have picked me specifically." She looked across me, catching Alien Drake's eye. "And I wouldn't want him to, I swear. It's just that for these few weeks, our world hasn't seemed quite so . . . so *little*." We laughed at her choice of words. We'd grown up here, laughing at but also loving our Little-ness. Still, Chloe was right; it was sometimes very small, and Adam Jakes had brought something bigger here for a few weeks, had widened our skies.

I glanced between them, each of them at my side like they always were. "I'm not going to ask you guys not to tell anyone. I don't feel right about that. Only I kind of hope you won't."

Chloe slapped my bare arm.

"Ouch!" I rubbed at it.

"We would never tell if you didn't want us to," she said, her eyes wide. "We're your friends."

"Thank you, guys." Leaning into them under the stars, I knew I would rather have a few people love me for who I really was than millions of people adore me for who they *thought* I was.

Just one of the many ways I was different from Adam Jakes, one of the many reasons why he and I were never meant to be.

✳ ✳ ✳

Early the next afternoon, I met with Parker one last time in the garden of The Hotel on Main. Minutes before, we'd stood on the porch, issuing a statement to the press, my sunglasses dark saucers over my face. I ended things, we explained, because I just couldn't find my place in Adam's world. It wasn't Adam, I told them. He'd tried. I just couldn't find the midpoint in our worlds. There'd been flashes and questions and then, after a few minutes, Parker had led me inside, past Bonnie's sympathetic face, into the garden in back.

Now, Parker handed me a check. The rest of the money. When I didn't reach for it, he said, "You earned it."

So I took it from him and tore it up.

Surprised, he took the torn pieces. "What about your brother?"

"He leaves tomorrow for his program. We'll figure it out as a family." John could finish recovering from his injuries at the in-patient program down in the Bay Area where Mom would drive him. We had no idea how to pay for it, but I couldn't take any more of Adam's money. Somehow, the money felt like the biggest lie of all. And Adam had already made that donation to Sandwich Saturdays. He'd called Investigator Meadows for help.

"We're even," I told Parker.

With sad eyes, Parker shook his head, pocketing the ripped pieces of check. "Someone else would like a chance to say good-bye, if you have a moment." He motioned to where Adam emerged from the shadow of a tree in the lower part of the garden. "Go easy on him," he said, leaving us alone in the cool green of the yard.

I walked down the sloping lawn to meet him. "Hi."

He had his sunglasses pushed into his hair and his hands in the pockets of his shorts. "Hi." He cleared his throat quietly. "So, you're pretty mad at me."

I shrugged, studying the fountain resting near the base of the tree. It had a frog spitting water into a pool. "Not really, not anymore." Because I wasn't. This was something else, a sort of hurt that burrowed deep and nested there.

He searched my face. "I'm sorry, though. I wish you could understand."

I put my hand on his arm, his nearness still affecting me, still sending those currents moving through me. "I want to, honestly. It's just . . ." I searched the leafy trees around us, as if their shade held answers. "I just don't think I can. I'm sorry."

Before he could say anything else, before I could change my mind, I walked away.

* ✳ *

At home, I found my parents reading a note from John at the kitchen table. Mom held it out for me to read, and I dropped into the chair across from them, tears welling.

DAD, MOM, & C —

I CAN'T GO TO THAT TREATMENT CENTER. I'VE BEEN THERE BEFORE AND IT FEELS LIKE JAIL. I KNOW YOU MEAN WELL TRYING TO SEND ME THERE, BUT I JUST CAN'T. SO I'M LEAVING. I NEED TO FIGURE THIS THING OUT FOR MYSELF — WITHOUT YOUR HELP. PLEASE DON'T TRY TO FIND ME.

— J

"I'm sorry," I whispered, as much to myself as to them. It was my turn to feel like a black hole, too much density in too small a space, too much debris sucked inside me with no chance of escape.

Mom reached across the table for my hand as Dad stood and

put his arms around me. The afternoon light played on the kitchen wall, shifting as the tree outside moved in the wind. The refrigerator clicked and hummed.

Dad sighed into my hair. "Me too."

*　✳　*

The Ghost of Christmas Future scene would be filmed back in L.A., so the last scene Adam Jakes would shoot in Little, in a narrow Victorian near downtown, was the famous Tiny Tim "God bless us, every one!" moment. In this retelling, Scott would visit a weak Cheryl at her home, and she would wake just in time to say, "God bless us, Scott, every one!" in front of a roaring fire and sparkling Christmas tree.

Late that night, while my parents talked quietly downstairs about John's flight, I slipped out of the house, the moon a slim wedge in the sky. I started in the direction of Alien Drake's, but I paused on the sidewalk, realizing that the one person I really wanted to see, the person I felt pulled to like a magnet, was shooting his last scene in Little in a house two streets away. I turned and headed down the hill.

When I got to the house, I knocked lightly and one of the crew guys opened the back door for me. A slender hallway spilled into a living room where I found Adam sitting on a red velvet sofa, studying a script as the crew hurried around him, the room a cozy Christmas scene.

When Adam saw me, he stood in surprise. "Carter?"

Seeing his face light, I crumbled, and he whisked me into a room they weren't using, the kitchen. Moonlight streamed through the wide window over the sink, glazing everything silver. Adam looked worried. "What happened?"

I showed him John's note.

"Oh no," he mumbled as he read. "I'm sorry."

"He's not going." I brushed at the tears on my cheeks, feeling ridiculous for being here.

Adam put a hand on my shoulder. "Where do you think he went?" He handed the note back.

"No idea." I slipped it into my bag. "We don't know where he is."

"Is there anything I can do?" he asked, his eyes concerned.

I shook my head. "There really isn't." I let out an awkward laugh. "Sorry, I know I shouldn't be here. It's just, it's so stupid of me."

Adam frowned. "What is?"

"I thought he'd get help, you know? I thought he'd get better." I took a deep breath. "I thought he'd finally figure it out."

"Relapse is part of recovery." Adam held up his hands against my sharp look. "I might not have been in real rehab, but I've spent plenty of time in therapy."

I leaned against the silvered counter. "I was just hoping he'd have his Scrooge moment, you know? Like Scott, like you do in the movie. Realize he'd been wrong, that he could change, and then fix it."

"He's an addict. It's not that easy."

"So was Scrooge. Addicted to selfishness, addicted to money." I motioned toward the other room, where the sounds of the scene echoed, spilled Christmas into the night kitchen. "But he fixes it.

He realizes he's wrong in two quick hours." I sighed. "Do you ever get tired of telling lies to people with all these Hollywood endings?"

Adam's expression softened. "Not lies. Possibilities. Isn't that what you and Alien Drake are always talking about with your stargazing? We have to keep telling these stories, just like we have to keep looking up at the stars at night, because we're human. We need steady reminders. We need to hope."

My heart tugged. Why couldn't he just be a boy who went to Little High, who took me to the movies instead of starring in them? Why did our lives have to be so different?

But he was right. We needed our ghosts to remind us.

"I think I'm going to start dancing again," I told him. "With Nicky. At Stagelights. I'm going to go see him tomorrow."

"That's great!"

"Nothing big," I hurried to explain. "Just for fun. And I'm going to look into some dance therapy programs. You know, for after graduation. For college."

He leaned forward, the moonlight catching his hair, bleaching his tan face, making him his own sort of ghost. "I'm going to take some credit for this epiphany."

I hoped my face showed how true that was. "You should."

"I can hear the sounds of roots ripping up as we speak," he teased.

"Mr. Jakes?" Tiny Tom stood in the doorway. "They're ready for you."

"I'm glad you came," he said, squeezing my hand. "I wish I could talk longer, but —"

"Go," I said, waving him on. "I totally barged in on you. Thanks for listening."

His body already morphing into Scott, he vanished into the next room.

Not wanting to go just yet, I followed Adam and found a chair near the back, watching everyone build the rest of the Christmas fantasy. In the scene, Cheryl was home from the hospital, recovering on the couch under a mound of quilts, snow falling gently outside her dark window. Scott had already been visited by the Ghost of Christmas Future, and had brought Cheryl a music box, one that had been broken and he'd repaired for her as a symbol of his new commitment to living a whole, good life. Blinking back tears, Cheryl held the music box aloft and blessed us, every one, the lights of the fake Christmas tree twinkling behind her, reflecting in the frosted windows.

I couldn't wait to see it when all the movie magic had been added, the music, the glowing lighting. But even watching from where I could see the cameras, see Hunter's back hunched as he directed the scene, see the crew moving silently about, I knew it would be a beautiful scene.

There was a reason this particular story kept being retold. We all had our own ghosts who visited us. We all had these reminders, these spirits sent to warn us, guide us, awaken us to things in our lives. Each of us had people who reminded us of our past or pointed out our present, who illuminated our future path in some way. I had them in Chloe and Alien Drake, in my parents, even in my brother.

And in Adam.

They guided us like night stars, nudging us, reminding us that so much was possible.

At one point during a lull in the shooting, Adam caught my eye, and he gave me a sad sort of smile.

After the shoot, he came to sit next to me in the back of the room. As we watched the dismantling of the tree, I realized I'd have to wait another five months before we built Christmas around us again, its spirit dormant in the hot days of summer.

"Parker said the announcement went well," he said, his eyes downcast, picking at some loose strings on the chair's seat. "I look like a prince — hooray," he added weakly.

"Yes, you're officially single and heartbroken. The world will love you again." I tried to keep my voice light, but it caught. Hearing it, he glanced up, his eyes searching my face. It sent a coil of sadness through me. It might have been fake, what we had, but I'd miss him for real. "Sorry, Adam."

"For what?"

"For not understanding why you needed to do all those things with the tabloids." I kept my voice low, knowing anyone could overhear us and, suddenly, the whole world would know. "I'm not saying that I agree; I'm just, you know, sorry."

He studied the photos lining the walls — another family, another set of stories playing themselves out in the world. "We're from really different worlds, aren't we?" His face darkened.

"That's an understatement." We were like two planets whose orbits should never cross.

"Still," he said, his gaze slipping to me. "I'm really glad I met you."

"Me too," I whispered over the thickness in my throat.

"Mr. Jakes?" Tiny Tom stood again before us. Behind him, the room had been completely cleared. Nothing left of Christmas. Just a house, dark in the middle of a July night. "We're done here."

In the small bubble of silence to follow, knowing an exit when it opened, Adam stood. "We should go."

I pulled a picture frame from my bag, the dark blue one scattered with stars that Chloe had given me in my survival kit. "This is sort of dumb, I guess, but I brought you this." I handed it to him. It held a quote I'd written onto a blank piece of cardstock. "It's from *A Christmas Carol*, the original novella."

I will honour Christmas in my heart, and try to keep it all the year. I will live in the Past, the Present, and the Future. The Spirits of all Three shall strive within me. I will not shut out the lessons that they teach.

He took it, his face unreadable. "Thanks."

I told him how glad I was they'd filmed the movie here, how much I loved how Dickens's little book had been so lasting, had been retold so many times. What I didn't tell him was how much he mattered to me. I knew my few weeks with Adam wouldn't really factor into the grand scheme of the world, but they had made a huge difference to me.

I didn't tell him because I was pretty sure he already knew.

"Keep watching the sky, okay?" He leaned to kiss my cheek, his lips the quick flick of butterfly wings.

"I will."

yesterday's sightings

Things Are Looking Up in Little, CA

Morning, sky watchers. In 1961, John Kennedy said that we should explore space because it "may hold the key to our future on Earth." It's been two weeks since Hollywood left Little, and since they left, we've been talking a lot about why we watch movies. Why are they and the lives of their stars so important to us? We think it's much the same reason as Kennedy suggested. They might hold the key to something in our own future, in our own lives. Whether we search for answers in space or in the books we read, in the music we listen to, or through the movies we watch, the essential thing is that we keep exploring, that we keep pushing ourselves to find our possible lives.

What possibilities will you seek out today?

See you tonight, under the sky.

twenty-three

a few weeks later, there was no trace of Hollywood in Little, CA. No more humming generators, no more blocked-off streets, no more crews scurrying around with snow-hoses and annoying the locals who found stray bits of fake snow on their cars. As much as I felt the hollow of Adam's absence, peace had returned to our small town, even if it left Chloe sort of sulky.

"Did you guys even try to talk?" she was asking as she stacked cups above the espresso machine. "I mean, I know he screwed up, but maybe you guys could have given it a real chance. You really liked him, Carter. Like, *really* liked."

"And how exactly," I asked her, "would we do that? It's not like my mom and dad would let their high school daughter fly off to Australia with a movie star." I wiped the counter with a rag.

"Maybe they would have let you," Chloe insisted. "They did tell you to keep your options open, to look for something for your life outside of Little. Well, Australia is outside of Little."

Over the past couple of weeks, I'd been sharing my ideas about post–high school plans with Chloe and she'd been sharing hers with me. No surprise, she was looking almost exclusively at communications majors in Southern California, Hollywood drawing her like a moth to its neon light.

"I'm pretty sure becoming part of Adam Jakes's entourage was not what they had in mind. It's not going on the list."

To my surprise, with Alien Drake's and Chloe's help, the list was getting longer and longer. There were plenty of schools near and far with programs in dance therapy as well as social work. I even found a few gap-year programs that would let me take some of the work I'd done with Sandwich Saturdays and expand it to a bigger level.

My eyes caught on something through the window. Cars piled up in a line, snaking up the street. A stalled SUV blocked the way, angled so cars couldn't pass. "Hold on, Chlo — we might need to call a tow truck," I said as I pushed through the door and out onto the patio.

The SUV wasn't stalled.

Adam Jakes lounged against the Range Rover, which he had parked crookedly in the middle of the street. Drivers leaned out of their cars, trying to determine the cause of the holdup.

All air escaped me. So much for Hollywood not blocking any more of our streets.

"What are you doing here?" I asked him over the fence separating our café from the sidewalk. The café diners paused. The man playing jazz guitar in our patio stopped. Silence leaked in around me. "Aren't you supposed to be in Australia?"

The patio door banged open behind me. "Carter, what —" I heard Chloe gasp. "Oh, WOW!"

Adam waved a sheet of paper in the air. "We have some unfinished business."

My face reddened. I waved a sort of apology at Mr. Murdoch, who was fuming in the car behind Adam. "What are you talking about?"

"Well, we were talking about how stories need to be retold, right? What about love being a risk worth taking even when it makes no sense? I'd like to discuss *that* story more." Two women diners in the patio gave out a simultaneous "Woo-hoo!" Adam grinned in their direction, then let his gaze fall back on me. "Take a risk, Carter. It's an old story for a reason. I know you're considering all your possibilities right now, and I'd just like to throw my hat in the ring."

Feeling all sorts of light-headed, I tried to fasten my mind to exactly what Adam was saying as Mr. Murdoch was attempting to push around him. Finally, an old-timer in a beat-up Chevy made a seven-point turn and sped back up the hill, giving Adam a not-so-friendly finger. I tried to hide my smile. "You need to get out of the street. People have jobs. You know, *real* jobs? They need to get to work." I nervously twisted the rag I was holding.

He held up the paper again. "I repeat: We have a tour to finish."

I realized with a start that it was my handmade Little Star Map. I couldn't believe he'd kept it.

Mr. Murdoch leaned on his horn. "Hey, Carter, can you get this jerk to move his vehicle?"

"I'm trying," I called to him, my heart thumping. To Adam, I said, "You have to move your vehicle, jerk."

He didn't waver. "You're kind of raining on my grand romantic gesture."

I grinned. "Grand? You don't even have a sound track."

He knew he had me. "I was going to have your dad's band play, but I thought that might be a bit over the top. I know you like your privacy."

"Yes, and this is so subtle."

He took a step forward and pushed his sunglasses into his hair. "I think people from two worlds sometimes just have to meet in the middle." He gestured to the car. "You coming?"

Mr. Murdoch made the turn like the Chevy had and sped away, but most were clearly enjoying the show, had gotten out of their cars to watch.

I chewed my lip, not answering, my body electrical, buzzing.

Adam didn't take his eyes off me. "You need to come kiss me, and then we need to finish our Star Tour. That's how this works."

"Carter, go to him!" Chloe hissed behind me. "You're ruining this."

I looked at her. Alien Drake stood next to her in the doorway. "Well, go on; don't drag it out. Some of us have things to do." He grinned.

Adam tossed the map into the rolled-down window of the Range Rover, then came to the fence. "People like a Hollywood ending, Carter."

"Not all people."

"But you do."

He was right. I did. I loved a Hollywood ending. Loved the montage where they figured everything out to the swell of music, the scenes from the beach or skyscraper where everything worked out the way it should. Simple, lovely — hopeful.

The way I wished the whole world could be.

If this moment were a movie, this would be the part where he kissed me, where the music would rise over the press of our lips, where the shot would pan away into the yellow light of afternoon, the credits starting to roll.

But this wasn't a movie. In life, we didn't get to have credits roll to tell us when we'd come to the end of our epiphany arc. To know when to applaud. In life, there were no credits, no sound tracks. In life, things often didn't work out. My brother might never get better. I might make the list for my parents but not choose the right answer. Because there were no right answers.

That was the great thing about growing up. We got to write our own endings, thousands of them, over and over. That *was* life. It was a million little endings. But it was also a million little beginnings. Even when other people thought we were writing them wrong. I didn't know if Adam and I could make our separate worlds work in the future, but for today — we had a tour to finish.

Not everyone liked a Hollywood ending.

But I did. As long as it was *my* Hollywood ending.

Adam tilted his perfect movie-star head and gave me his signature brand of puppy-dog eyes. "Come on. What can I say, Carter Moon? I missed you."

I melted. "Where's Mik?" I tossed the rag I'd been holding onto a nearby table.

"I gave Mik the day off."

"Isn't that a security problem?"

"I'll risk it." He held out his arms, and I walked through our gate and into them.

Adam pulled me to him, and his scent of spice and clean soap engulfed me. I inhaled as he bent down to me. When he kissed me, his lips covered mine, warm and real, my body, my heart, everything — fireworks. And I knew this kiss was real. That it was meant for me. Not Small-Town Girl. Not Tabloid Girlfriend. Me.

No, this moment wasn't a movie.

It was better.

Because this moment was mine.

So I leaned into him and kissed him back.

acknowledgments

In life, we have our little galaxies sparkling with the stars who love and support us. And I couldn't have written *Catch a Falling Star* without my shining stars. . . .

First, a huge thank you to my agent, Melissa Sarver, who, when I said, I want to write about a small town, and our cultural obsession with fame and achievement, and, oh yeah — I want to make it a love story . . . and feature Christmas . . . and stargazing, didn't blink before encouraging me, and then guided me through so many drafts of this novel. You're amazing, Melissa. I'm also grateful to Molly Jaffa and everyone over at Folio Literary Management for their ongoing support.

I found my dream editor in Jody Corbett. Jody, you elevated this book in your own swoon-worthy way. Also, thanks to the whole team at Scholastic, with a special shout out to Roz Hilden, Elizabeth Starr Baer, and Yaffa Jaskoll. As Jody says, it truly takes a village to make a book. This has been an exceptionally nice village to dwell in.

And to my first readers: Michael Bodie, Gabrielle Carolina, Kirsten Casey, Erin Dixon, Tanya Egan Gibson, Alison Jones-Pomatto, and Loretta Ramos — you were all generous and honest and kind in your early feedback of this book. I'm so grateful.